D1098295

r(

or before the date shown

Ticke~

to

Paris

ALSO BY EMMA ROBINSON

The Undercover Mother
Happily Never After

EMMA ROBINSON

One Way Ticket to Paris

bookouture

Published by Bookouture in 2018

An imprint of StoryFire Ltd.

Carmelite House
50 Victoria Embankment
London EC4Y 0DZ

www.bookouture.com

ISBN: 978-1-78681-699-3
eBook ISBN: 978-1-78681-698-6

For William
I love you as much as the gravity of a neutron star

PROLOGUE

When I was a kid and I'd lost something, my dad always said, 'Go back to the place you last had it.' That's why, when I found myself (aged forty-one, married with kids, a house and an unreliable Renault Clio) missing something, I decided to take his words literally.

The problem was that what I'd lost was... me.

CHAPTER ONE

Kate

Insomnia at three a.m. is not the ideal time to purchase an unplanned train ticket to Paris. Without telling your husband. Or having any clue who will look after your two children while you were away.

It was now 7.30 a.m. and Kate was in the bathroom, cleaning her teeth whilst undertaking covert surveillance on four-year-old Thomas doing a stand-up-wee-like-daddy. There weren't enough bottles of bleach in the world to keep up with that boy. She spat toothpaste into the sink. 'Thomas, please at least *try* to point your willy somewhere near the toilet.'

Luke shouted up the stairs. 'Love, do you know where my car keys are?'

She gritted her newly-brushed teeth. Of course she knew where they were; she was the only person in this house who put things where they should actually be. 'Look by the side of the kettle!'

Kate had woken at the usual three a.m. and, between her stowaway daughter's determination to sleep like a star fish and her husband's snoring, she hadn't had a snowball in hell's chance of going back to sleep. Then her brain had started its night-time cycle: shopping lists, upcoming birthday parties, school events, missed dentist appointments, things she'd forgotten, or might forget, or… Somehow, she'd wriggled caterpillar-like from under the duvet without waking either of them and had gone downstairs for a glass of water. Which is when she'd found Luke's keys.

Alice wandered into the bathroom. 'What do you think of my hair, Mummy?'

Kate's six-year-old daughter was adorned with the entire contents of the box of hair accessories. 'You look beautiful, darling, but I think it might be better to save that look for the weekend.' Or a Boy George lookalike convention.

Alice flounced off to her bedroom and Kate turned her attention back to the boy child. 'Pants up, Tom-Tom. Let's give those hands a good scrub.'

The glass of water hadn't really cut it last night, so she'd stepped it up to a cup of camomile tea. So rock and roll. The keys had been by the side of the kettle on top of the Eiffel Tower postcard. When they'd bought the house in Kent, Luke had waxed lyrical about the fact they would be so close to the Eurostar station at Ebbsfleet. But they hadn't been to Paris since their honeymoon. Moving the keys, Kate had flipped the postcard over to reread the familiar handwriting: *When are you coming?*

Luke stuck his head into the bathroom. His thick, blond hair was still tousled from bed. He winked at her. 'Found the keys, thanks. Are you done in here? Can I get in to take a shower?'

He disappeared into the bedroom before she had a chance to say anything. But what was she going to say? Kate put a hand up to her own, dark hair and looked in the bathroom mirror. She still missed having hair which reached past her shoulders. But it had been the right decision to have it cut shorter. So much easier now she had the children to worry about. Practical.

Whether she stayed or went, the kids would still need lunch. Kate consulted the school lunch choices sellotaped to the door of the cereal cupboard, praying for pizza. No such luck: Beef stew. Fish stew. Vegetable stew. Fabulous. Did *anyone's* child eat that?

'Alice, Thomas. There's a yummy stew for lunch today!' The enthusiasm in her voice sounded fake even to her. But she really wanted them to have a hot meal at school. They might be eating later than usual tonight. Something else to feel guilty about. *Just add it to the list.*

Both children clutched their stomachs and pretended to be sick. Then Thomas looked up with his beautiful blue eyes. 'Chocolate spread sandwiches?' You had to admire his optimism. Kate got out the bread to make packed lunches – ham, not chocolate spread. Obviously.

Last night, she'd carried the postcard through to the lounge, putting it on top of the ever-growing pile of papers on her piano. Luke called it the most expensive letter rack in the country. She'd sat on the piano stool, sipping the disgusting tea and just staring at the postcard. Paris. And Shannon. If Shannon was awake at three a.m. it would be because she'd just got home from a glamorous night out, not because she was drinking camomile tea and turning over in her head whether or not she had made a fool of herself in the school office yesterday because she couldn't for the life of her remember the name of her daughter's class. Or worrying whether her husband would find out where she'd been. Or who with.

Kate had given up on the tea and hunted through the mountain of papers on the piano until she found the old photo Shannon had sent her the month before: the two of them drinking virgin marys, complete with celery sticks, at The Albert on Victoria Street. It must have been one of the many Mondays they had pledged to start a health kick. She peered at her thirty-year-old self. Where had that girl in the photograph gone?

Right now she was squashing an apple into each of her children's lunchboxes – apples which would undoubtedly come back uneaten but would prove that Kate encouraged healthy eating. When she put the lunchboxes inside their backpacks, she found a letter in Alice's informing her that an 'optional' homework for last night had been to draw their hero. 'Shit.'

Alice was right behind her. 'Mummy, is *shit* a square word?'

Perfect timing. 'Alice, who is your hero?'

Alice considered for a moment. 'I would say Daddy.' Of course he was. It didn't matter that Kate was the one running herself into the ground making healthy lunches, arranging excruciating playdates, supervising hellish craft activities. It was Daddy – who would come home late, feed them secret sweets and throw them in the air – who was the hero of the house. It wasn't fair. Nothing had been fair lately. Nothing.

It had been that photograph which had started it. Or the girl in the photograph. Looking at it, Kate had had a sudden urge to find her; to bring her out again. And if anyone could help, it would be Shannon. Still wide awake, Kate had passed the time searching her mobile for Eurostar train times. By chance, there had been a £29 one-way ticket for the 10.30 a.m. later that morning. She'd screwed up her eyes and done the calculations. Eight forty-five drop off, plus fifteen minutes to get the car, plus half an hour's drive… Yes, she would be able to do the morning school run and still make that.

Was it meant to be?

Showered and dressed for work, Luke now appeared. He always looked handsome in a suit. 'I'm going to make myself a coffee for my travel mug. Do you want a proper cup of tea?'

Should she just tell him? No. It would spoil everything. 'Actually, I'll have a coffee, too.'

Luke stopped mid-spoon in the coffee jar and looked at her. It was the same expression Thomas wore when she explained he had to put on new pants *every* morning. 'Really? That's not like you.'

If changing her morning drink to coffee was surprising, Luke had better hold onto *his* pants when he found out what she had planned for the rest of the day.

Last night, she'd sat for at least five minutes as her thumb had hovered over the online payment button. It was the longest she'd sat on the neglected piano stool in years. The camomile tea had done nothing for her pounding heart. Was she actually going to do this? Going to another country on a whim – without booking a return ticket – was the kind of thing the old Kate would have done. The single Kate. The reckless Kate. The fun Kate. The new Kate didn't do things like that. The mother Kate. The sensible Kate. The bloody boring Kate.

She'd pressed the button.

If she was being transparently twitchy this morning, Luke was his usual oblivious self. 'Anything nice planned for today?'

Anything nice? Did he really think she spent her days lunching with the cast of *Desperate Housewives* whilst the housework and shopping fairies did their thing? 'Nothing much, dropping the kids to school and then some cleaning, maybe a trip to the supermarket.' *Running away to Paris for the night.* 'Have you got a busy day today?'

'Not really, I'll try and get away early if I can – we could get a takeaway tonight, save you cooking.'

'Mmmm, maybe.' She wandered into the lounge to check on Alice and Thomas, who were about fifty centimetres from the TV, glued to *Everything's Rosie*. If only it was.

Thomas, with his thumb in his mouth and his pudgy finger twisted in his hair, leaned in to Alice and she put an arm around him. Tears pricked in the back of Kate's eyes. This was crazy. She couldn't just drop them at school and skip off to another country. What if they were sick during the day or she'd forgotten something they needed and the school had to call her? She couldn't just say, *Sorry I'm in Paris, might be a while.* What the hell would the school think?

She could just tell them to call Luke. He was their father, after all.

Luke wandered into the lounge with her coffee and put it on the dining table. 'Okay, that's me off.' He kissed Thomas and Alice on the tops of their heads, and Kate on the cheek, and left for work. He was always the one who got to leave. Today he might not be the only one.

Kate's heart started to pound again. Was she really going to do this? The ticket was only £29, so she wasn't losing a huge amount if she chose not to go. She would just call Shannon. That would be the decider. Funny, clever, and too sensible to have children, Shannon was exactly what Kate needed right now. Shannon would understand how Kate was feeling. She'd help her to work this all out.

If Shannon was too busy to see her, Kate wouldn't go. But if she was free and up for it, Kate would pack, take the kids to school then head straight to the Eurostar. Kate's stomach fluttered as she listed to the warbled ringtone three times before the line connected. Voicemail. Dammit.

She would have to take a chance. The small purple suitcase was still under the bed from Luke's last work trip. Underwear first.

In the underwear drawer were about twenty pairs of black knickers and ten bras, only three of which actually still fit. There were even a couple of grey maternity bras still kicking around in there like teenagers with nowhere to go. She pulled out the least pathetic-looking items. Maybe she could buy something new once she got there? Something sexy, even.

Next, she opened her wardrobe. What clothes should she take? These options filled her with even less enthusiasm. A row of loose-fitting tops and leggings. Her uniform was worse than the kids'. Maybe she should be the one raiding the hair accessories? Downstairs she could hear the beginning of an argument; there were probably only about five minutes before tears and/or bloodshed. She grabbed a daytime dress, an evening dress, a couple of T-shirts and some Capri trousers which she prayed still fit.

Hours sitting by a hospital bed eating sweets had done nothing for her waistline.

CHAPTER TWO

Shannon

Shannon had been begging Kate to visit her in Paris for the last year. Why, oh why did she have to pick this weekend?

She'd missed Kate's call due to an urgent need to vomit the contents of her stomach into the toilet. If only this had been self-induced by a wild night out. Ironic that the last time she'd clung to a toilet quite like this had been her first week in the UK after arriving as a fresh-faced Yank who couldn't hold her ale. At least, that's what Kate had called her as she'd held back her hair and laughed. They'd been 'mates' ever since.

Dragging herself away from the comforting coolness of the bathroom tiles, Shannon crawled back to the bedroom. There were six territory managers coming for a sales conference today and she was supposed to be the friendly face that put them at ease whilst organising everything within an inch of its life. Very much like a jovial duck, she had to be serene on the surface, paddling like a madwoman underneath. How the hell was she going to do it?

The mirror confirmed that her face wasn't looking friendly so much as frazzled. She dragged the hair band from her ponytail. It had been a good idea to leave a pile of them in a pot by the toilet for puking purposes. Chunks of carrot did not coordinate well with rose-gold highlights. She rubbed at her face to generate a bit of colour. Did she have time to reapply her make up?

Probably best to get dressed first in case there was another wave of stomach lurches. She paused and put a hand to her stomach. Was that another one coming? No, she was okay.

Sitting on the side of the bed, Shannon tried for the second time to put on pantyhose, managing to get her feet in before flopping forwards as she summoned the energy to pull them up. How could she be so exhausted when she'd only been awake for thirty minutes? She felt across the quilt to where her mobile was and listened to Kate's voicemail, upside-down. The surprise made her sit back up.

Wow. Kate was coming. And on her own. On any other weekend Shannon would have been psyched to have Kate just turn up like this. It was the kind of thing the old Kate would have done. They'd done some totally crazy stuff back when they'd worked together in London. Once, they'd gate-crashed a really posh New Year's Ball. It had been a huge deal in a marquee, with free champagne and waiters laden with canapés. There were so many people there, they'd thought they'd never be discovered. Everything was going well until Kate whispered to the man she was dancing with that they hadn't actually been invited. 'I know,' he'd said. 'It's my party.'

Shannon lay back and wriggled the pantyhose up over her hips. A couple of weeks ago it had been still warm enough to go without them – and her legs tanned at the first sight of sun – but now autumn had brought a cool breeze. It was true what they said about Paris in the springtime, but autumn was a close second. She'd fallen in love with this city and its parks and open spaces and sprawling cafés. If Kate had just left her visit until later this month, they could have spent the whole weekend together. Now Shannon would have to try and see her around meeting times and meals out with the team.

Sales meetings were busy but a lot of fun. Every quarter they would meet at a different European office and this time they were hosting in Paris: the European HQ. She'd planned some nice things for them to do today as a counterbalance to what was coming from Robert: he was on the warpath about sales figures. He'd been stomping around the office like a bear with a sore head since his conference call with the US last week – even Shannon hadn't been able to stand him. He was pretty cute when he was angry, though. A bear crossed with George Clooney. Although she knew better than to say that to his face.

Fabienne, the office manager, did most of his PA stuff now that Shannon's role had morphed more into… What was she, exactly? Sales Manager Coordinator with extra responsibilities? Whatever. She still liked to coordinate events like this, though. The sales guys were a great gang and she was looking forward to seeing them. She was looking forward to seeing Kate, too. Her lovely Kate; she'd missed her.

Why had Kate decided to just book a ticket and come without any warning? Since children, the new, sensible Kate just didn't do stuff like this. Whenever Shannon had asked her to visit, she'd always had some excuse. The children were always breastfeeding or teething or had just had injections. Was it that she *couldn't* come or was it that she didn't want to? People always changed when they had kids. Suddenly their lives revolved around their children and they got new friends who also had children and all they *talked* about was their children. Which is part of the reason Shannon had never wanted them. Part of it.

The tights were on. Now, where had she put her skirt? It had been thrown to the floor in her haste to make it to the bathroom in time. At least that was one benefit of this tiny Parisian apartment: less distance to run. This lounge was the size of a hotel bedroom back in Chicago, and the kitchen area was almost an afterthought. Shannon found her skirt dangling from the back of a chair and slipped it on. Was she imagining it or was the waistband a little tighter than usual? Hopefully it had just shrunk in the wash. *Don't think about it till you know for sure. Think about Kate instead.*

Something big must be up if Kate was coming out to Paris alone. Hopefully there wasn't some problem. It couldn't be her marriage, surely? Luke was a cool guy; the two of them always seemed real happy together. He was funny. And kind. And he looked at Kate as if she was the most fabulous woman on the planet. It was almost enough to make a woman jealous. If she was looking for that kind of thing.

But maybe things had changed. Shannon hadn't seen them in a year. Even when she'd gone to the UK with Robert six months ago, she hadn't looked them up. Hadn't even told Kate she was there. Of course, it had been a business trip. There hadn't really been time to leave London to visit Kate. But she should have made time. You didn't find friends like that everywhere. Kate was a keeper.

Now the skirt was on too, it was time to get going. Although, maybe she should try and force down a couple of ginger cookies before heading for the Métro. The cookies were in the cupboard in a jar she'd bought especially a few days ago. Before that, she hadn't allowed confectionery of any type in the house. Now it was her best friend. Speaking of which, she'd better call Robert and tell him she was going to be late.

He picked up on the first ring. 'Hi.'

Was he still mad at her from their argument last night? She'd been pretty mad too, but right now she was too wrung out to carry it on. 'Hi, I'm going to be late.'

There was a long pause at the other end. He *was* still mad. 'Why?'

Shannon took a small bite of the ginger cookie, chewed and swallowed. Two could play at this pausing game. 'Just running late.'

At the other end of the line, Robert took a deep breath and let it out slowly. Maybe it was her excitement at seeing Kate again, but it almost made Shannon laugh. He could be so dramatic. So deliciously French. 'You know we are meeting the sales team at one thirty at the hotel? It was your idea to waste time *sightseeing*. As if strolling around the Louvre staring at paintings is going to help them get anywhere near their targets.'

Of course she knew. She was the one who had booked everything. The conference room, the hotel, the minibus and the tour guide for the Louvre. 'Yeah. About that. I need an hour at lunchtime to meet an English friend at Gare du Nord.' She purposefully enunciated the 'd' at the end of 'Nord'. It really irritated him.

But Robert was more interested in who she was meeting. 'What English friend?'

Shannon took another bite of her biscuit. She could picture him right now, frowning into the phone, running an irritated hand through his thick, dark hair. He was too easy. 'Oh. No one you know.'

'A man?'

Fun though it was to make Robert jealous, Shannon didn't have the energy this morning. 'No. A girlfriend. Kate. We worked together in the UK. I have mentioned her before.'

Despite the short notice, it *was* going to be great to see Kate. Shannon had been so busy since she came to Paris to work for Robert that she hadn't had time to make any friends here. Of course, dating him made that even more difficult. He didn't have a large social group himself. Although his divorce had happened a long time before he met Shannon, his ex-wife seemed to have won most of their mutual friends in the settlement. He also had two almost-adult daughters. Shannon hadn't met them either; families weren't her thing.

Robert's voice was so sharp he was in danger of cutting himself. 'Why didn't you tell me this before? Why is she coming this weekend? We have work to do.'

Shannon took another cookie and snapped it in half. If he was going to talk to her like that, he didn't deserve an answer. This was why she hadn't let him stay over last night. He'd started on at her about meeting his girls. She'd tried — again — to make him understand that she just wasn't the maternal type. With any luck, God had got that memo too.

Finally, when he didn't get a response, Robert's voice softened. A little. 'Okay. Meet your friend from the station. I can do the Louvre on my own. I'm in the office now. How long before you get here?'

This was usually how their disagreements went. He would blow up and then back down. But he'd irritated Shannon now. 'Actually, I have my laptop, so I may as well work here until I go and meet her. Otherwise, I'll be wasting time on the Métro. If I come in to the office, I'll only have an hour before I have to head to Gare du Nord.' She pronounced the 'd' again.

But he didn't bite. 'Well, I'll see you at the Louvre later, after the tour. Maybe we can have coffee together when they have their free time this afternoon?'

The ginger snaps were doing their thing and Shannon felt less like she'd just come off a rocky sea voyage. 'Maybe.'

Her laptop was charging by the apartment door, beside a full-length mirror. Shannon stood in front of it and straightened her skirt. There was a definite pull in the fabric across her stomach, even though she had eaten hardly anything in days. For the last two weeks, she'd barely been able to keep her breakfast down. She couldn't put this off any longer. She would find out today. Like she told the sales guys when they panicked about cancelled orders, there was no point worrying about it until she knew for sure.

CHAPTER THREE

Kate

Despite the taxi driver's penchant for Kiss Radio, it was quite nice to be a passenger without being responsible for crowd control on the back seat. Most long car journeys for Kate these days involved alternating between threatening 'don't make me come back there' and throwing packets of sweets over her shoulder.

Kate had caught Nina — the one school mum friend she'd managed to make — and Nina had kindly agreed to collect the kids from school with hers if Luke couldn't make it back in time.

Kate had almost made it back to the safety of her car, when a familiar strident voice rang out. 'Kate! Kate!'

Could she ignore her? Just keep walking? No, she couldn't do it. Kate took a deep breath, plastered on a smile and turned around. 'Melissa?'

'Gosh, you can move fast when you want to, can't you?' Melissa put a hand to her throat. 'Just checking whether we can rely on you for a cake for the bake sale?'

There was something overwhelmingly irritating about people who spoke about themselves in the plural. The damn bake sale. Kate had forgotten all about it. Why the bloody hell would she want to make a frickin' cake on top of everything else? She'd rather boil her own head in baby oil. Kate swallowed. 'Of course, Melissa.'

Melissa smiled. 'Great. I'll ping you an email with the deets.'

God, she was irritating. Kate wished she could ping her and her flippin' 'deets' into outer space. 'Great. Sorry, I have to dash off.'

At least the traffic wasn't too bad, and the taxi driver seemed as keen to get to the station as Kate was, so being caught by Melissa wouldn't make her late. She checked her mobile again. There was a reply from Shannon: *Can't talk but would love to see you. Text me your train details. I'll meet you at the station x.* While she had her phone out, she thumbed through Facebook. Melissa had already posted, obviously. Apparently her daughter had gone up to the next stage reading book. This was a relatively tame piece of self-promotion when compared to Melissa's recent epistles in which her child was 'eating a home-grown strawberry' and 'discussing Brexit'. At five years old.

Kate never actually posted anything on Facebook. She just crept around it reading other people's updates about their perfect lives: a bit like self-flagellation without the need for extra equipment. It was surprising how bad you could make yourself feel just by checking the profiles of your high-achieving, Tough Mudder-running ex-schoolmates. Or your career-driven, designer-clad ex-work colleagues. Or indeed your good-looking, saxophone-playing ex-boyfriends.

She'd bumped into Tim again at the hospital. Wandering round those soulless corridors, trying to remember which colour signs she was supposed to be following. She hated it: the smell, the squeaky floor and the hushed voices everywhere. Nosocomephobia, it was called – a fear of hospitals. Another useless nugget of information gleaned from her parents' love of quiz shows. Between them they could have answered the whole of a Trivial Pursuits box; even the Arts and Literature questions.

Tim had spotted her first. 'Kate? Kate, is that you?'

She'd turned and seen him down the corridor. Her traitorous heart had flipped. Thirteen years and he didn't look any different. Thick, dark hair, tight jeans, black shirt and some kind of metal symbol on a leather thong around his neck. Wasn't he a little old to still be dressing like that? The young nurse checking him out as she walked past hadn't seemed to think so. *Don't waste your time on this one, love.*

Kate swallowed. Frowned. And pretended she was running through a mental Rolodex to work out who he was. 'Tim? Tim Watson? Oh, my gosh! How are you?'

When you meet up with your ex-boyfriend from ten years ago, you are supposed to look fabulous. Kate, on the other hand, had looked like a crap-bag. She'd just arrived at the hospital after wrestling Thomas in and out of the shower before lying next to him in bed, praying for him to go to sleep before the end of visiting hours. Luke had told her to leave Thomas to him, but how could she leave the house to the soundtrack of her son crying for her? It made her stomach hurt. Besides, Thomas always went to sleep quicker with her than Luke. He'd twiddled her hair into a set of complicated knots that she hadn't had time to brush out properly before dashing to the hospital to spend the next two hours sitting by her dad's bedside, willing him to wake up.

Tim had walked over with a huge grin on his face and kissed her on the cheek. Like they'd only seen each other yesterday. 'How great to see you. I'm just visiting my sister; she's had surgery on her foot. What are you doing here?'

Wasn't that one of the questions you should never ask someone in a hospital? 'It's my dad.'

The heart attack had come completely out of the blue. Her dad had just retired, had bought himself a new set of golf clubs whilst her mum stockpiled cruise brochures and left them in the toilet for him. Guerrilla marketing for the over-sixties.

The call had come on a Saturday. Just after lunch. Kate had been home with Luke and the kids. Her mum was at the hospital. Could Kate come? She'd been too shaky to drive herself, so Luke had driven her with the kids strapped into the back of the car.

They'd been squabbling and fighting over a broken yo-yo and Kate had had to squeeze her fingernails into the palm of her hands not to scream at them. *My dad could be dying! Stop arguing about a stupid piece of plastic! Shut up! Shut up! Shut up!*

The shock of seeing him in that bed. He'd looked old. And vulnerable. And not like her dad. She'd just wanted to run. Her mum had gripped her hand. 'Come on. We have to be here. He would do this for you.'

The taxi arrived at the station, jolting Kate out of her reverie. It was busier than Kate had expected. She made it through customs to the concourse, which was mainly full of adults in ones or twos – but there were a couple of families. She felt a slight pang watching one of the mothers peeling a banana for her little girl. Alice loved bananas. The pang lessened somewhat as she watched the little girl pluck the fruit from its skin and mash it into her mother's trouser leg.

According to the departures board, her train was leaving shortly, so she headed straight for the platform. About to step on the train, she paused. Was this a ridiculous thing to do? Before last night, this trip to Paris had been a pleasant daydream. Surely every mother of young children fantasised about jumping on a plane or a train – or even a bicycle – and escaping for a couple of days? During long evenings lying next to Thomas, waiting for him to stop rotating 360 degrees and go to bloody sleep, she had mapped out the whole thing in her brain. The secrecy. The clandestine arrangements. The Eiffel Tower. She'd never thought she'd actually go through with it.

It would be so easy to turn around and go home. She hadn't even sent a text to Luke yet. She could spend a couple of hours up here shopping and be back in time for the kids leaving school. No one would know what she'd planned. Nothing would change. Life would go on as normal.

She got on the train.

*

The train carriage was stuffy and every seat was filled. Kate stowed her bag overhead and got comfy. There was a young woman sitting in front of her: probably in her late twenties or early thirties. Pretty, in a wholesome way; shoulder-length glossy brown hair, well put-together; she looked like she had a facial every month rather than when a friend bought her a voucher for her birthday. Tapping away into a small computer; checking a folder on the table which looked like it was full of sales figures or something similar; she was so absorbed in what she was doing that she hadn't even looked up when Kate had slipped into the seat opposite.

Hitting the return key with a final flourish, the girl sat back with a sigh and picked up her water bottle. Ten years ago, Kate had worked at a computer like that. She'd had manicured fingernails. Had worn suits and shirts and high heels. She'd left it all behind without a backward glance when Alice was born. Child rearing had been the perfect excuse to leave a job which bored her sideways. But now?

She smiled at the younger her opposite. Might as well make conversation. 'All done?'

The girl sipped at her water and pulled a face. 'Yes, I have a big catch up with my boss tomorrow morning and I'm just trying to make sure I've got all my figures straight.'

'What do you do?

The girl wrinkled her nose and shut one eye. 'Sales. Computer printers. I know it sounds completely boring. I mean, I get to travel quite a lot, which I like. But it's a bit stressful at the moment – sales are slow.' She shrugged and put out her hand. Those fingernails looked fabulous. 'I'm Laura.'

Kate shook her hand – her own fingernails were short, rounded and practical. 'I'm Kate. And I used to work for an IT company, too. Before I had my children.' Those had been the days when life was more organised. When they'd called her the Queen of the In Tray. It was where she'd met Shannon. And Luke.

They'd got together one Friday night at the pub. Kate had been single for six months. Shannon – only an admin assistant in those days – had been the one to introduce them. 'You are gonna *love* him! He's so cute! And such a gentleman!' Kate had wondered why Shannon hadn't gone for him herself. 'He's a settling-downer,' she'd said. 'More your type than mine.' And she'd been right.

The girl, Laura, nodded slowly. 'Oh, you have children? How lovely. Girls or boys?'

'One of each.' And then, before Kate could stop herself, she was doing that thing she hated when other people did it. Getting her mobile out and showing Laura the most recent pictures of Alice and Thomas. Pictures, plural. Because, clearly it wasn't enough to bore her with just one photo of children who she didn't know or would ever be likely to meet. And what was she going to say? What could she say, except:

'They're very cute.'

'Thanks. Every wrinkle is their fault though. They've made me look *way* older than forty-one.' Kate laughed with more humour than she felt and slipped her mobile back into her handbag. She still didn't know when she should text Luke to tell him that she'd left. She wanted to leave it as late as possible, but needed to give him time to ensure he didn't agree to work late. Or get 'pulled along' by the Friday night pub gang. Again.

Laura shook her head and smiled. 'You *so* don't have wrinkles. But how come you're travelling to Paris without them? Are you on holiday?'

'I'm visiting an old friend.' An old friend who hadn't even known she was coming until a couple of hours ago. This was quite possibly the most hare-brained thing Kate had ever done. And the most exciting. Shannon would be proud.

'Unfortunately, I'm getting the train back tomorrow.' Laura picked up her water bottle again; it was one of those trendy metal ones. 'Which is a shame as I haven't been to Paris before. Actually,

I need more than this water; I'm going to get a coffee from the snack bar. Would you like anything?'

'No, I'm fine. You go ahead.' As Laura left, Kate fished her copy of *The Catcher in the Rye* from her bag. But the train was busy and loud and it was difficult to concentrate on Holden Caulfield and his nervous breakdown. Should she text Luke yet? How was he going to react? How would she have reacted if the tables were turned? Actually, she'd have been excited by such a display of spontaneity. Before the children, Luke would often surprise her with a Groupon hotel break or a bunch of her favourite white roses. Now she was lucky if he brought home a Starbar from the garage without being asked.

She should definitely text Shannon with her arrival time. After sending the message, she managed to resist checking Facebook again. But made the mistake of looking at her email.

Re: School Bake Sale

Dear Mums!

*I think I've spoken to you all about the cake sale but just wanted to follow up on a few items so that we're all on the same page. PLEASE READ CAREFULLY AND **THOROUGHLY**!!!!!*

1. *We do accept shop-bought cakes but home-made cakes are preferred. I know that we lead busy lives but a small amount of effort makes all the difference, don't you think?*
2. *The cakes must be delivered to the Junior School reception by 2.30 p.m. AT THE LATEST. My helpers and I will need thirty minutes to cut and display the cakes and late delivered cakes will mean the overall presentation will be affected.*
3. *Absolutely NO NUTS! (I know you are all aware of the implications for pupils with a nut allergy but we all need a little reminding sometimes.)*

4. Provide a label for your cake so that we know what it is (some of the ones we were given last year were undetectable, even after a taste test – ha ha!) A plain hand-written label is perfectly acceptable but if you have time to design and make a more eye-catching name card that would be super. If you need inspiration, I am making flags from coloured paper and cocktail sticks with my daughter for the cakes we are making.

Thanks in advance to everyone who is making a cake. Remember that all funds from the bake sale will go towards new cushions for the school library.

Happy baking!
Melissa x

Making a bloody cake. The cost of the ingredients was more than the profit generated by fifty pence a slice. Last time, Kate had forgotten until the night before and had had to go to the twenty-four-hour Tesco for ingredients, then sit up late while the damn thing cooked. Luke had gone to bed shaking his head. 'Why don't you just give them a tenner and say you bought and ate your own cake?'

This time she'd make her dad's old favourite: pineapple cake. It involved chucking all the ingredients into a pan until they melted and then sticking it into the oven for forty-five minutes. Easy. Her dad had always enjoyed cooking as long as everything went into the same pan.

Tim had offered to visit her dad the second time she'd bumped into him in the hospital corridor, but she'd declined. It would have been too weird. Her dad still hadn't forgiven Tim for 'stringing you along all those years'. Plus, he was a very proud man and wouldn't want Tim seeing him in bed in his pyjamas. It had been kind of Tim to offer, though. Maybe that's why she'd agreed to go and get a coffee with him in the hospital canteen instead.

CHAPTER FOUR

Laura

Photographs of other people's children made Laura anxious.

She tapped her fingernails on the counter whilst she waited for a coffee. She didn't usually get them manicured but had thought a perfect finger to point at her PowerPoint would make her feel more confident. Who was she trying to kid? *I missed my target but don't my nails look pretty?* Idiot.

The woman sitting opposite her back there had seemed perfectly nice with her short mum bob and smiling face, but the pictures of her children smiling up from the phone screen had twisted something inside Laura. The woman – Kate? – had said she was forty-one, and her oldest child looked about six. Therefore, she must have been about thirty-five when she had her first child, which meant she fell pregnant when she was thirty-four. That gave Laura three years. Which sounded a long time. But wasn't.

There was a display card on the counter advertising the free Wi-Fi on the train. Laura entered the lengthy password on her mobile; it looked like the coffee machine might take a while to regurgitate her drink. A circular icon spun around and around as her email tried to connect, and she issued another silent prayer. *Please don't cancel the order. Please don't cancel the order.*

A WhatsApp message rolled up her screen. Her mother. Laura didn't need to read it to know what was in the message: *Look*

at this one – it's got a fabulous hallway! Xxx Her mother's new
hobby was finding her daughter a home on Rightmove. It was
practically an addiction: online real estate porn. It hadn't helped
when Laura had told her that she and James couldn't afford to
buy a house in South London. Her mother had happily said that
houses were 'a lot cheaper near us' and had started to send links
to three-bedroom semi-detached houses in Kent. Three bedrooms
for an obvious reason.

That woman back there – Kate – had looked serene and happy.
Is that what life was like when you gave up work and became a
full-time parent? Lunch dates with your friends whilst the children
played happily together. Must be bliss. Laura had to stop doing
these mental timelines, calculating the age that someone would
have had their first child. If it was thirty-six or more, though,
it was strangely comforting. She used to pick up those trashy
magazines with exclamation marks in their titles just so that she
could read about celebrities who had had their first pregnancy
well into their forties. Then her friend Tina had said that a lot
of them had to do IVF or use donor eggs. Not that there was
anything wrong with that, but there were lots of needles involved
in fertility treatment and Laura had once passed out in the middle
of Claire's Accessories trying to get her ears pierced. She'd been
revived by a very kind seven-year-old patting her hand.

Alongside the birth age calculating thing, she'd also developed
an unhealthy bitterness towards people who were getting married.
Up until recently, every time an old school mate announced their
engagement/marriage/second child, Laura would email Tina, her
last single school friend. *Can you believe it! Rhys Hereford is getting
married! Rhys Hereford! He couldn't even put his shirt on the right
way round after PE!*

In those days, Tina would commiserate. *ANOTHER ONE!
How come all these people can manage it and we can't? Where do
they meet these people?*

But now Tina was one of them too. After a whirlwind six months in which she and her now-husband had met, moved in and married. And Laura had been forced to live at the centre of it all. A week-long hen-do in Ibiza where every other woman had been married and had recounted their own wedding day in excruciating detail; a bridesmaid dress which had made Laura look like Bo Peep's slutty sister; a wedding reception from which James had excused himself at 9.30 p.m. citing a headache, leaving Laura dancing with Tina's slightly dodgy Uncle Bill.

Since the wedding, other than a painful evening when all the hen-attendees had had a girl's night at Tina's to watch the wedding DVD (and two of the freaks had actually come wearing their own wedding dresses for a 'laugh'), the whole thing seemed to have calmed down. But who the hell was Laura going to email now?

There were still no emails from the distributor, Machon UK. Who knew the world of selling computer printers could be so stressful? Managing the distribution channel from manufacturer to distributor to retailer to end user. She might have more luck opening a stall outside PC World and flogging the damn things to passers-by herself.

Maybe her buyer wasn't in? Off sick? Dead? Laura shook that thought from her head; that was not nice. And anyway, if they were dead, someone else would just take over and return the two thousand units of unsold printers in their warehouse. No, better they were just off sick long enough for her to get home from the sales meeting. Robert's wrath would be easier to deal with over the phone than in person. Maybe. At least she wouldn't have 'the stare' over the phone. Heaven help her from that. It made her want to frantically confess everything she'd ever done wrong, from missed sales opportunities to nail polish stolen from Boots on a dare when she was fourteen.

A dubious-looking coffee materialised and Laura edged back towards her seat. James had pronounced his advice on dealing with her distributor last night in his usual condescending way. 'You just need to be firm, Laura. Show them that you are in control of the situation. Don't give them an opportunity to disagree with you.' She'd tried to let it go over her head. Her boyfriend might be the darling of his accountancy firm, but he knew nothing about sales. The advice obviously came from a place of love, but when he used his 'I know best' tone she wanted to shove his advice right back up that place of love. Quite forcefully.

How he could do his job day in, day out was a complete mystery to her. They'd left university with the same accountancy qualification, but Laura had sworn she'd rather read the entire works of Shakespeare backwards on a continual loop than scrutinise someone else's bank statements and receipts for the rest of her life. It wasn't the numbers – that part she liked – it was the sheer repetitiveness. James, on the other hand, had followed his life plan to apply to the Big Six accountancy firms and had slid straight into a fast-track graduate scheme. Since then, he'd climbed up and up, while Laura had fallen rather more haphazardly into the world of IT sales with Sentek, a US company with a small UK office, reporting in to the European head office in Paris. And the force that was Robert Fournier: European Sales Director. She shuddered.

And now she and James were living together. Sort of. Laura was living in James' flat in Peckham. Tina had used to point this out in the days when she'd still been single – *at least you're living with someone* – but then Laura would argue that there is a world of difference between sharing some space in a rented house where you weren't even allowed to change the layout of the kitchen cupboards, and actually buying a place together. Her living situation was so temporary. Only one step up from her student house because they didn't have roommates in the second bedroom or a sink full of three days' washing up.

It had all come to a bit of a head again last night. It didn't help that Laura had made the fatal mistake of flicking through

Instagram while preparing dinner. Tina had posted pictures from her honeymoon in the Maldives along with some candid shots from the wedding reception. Nothing wrong in that. Deep down, Laura was made up for her lovely friend; Tina's new husband, Phil, was a great bloke and Tina deserved to be happy. It was the comments on the photos that had bothered her: **KTB87:** *One of us now!* **CopperTop:** *Welcome to the Mrs Club!* **SadieSmith:** *Babies next!*

Laura had taken the meat tenderiser to the two pieces of fillet steak like a psychopath who'd had a really bad day.

James had come home in a buoyant mood, carrying a bottle of champagne from a grateful client. He'd poured them a glass each, then put the rest of the bottle in the fridge with a spoon in it to keep the bubbles; he wouldn't have more than one on a work night. Over dinner, he'd mentioned that his colleague, Peter, was getting married.

'That's nice. How long has he been with his girlfriend?' Laura had focused her attention on cutting a slice of steak and keeping her voice neutral. They'd probably been together for years. Childhood sweethearts, etc., etc.

James had shrugged. 'I'm not sure. He definitely wasn't with her when he started with the company, which was about… er… three years ago, I guess.'

Which meant that this Peter had been with his girlfriend – *fiancée* – for a quarter of the time that Laura and James had been together. She'd stuck her fork into a fat chip rather forcefully. 'And how old is Peter again?'

James clearly had no idea what he was walking into. He'd finished a mouthful of steak and picked up his champagne glass before answering. The glasses had also been a gift from a client. There were a lot of grateful people in James' life. 'I think he's about twenty-seven or twenty-eight. Definitely younger than me.'

At least four years younger than him. Laura had stabbed her steak with her fork and pressed her knife down hard until a little blood oozed out. When she could trust her voice again, she spoke. 'And did that make you start to think about when you'd like to get married?'

James put an elbow on the table and rested his forehead on his fingertips. 'Oh, for God's sake, Laura. How does every conversation come back to this?'

How? A conversation about a colleague getting engaged was hardly a 180-degree turn from her question about them doing the same thing. This kind of comment from James used to be her signal to back down. To stop 'banging on' about it. Not any more. 'Because you *never* give me an answer, James.'

It was true. His refusal to just sit down and have a grown-up conversation about their future was turning her into a pathetic, nagging whiner. And that made her even angrier. But what else could she do? *Not mention it* and keep on *not mentioning it* until they were still *not mentioning it* in their retirement home?

James raised his head and brought his other elbow onto the table, pressing his fingertips together as if he was about to conclude a financial summary. 'If I *was* ever planning on proposing, do you not think you would be ruining it by constantly bringing the subject up? The more you go on about it, the less likely it is that I will be able to surprise you. You need to just leave it alone, Laura.'

The first five or so times Laura had heard him say this, she had been excited to think that he had a plan in mind. Nowadays, she knew it for what it was: a well-rehearsed feint. Except they weren't playing a game of James' beloved rugby; this was her life.

Even though Laura had technically started it, she could really have done without another argument like that the night before a sales meeting. Robert – he of the intimidating stare – was hosting this meeting at a hotel near his office in Paris, and all the regional sales managers like Laura were expected to fly in from wherever they were in Europe and prostrate themselves before him. That was probably a little unfair: he had at least promised them some sightseeing today in return for giving up their Saturday, but he could be a bit of a tyrant. They also had a dinner out tonight, before, first thing tomorrow, getting down to the nitty gritty of whose territory was performing in line with expectation and whose wasn't. It had been a tough quarter for most of them and Robert had made no secret of the fact that sales needed to improve soon. Very soon.

As she made her way back to her seat, Laura saw herself reflected back in the train windows. Reddish-brownish hair, no make-up and a T-shirt and hoodie; she hadn't changed much since she'd graduated ten years ago with the vague plan that she would do some travelling, find a job she loved and then settle down with James and two-point-four children. How had she ended up here? Her career had started as a temp job in the finance department when she'd finished university. Somehow, a *decade* later, here she was, heading up the UK sales team. Badly.

When Laura slid back into her seat, Kate was engrossed in a book. What was it? Laura had almost broken her neck a few times, craning it at an awkward angle to try and find out what someone on the train was reading. *The Catcher in the Rye*. Good choice. James didn't read at all. One of the many things they didn't have in common. Maybe that's why he didn't want to marry her? Or *surprise her* with a proposal.

Lots of people around him did seem surprised: surprised that they were a couple at all. The girls in his office were blatant about looking from Laura to James and back again in amazement on the rare occasion she visited him at work. They were probably expecting someone special – and then Laura walked in. It was true that he looked good these days, with his expensive, well-cut suits and salon-styled hair. Though his mother said to her once, 'I don't know why he hasn't popped the question, Laura. What is he waiting for, a supermodel?' How was she supposed to react to that?

Kate looked up from her book and smiled. 'How's the coffee?'

Laura pulled a face. 'Pretty grim, actually. It's my fourth one today. My boyfriend says I drink too many.'

Kate nodded. 'I used to drink a lot of coffee, but now I can't have any caffeine after about three o'clock or I can't get to sleep. It's a shame your first trip to Paris is on business. Could you not get your boyfriend to come out and meet you tomorrow after your meeting with your boss? Make a romantic weekend of it?'

Laura had had the same idea. But James wouldn't even consider it. 'He's not keen on Paris. Says it's full of cigarette ends and dog crap.'

Kate raised an eyebrow. 'Maybe he should look upwards a little more often. There's considerably more to see *above* the pavement.'

Laura laughed, but she felt disloyal. James had taken her to lots of nice places in the last year and they *were* happy together. Twelve years was a long time to be with someone and, apart from the 'Where is this going?' argument they had every few months, she and James rubbed along together well. Sometimes men just needed longer to get used to the idea of settling down, didn't they? Even Laura hadn't started worrying about it until a year or so ago. Now it was all she could think about. Well, that and not losing her job.

Kate had returned to her book. Laura couldn't face opening her spreadsheet again and creating another colour-coded graph, even if she did find it strangely soothing. Maybe Excel could help her sort out the buzzing in her head. A pie chart, perhaps? James and commitment (35%), worrying about job (30%), life left in ovaries (20%), finding clothes that make her look thinner (10%), seeing Paolo again (5%).

Actually, the 'seeing Paolo again' segment was getting bigger the closer she got to Paris. She'd been actively *not* thinking about their conversation at the last sales meeting, but that meant she hadn't formulated a strategy for how to act when she saw him today. Technically, nothing had actually happened between them, so she should just act normally. They were just two colleagues, meeting up with a lot of other colleagues at a sales meeting. Everything was normal.

Except, acting normally was quite tricky when you thought too hard about it. Like when you were a teenager and you came home to your parents' house a little drunk. The sensible (and normal) thing to do would be to call out 'goodnight' and go straight to bed but, no, in the spirit of 'acting normally' you would decide now was the time to sit down with them as they watched *Inspector Morse* and try to have a full-blown conversation which 'proved' you hadn't been drinking.

That was the kind of 'acting normally' she worried she might do when she met Paolo again. Minus the slurred speech. Hopefully.

CHAPTER FIVE

Shannon

If Shannon was going to find out her life was totally ruined, it might as well be sooner rather than later.

There were pharmacies on every street in Paris. Each one advertising some super cream that would remove cellulite from your thighs and the last twenty years of your life from your face. Right now, Shannon would settle for removing the last two months. How had she let this happen? By letting down her guard, that's how. And she had sworn that she would never do that again.

It was impossible to get any work done at home with this on her mind, so she'd hailed a taxi outside her apartment to take her to Gare du Nord in plenty of time to find a pharmacy, buy a test and get it over with before she met Kate. Like she'd tried to tell Laura about her order being returned, there was no point worrying about something until it actually happened. Now was as good a time as any to find out if it had.

Five minutes into the journey, she changed her mind. The toilets at Gare du Nord were on a par with a dystopian sci-fi film. There was no way she was going to do the test there. She stopped the cab, jumped out and ducked into the first pharmacy she came to.

Her stomach was flip-flopping as she browsed the boxes on the busy shelves, straightening them as she went, reorganising the ones that had been put back in the wrong spot by a lazy customer. Careless. Though, who was she to judge right now?

How had it happened? Taking the contraceptive pill had been a religious ritual since she was twenty: ten p.m. every single night. Why had it suddenly malfunctioned? It must have been that time she'd had dubious seafood and been in bed for three days afterwards. Why hadn't she just got the implant done? Or got herself sterilised? Or become a nun?

She stopped tidying and focused on the job at hand. Hopefully, she'd locate the right section in a minute and just take one from the shelf. Otherwise she was in danger of having to re-enact the scene from *Bridget Jones's Diary* in the ski resort pharmacy, as her French did not run to 'pregnancy test'. Should she google it?

Thank God. There *was* a section for contraception and tests. Strange to merchandise them together. Maybe they should also display them alongside a bottle of wine and a packet of hangover pills?

There was so much choice! Did she want digital? To know how many days pregnant she was? What colour hair the baby was likely to have? Okay, so she'd made up the last one, but seriously? What had happened to a simple yes or no?

Kate's train was due real soon; Shannon had no time for procrastination. She grabbed a mid-priced one and took it to the counter. Should she buy a pack of condoms at the same time to show the totally uninterested shop assistant that she was a responsible person? The words *horse* and *bolted* came to mind. Keep your head down. Pay for the test. Get out.

Once the test was safely stuffed into her handbag, there was a second dilemma. Where was she going to do it? She couldn't go to a café and use their toilet – they might wonder why she was taking so long. If she didn't do it now, who knows when she would get time today. And she wanted to know for sure. She *needed* to know. There was a department store opposite. They must have a ladies' room.

Somehow, Shannon negotiated her way through the cosmetic counters and the impossibly tiny and beautiful French women who manned them. Shannon was slim and pretty fit, but she hadn't had a waist like theirs since she was seven. No wonder it was so difficult for her to buy clothes over here. And that was potentially only going to get worse. Heavy perfumes fought each other for supremacy; she could barely breathe. Where were the damn toilets?

When she found them, there was such a long queue that she almost lost her nerve. For a start, she was now going to be late meeting Kate from the train – she hated being late – and there was also a rather unpleasant aroma in the vicinity. But the alternative – waiting another day – was unthinkable. Just do it.

She tapped her foot. She could use the time in the queue wisely by getting the instructions out of the box and reading them through. But they didn't look to be a very tolerant crowd and if she did that she may as well write 'whorebag' across her forehead. Or whatever the French equivalent was. *Le whoresac?*

When she was first in the queue, a woman with a small child emerged from a cubicle, taking an *interminably* long time to get out of the way. *Come on. Come on.* Then the child realised she had left her toy behind and they went back for it. Very slowly. Shannon hoped her frustrated scream had stayed inside her head.

Finally. She was in a cubicle. She located the test box in her bag and pulled out its contents. Of course the bloody instructions were in French. Shannon had decent business French, but specific vocabulary still tripped her up. She knew *première* meant *first* and *matin* was *morning*. Was she supposed to do this in the morning? According to her watch it wasn't quite midday, so that should be fine. Shouldn't it? Now she just needed to work out what to do. There were black and white drawings to help. Take the tip off. Wee mid-stream. Wait five minutes. Didn't look too difficult. It needed a final sketch of a woman with a big smile – either ecstatic to be pregnant or overwhelmingly relieved not to be.

Shannon had been taught from a young age to hover in public lavatories so as not to make contact with the potential diseases on the seat, but that was far too difficult to manage at the same time as urinating on a plastic stick. A bout of VD was the least of her worries right now. She sent a silent apology to her mother and sat down on the toilet.

The wee wouldn't come. What with the throwing up and the three kilos of ginger biscuits, her bladder was drier than the damn Sahara. She took a deep breath and breathed out slowly. Just relax. Think about a stream of water. A bubbling brook. The soda siphon at a frat party. There you go.

Now she needed to put the stick in mid-stream. How mid was mid? Did it have to be exactly halfway through? How would she know? Shit, it was starting to slow down. She needed to get it in there. Was it in the right place? Was she weeing in the right place? Dammit. She'd peed all over her hand. Nice.

Now she had to wait. Patience did not come easily to Shannon. Especially when her whole life was in the balance. Outside the cubicle, the queue of annoyed shoppers was mumbling and shuffling their feet. Let them use one of the other cubicles; she needed to get this done. After laying the test on the back of the cistern on a folded square of toilet tissue – she had some standards – she turned her back on it. How could her whole life be decided by a thin strip of plastic and a chemical reaction? *Please be negative. Please.*

The test took five minutes. She set the timer on her phone. *Do not look at it until the timer beeps.* But she couldn't just stand here. Doing nothing. With her non-urine-spattered hand, she scrolled through the photos on her phone. Her and Robert at dinner. Her and Robert watching the Superbowl on TV when she had cooked hotdogs and made him wear an American football shirt and huge foam hands. She smiled, in spite of the fact she was standing in a public toilet drenched in her own pee. If his colleagues had seen him that night, they would never have believed it. Such a doofus.

But if she was pregnant, and it looked very likely that she was, what was he going to say? This was never supposed to be a serious relationship. It was just fun. Starting a relationship with your boss was a completely ridiculous thing to do, but it didn't matter if you weren't planning on staying with the company – or even in the country – for that long. She had been very clear with him from the beginning. Keep it light and uncomplicated. He had agreed. It was just a casual thing.

Four minutes to go.

The row last night. The reason he hadn't stayed over at her place. It was the same discussion they'd been having on and off for the last two weeks. Robert had first mentioned her meeting his daughters about two months ago, but the pressure had started to mount the closer it got to his eldest daughter's birthday party. He wanted Shannon to come with him. To meet his daughters and the other members of his family. He was so deluded that he had even suggested she might get on well with his ex-wife. The French and their mature attitude towards relationships. That would never happen in the States. Back home, your ex was usually an ex for a good reason. A very good reason.

The birthday party wasn't even the real issue. It was Shannon's feelings for Robert. They were getting out of control. She hadn't even liked him when she'd first met him – stern, unfriendly, demanding, and he came down so hard on those poor sales guys. Fixing them with his steely glare and waiting for them to start babbling their excuses before pronouncing his decision. But then, it was this steel that she had also found interesting. It was a challenge.

Three minutes.

And beneath the steel was a real sensitive side. Of course she had been totally attracted by his looks: dark floppy hair, broad shoulders, an intense frown which could flip in a heartbeat to a raised eyebrow above a wide smile. But as she'd got to know him, it was his gentleness that had reeled her in deeper than she'd wanted to go. Deeper than she'd planned to go with anyone. Ever.

And he was thoughtful. He'd searched Paris to find a store which imported Lucky Charms so that he could surprise her with his idea of an American-style breakfast on her birthday. He would listen to her stories from home with an intensity that made her blush. And in bed… Well, that's what had landed her here.

Two minutes.

But Robert had *had* babies. He had two grown-up daughters who he clearly adored. The eldest of which was turning twenty soon – twenty being the coming-of-age birthday in France – hence, her party. But he was very clear that he liked his daughters a lot more now that they were grown. He even blamed the break-up of his marriage on the fact his youngest daughter hadn't slept properly until she was seven. What if one of the things he found most attractive about Shannon was her absolute certainty that she didn't want a family? And she didn't. She really, really didn't. This was not something she was going to change her mind about. Some women were born maternal. Some women became maternal. Some women had pregnancy thrust upon them and… Whatever the maternal gene was, it had been missed out of Shannon's DNA. And that was just fine and dandy.

One minute.

Shannon turned and confronted the damn stick, staring it down. Willing it to remain unchanged. Willing that second blue line to not appear. Why was the line on the maternity test blue? Not pink. Or red for danger? Or black for *What the hell do I do now*? Blue for a boy. After his two daughters, would Robert be more interested in having another child if it was a boy? A son?

Would she?

Maybe her period was just late. Maybe she had some weird virus. Maybe she just needed to stop being such a huge wuss, woman up and find out what she was dealing with. She took a deep breath and turned the stick over.

Two lines.

Merde.

CHAPTER SIX

Laura

Gare du Nord at midday was a maelstrom of bodies and noise and… rather unpleasant smells. The rumble of trains, crowds of commuters and bedraggled beggars waving frayed cardboard signs didn't really fit with Laura's romantic expectations. It was less *Three Colours: Blue* and more three colours grey and grubby. Maybe James was right.

She said a brief goodbye to Kate and made her way off the international platform. At the gate was a group of people similar to those you find at airport arrivals: a mixture of bored taxi drivers holding placards, and families waiting to throw their arms around relatives. Laura had neither of those waiting for her, so she headed towards the signs for the Métro.

Her team coordinator, Shannon, had sent instructions that were precise and accurate as usual, and Laura managed to navigate the Métro and the short walk to the hotel with ease. When she'd first started coming to these team meetings in Europe, she'd loved the sophistication of being a business traveller, but the novelty had definitely started to wane. Hotel rooms were becoming hateful places. Anonymous, lonely boxes where you had nothing to keep you company except your own thoughts and CNN. Both of which were on a repetitive loop.

As soon as she got to her room, Laura checked the Emergency Evacuation instructions on the back of the door, opened the window to let in some air and connected to the hotel Wi-Fi. Her email account still showed nothing from her buyer at Machon. Thank God.

Should she call James? Normally, she'd call him as soon as she arrived, often having to leave a message because he was busy. He liked to know that she'd arrived safely. So, he must care about her, right? But after last night, calling would feel as if she were the one apologising and she *wasn't* sorry for trying to get him to talk about their future together.

It was okay for him, he could wait to have babies until he was as old as Mick Jagger. Women didn't have that luxury. Perhaps it wasn't a good time for either of their careers, but it wasn't like Laura was asking for a baby right now, she just wanted to plan for it. Once they decided to get married it'd take at least a year to plan a wedding, then it would be nice to enjoy being married for a little while before they started to try for a baby – and even then, it was not a given that they'd even fall pregnant straight away.

And that was the other problem. Laura was more than a little worried that they *wouldn't* fall pregnant straight away. And that would mean it would take even longer. Or even that they might need some help. But she couldn't tell James that without telling him the whole story. And that wasn't going to happen.

She shut down the screen of her laptop. No point sitting here, staring at her email inbox waiting for the Returns Authorisation bomb to hit. Might as well check out the room. Bathroom first. White. Chrome. Plain. Anonymous. There were two sets of towels, two flannels, two beakers. But there was only one of her.

Next, she paced out the bedroom. It took roughly three seconds to get from one side to another and back again. She needed to find something to do. Anything. What was in the minibar? Did she want Toblerone? Orangina? Maybe not just yet.

In the absence of a better plan, she might as well text James to tell him that she'd arrived. Be informative but cool. As soon as the text was sent – *Arrived safely at hotel. I'm in room 365* – her mobile rang. That was quick.

'Hello.'

'Laura! It's Paolo. Are you here yet?'

Laura's heart started to race; she hadn't had time to prepare her nonchalant voice. Paolo's Italian accent always made her stumble over her words like she didn't even know her own language. But if she paused too long, that was like saying something without saying anything. *Just speak.* 'Yes, literally just arrived. You?'

His voice poured down the line. 'Same. I'm going to try and find somewhere to get good coffee before we meet up with the others. Do you want to join me?'

No way was she ready to see him yet; especially on her own. What if he picked up the same conversation from the last time they'd met? She crossed her fingers behind her back. 'Actually, I was just about to jump into the shower. I'll catch up with you when we meet at' – she glanced at the itinerary where she'd left it on the desk – 'one-thirty in the lobby.'

'*Bene*, okay. No problem. I'll see you soon. *Ciao.*'

'Bye.'

Did he sound disappointed? Or was she just imagining that? James always complained that she had an overactive imagination. Especially when she commented on his tone of voice. He would look at her as if she was crazy. Although sometimes he *was* overly sharp. She'd remind him he was speaking to his girlfriend. 'I'm not one of your minions.' Not that he'd ever speak to his PA like that. He was charm personified when he spoke to anyone from work. Especially the women.

She opened the minibar again. Maybe just one triangle of the Toblerone. Paolo probably wasn't disappointed. Other people would have arrived early and he would just call them instead. It wasn't even as if their last conversation had been that big of a deal. It was just embarrassing because he was a work colleague. It had been unprofessional. And a bit pathetic.

One more triangle of Toblerone wasn't even a quarter of the bar.

It had been late in the evening on the final day of their last sales conference. Everyone had been tense; the main man from the US had flown over to Munich and they'd all been under huge pressure to impress. Once he'd left to catch his flight, the entire team had headed out for drinks at the Kunstpark. Robert had opened a tab at a bar and told them to do their worst.

The bar was very dark and busy. European pop music thumped out of the speakers. There weren't many available tables, so Laura and Paolo ended up alone in a corner, having bought double drinks at the bar to avoid having to queue twice. She'd had another row with James the night before – he had refused to go out on a double date with Tina and Phil because he was too busy at work for the next few weeks – and she'd had to push down her frustration and anger all day to focus on work. So when Paolo said that she didn't seem herself, it all spilled out. James' refusal to plan anything more than a couple of months into the future in case he needed to work; her worry about his reluctance to talk about marriage and children; that she didn't want to be one of those women desperate for commitment, but that he was turning her into one. The words 'biological clock' had featured quite heavily.

Paolo had sat patiently, nodding and waiting for her to finish. When she did, he looked her straight in the eye. 'He must be insane.'

Her heart had flipped. It sounded like a line from a Richard Curtis film, but he'd been completely serious. She'd tried to bat it away, thanking him for being kind, but he wasn't fobbed off so easily.

'I mean it.' He'd looked at her with those dangerously dark brown eyes. 'You are lovely, Laura. He should beg you to marry him. Before someone else makes a move.'

The 'before someone else makes a move' had been accompanied with a raised eyebrow which had given Laura the urge to cross her legs. She'd been well into her second double vodka tonic by this time and hadn't eaten anything since breakfast, so her radar could have been a little off. But then he'd followed it up by reaching over and taking her hand.

'Are you sure he is the right man for you, Laura?' He always used her name at the end of every sentence like this. Was it an Italian thing? If it was, it was definitely effective. Her name seemed to have extra syllables on his tongue. 'Does he make you happy?'

That particular week James hadn't made her happy at all. Late home most nights with no real apology except, 'It's work, you know how it is' and the final decision that he wasn't going to come to her parents' for the weekend because he 'just needed some time at home to relax.' Before she'd had a chance to answer, Paolo had stood up and was holding out his hand.

'Come on. Dance with me. We need to make you smile.'

Thankfully, he didn't take her in his arms and sweep her around the dance floor. Which was a relief, because she'd never been good at couple dancing. Some of their other colleagues were on the dance floor and they joined them, the abandon in their dance styles driven by the pressure of the day they'd just had. Paolo was laughing and joking with everyone as he usually did and Laura felt a curious mixture of relief and disappointment. Then he leaned in towards her as he passed on his way to the bar and said, 'I think you are absolutely beautiful.' And her stomach flipped again.

Somehow they had ended up in different taxis getting back to the hotel and then everyone had headed up to their rooms, but the next day there had been this kind of a… crackle between them. Paolo had caught her eye more than once and her face had burned every time he discovered her looking at him.

Once they were back at their respective local offices, their contact had been purely professional: conference calls and threads on Slack. He always had her back in the weekly virtual sales meeting with Robert and the rest of the team, though. Supporting her against an interrogative Robert when she argued that it was the consecutive sunny weekends which had caused a dip in retail sales, and emailing her with his contacts at software companies for bundle promotions.

There had been no private conversations until the brief one they'd just had on the phone. But she'd been thinking about him. A lot.

This was ridiculous. She'd been speaking to James less than twenty-four hours ago about their future and even the possibility of starting a family, and here she was daydreaming about a man she hardly knew. Now it was her who was being unfair and unreasonable. James didn't deserve this… this… mental unfaithfulness.

Paolo was just a man she worked with. A man she had only met on a handful of occasions and for only two days each time. A handsome Italian man. What a cliché.

Laura put the rest of the Toblerone back into the minibar, surprised to find there were only two triangles left. There was just enough time to call Shannon quickly before she met up with the others. She needed to focus on damage limitation on her sales figures and Shannon would help. Calm, clever, comforting Shannon. Laura wouldn't have survived at all in this job without her. As she picked up her mobile, there was another WhatsApp from her mother – *Look at the length of the garden on this one! Xxxx* – but there was no reply from James.

CHAPTER SEVEN

Kate

The platform behind Kate had completely emptied out. Even the family of twenty people who had all wanted to kiss and hug each other several times had disappeared, and Kate was starting to feel nervous. Shannon had said she would meet her, hadn't she? What would she do if Shannon didn't turn up? Kate had no actual plan other than to meet up with her friend. What if she was stranded here alone and couldn't find a hotel, or get a ticket back, or… Then she saw her.

Shannon, walking so fast she was almost running in Kate's direction, was waving frantically. Men were turning their heads appreciatively. Shannon was obviously as popular in Paris as she had been in London.

'I can't believe you're actually here!' What was it about an American accent that made people sound instantly cool, like they had just stepped off the set of a sitcom? Jokes just sounded funnier when Shannon told them in her smart East Coast accent. 'How long have I been asking you to come, and then you just turn up without warning and expect me to drop everything and change all my plans to collect you from the train station!' She grinned, threw her arms around Kate and squeezed hard.

Her hug was so tight that Kate could hardly breathe. 'I know, sorry. It was a spur of the moment decision.'

Shannon kept hold of her for longer than Kate was expecting and, when she pulled away, her eyes were bright. If she hadn't known that Shannon never cried, Kate would have sworn there were tears there. She still had hold of Kate's arms as she frowned into her face. 'Is everything okay?'

No. Everything was not okay. Looking into Shannon's kind blue eyes made Kate want to cry. But how could she explain how she was feeling without sounding like a petulant child? Shannon would think she was crazy. Or pathetic. Or ungrateful. Maybe she was. 'Yes, everything's fine. I just wanted to surprise you. Spend some time on our own. Have a girly dinner like the old days.'

Although Kate hadn't actually asked, she was hoping that she could stay overnight with Shannon. She hadn't booked a return ticket yet and, in the last half an hour, had formed the beginnings of a plan for tomorrow. Tonight she would hang out and have fun; tomorrow she would sort out her other problems. Once she'd worked out exactly how to do that.

Shannon stuck out her bottom lip. Close up, she didn't look that well herself. She was terribly pale. 'I can't do dinner tonight; I have a work thing, I'm so sorry. Although I don't know why I'm apologising as you are the one who has given me absolutely zero notice. How long are you planning on being here? Maybe you could come and meet me at the hotel after dinner?' She looked at her watch. 'I can't even stay very long now; I have to meet our team of sales managers at the Louvre.'

Kate felt a stab of jealousy. Shannon's life was clearly a world away from her own 'meetings' at Jungle Madness soft play and adult torture centre. Shannon's life was probably a whirl of stylish bars and clubs and nice restaurants which didn't supply free activity sheets and crayons. What the hell was she going to do tonight if Shannon was busy? And where would she stay now? What had she been thinking, just turning up like this? Should she just turn around and try and get a ticket straight home? A familiar heat rose up in her. *Just breathe. And smile.* 'That's okay. I know your life is crazy busy. I was kind of hoping to stay until tomorrow, maybe get a late train back in the evening? I haven't really… Do you have time for a quick coffee?'

'A super quick one. This is not a great area but there's a tolerable café just around the corner, where the waiters don't roll their eyes at you if you pronounce things wrong. Let's go there.' Shannon pulled Kate's arm through hers and started to lead her towards the road, 'And when we get there you can tell me what this is all about. I'm not buying this surprise story.'

That was easier said than done. Kate didn't really know herself. Unhappiness wasn't the right word, but she wasn't sure what the right word was in English, American or French. The Germans would have a good word for it – they seemed to always have a perfect word for everything. But as her one year of school German had left her able only to say how many brothers and sisters she had and to order a cup of tea, she didn't know what the word was in German either.

The café was typically French: small round tables and wooden chairs packed together inside and spilling out onto the pavement, followed by the aroma of strong, dark coffee and the strains of Bruch's *Violin Concerto No. 2*. Kate closed her eyes for a moment to absorb the warm, smoky smell and mournful sounds – the violin was not her instrument but no one could listen to this particular concerto and not be moved. It touched you. Her heart rate started to slow and her shoulders moved down from her ears. *Breathe.*

Shannon smiled at her, then leaned back in her chair and raised an eyebrow at a young handsome waiter. He came straight over. They always did for her.

'*Qu'est-ce que je vous sers?*' Even the most ordinary-looking man could be transformed into an object of desire when he spoke like that. How could Kate have left it so long to come back to Paris? The language, the music, the food: she loved it all.

Shannon ordered two coffees and a croissant for Kate – apparently she'd just eaten and wasn't hungry – and the waiter nodded and left. 'So, come on, spill. What's going on? The last time you did something this impulsive, I ended up cutting my head open on the glove compartment of your car.'

A giggle bubbled in Kate's stomach. That had been pre-Luke. Convinced the guy she was dating was two-timing her, she'd made Shannon accompany her on a stake-out of the pub he'd gone to. When he'd come to the door of the pub, Shannon had shouted 'Go! Go! Go!' and Kate had stuck her foot on the accelerator so hard that Shannon – who had been crouching forwards, taking her undercover role seriously – had ended up headbutting the glove compartment.

'I'd forgotten about that! Your poor eye!'

'Yeah, well. It wasn't the only time a night out with you ended in physical harm. Good job I love you.'

This was what Kate needed. Less than an hour in Shannon's company and she already felt better. It had been a good idea to meet Shannon and talk things through, get her head straight, but she couldn't do it on a time limit. What was she going to say? That she felt… lost? Finding yourself was something that happened on a gap-year break in Asia at eighteen. It was more than a little careless to be forty-one, married with kids and a mortgage, and realise you'd lost yourself again.

'Let's talk about that later. Tell me about you: what have you been doing since you moved here? How's the job going? How's it going with Robert? It's been a year now – isn't that a record for you?'

Shannon blew on her coffee. She hadn't actually drunk anything yet. 'Yeah, everything's great. Work is good – super, super busy, but good. Weekends are lazy, though. I still haven't found a gym I like here so I seem to spend most of the time drinking coffee and reading.'

Kate felt a wave of unbridled jealousy. This was what she missed. This easiness, this ability to do what you wanted, whenever you wanted. To be able to get up late on a Saturday, wander out for breakfast and spend all morning with the newspaper. When was the last time she'd read a newspaper? Not counting reading the headlines whilst in the queue in the supermarket. Sometimes Luke would come home and ask what she thought about some international disaster and she hadn't even been aware that it had happened. The country could be at war and she wouldn't even know until the tanks drove up the path.

Shannon reached forward and squeezed Kate's arm. 'I haven't met any good party buddies though. I've missed you so much. I can't find anyone here who wants to take their heels off, walk home, cut their foot on a broken glass, end up in A&E and serenade the cab driver on the way home. I mean, these French chicks, they just don't know how to enjoy themselves.'

Kate screwed up her eyes and laughed. Had that really been her? If felt like another life. 'I'm amazed we're still alive sometimes. When Alice gets to that age I'm going to put a GoPro on her head and watch it like a hawk. What about Robert? I bet he takes you out to some fabulous places. Or do you *stay in*?'

'He does take me to fabulous places. Although, there's only so much champagne and oysters a girl can take,' Shannon winked at her, her eyes bright, then took a deep breath and leaned back in her chair, stretching her long legs under the table. 'You were absolutely right about Paris; it's a great place to live. The fashion. The art. The amazing food.'

At the mention of food, Kate felt a cold trickle down her back. Dinner! She hadn't got any food out of the freezer for dinner. She smacked her forehead with the palm of her hand.

Shannon put her head on one side. 'What's the matter?'

Kate groaned. 'You talking about food made me realise that I haven't got anything out for the children's dinner.'

Shannon frowned. 'Surely Luke can feed his own children?'

Kate shook her head. 'Well, yes he can *feed* them. It's *what* he will feed them that's the problem. He'll probably take them to Café M's.'

Shannon raised her coffee cup to her lips and took the tiniest sip before putting it down again. 'Well, that sounds civilised.'

'It's not. Café M's is *McDonald's.*' Kate paused for emphasis. She'd discovered this code name by accident when Alice had been overly keen for Luke to 'take us to Café M's again, Daddy'. Kate had asked Alice where Café M's was and had been told, 'It's the place with the big yellow "M" on the front.' After that, Luke had sheepishly confessed.

Shannon didn't seem shocked. 'Surely that's okay now and then? Anyway, how is lovely Luke? How are the children?'

'Yeah, good, great.' Kate fumbled in her bag for her mobile as her brain ran through dinner suggestions she could text to Luke. She also knew better than to get her phone out and show photos to Shannon. Of course Shannon would pretend to be interested, but...

Shannon leaned forwards. 'Have you got any photos of the kids?'

That was a surprise. 'Of course.' Kate thumbed through her mobile and found a really cute one. The two of them at the bottom of a slide, Alice holding Thomas between her legs. They were so beautiful. *Stop feeling guilty.*

'They're gorgeous, Kate. Like mini versions of you and Luke.' Shannon continued to stare at the photo as if she was searching for forensic evidence. 'How did you know that you wanted kids?'

How had they known? They'd been married for three years. Luke had his promotion in the offing. Kate had been bored senseless with her job and more than happy to have a reason to leave. 'I don't know, really, Shan. We just kind of thought it was a good time. Why?' Kate narrowed her eyes. 'Don't tell me you're getting *broody?*'

Shannon snapped her attention away from the screen and handed the phone back. 'Me?' She frowned and shook her head. 'Don't be silly!'

Kate's phone pinged. A text from the school. Her stomach plummeted. She sucked in a long breath and let it out slowly. *Be rational.* If one of the children had nose-dived off the play equipment or caught norovirus they would be calling, not texting. *Don't panic.*

But when she saw the message, it was almost as bad. She let her head fall down on the table.

'What's the matter?' Shannon put her drink down and her hand on Kate's arm. 'Is everything okay?'

Kate lifted her head and groaned. 'It's a text from the school ParentCall system. To remind all the crap parents like me that it's dress like a frickin' farmer day on Monday.'

Shannon sat back in her chair and laughed. 'What the hell is that craziness?'

Kate pressed her fingers into her eye sockets. How the hell had she not known about this? She had a vague memory of some paper mashed up in the bottom of Alice's bag last week, sodden from a leaky water bottle accident. She'd been swearing about it under her breath – *Why the hell do they have to bring those bottles to and from school and not just leave them there? They've got taps, haven't they?* – and she definitely remembered scraping out the bottom of the bag and slapping what had looked like a failed papier mâché project into the recycling bin. There had been some choice 'square words'.

She split her fingers apart and looked through them at Shannon. 'Apparently they are planting seeds and the kids are dressing up.'

Shannon screwed up her face. 'In heaven's name, why? I mean, the planting thing I get, but why do they need a costume?'

Kate took her fingers away from her face and shrugged. 'To make it fun, I guess. Or possibly just to torture the parents who now have to run around like headless chickens to find a damn costume.'

Shannon picked up her coffee, sniffed it and put it down again. 'What do farmers even wear? Jeans? Overalls? Doesn't she have a pair of jeans?'

Kate shook her head slowly. 'It's not as easy as all that. I'll need to get a checked shirt from somewhere. A straw hat, maybe.' She started to tap on the desk. 'It's too late for eBay. And if I get the last train home tomorrow our local Primark will be closed and I don't think it's open on a Sunday. I wonder if Sainsbury's would have something suitable? And cheap.'

Shannon laughed. Kate had forgotten how deep and sexy her laugh was. It wasn't wasted on the two guys who looked over from the table by the door. 'Are you insane? Why has she got to have a checked shirt and a *hat*?'

Kate sighed deeply. It was like explaining it to Luke. 'Because I would stake my life that the rest of the children will have that already sorted out. And hair! What do girl farmers do with their hair? Plaits? I am totally crap at doing plaits.' And she would also stake her life that Melissa's daughter would have some sheaves-of-wheat-entwined hair construction. Harvest festival hair. Dammit.

Shannon leaned forward and patted her hand. 'Okay, crazy lady. That's enough now. Stick her in jeans and a T-shirt and be done with it.'

Kate didn't try to explain. Shannon didn't have kids. She wouldn't understand. She pressed down the butterflies in her stomach. She'd call Nina as soon as she got to her hotel. Or as soon as she actually found a hotel. This last-minute thing was a little bit stressful.

Shannon reached over and squeezed Kate's hand. 'What are you going to do tonight on your own? I feel really guilty leaving you, and we haven't even talked properly yet.'

Kate opened her mouth to reassure her that she'd be fine, when a rather tall gentleman made his way over.

'Well, well. Shannon Ryan! How are you?'

Shannon stood and hugged him. 'Graham! I'm great, this is my friend Kate – she's from England, too. Kate, this is Graham Sparks. He used to work in the office on the same floor as mine.'

Graham nodded hello at Kate. 'I'm back in the UK now. Although I seem to be over here more often than when I lived here. Do you live in Paris?'

Kate shook her head. 'No, just here for a short break. Trying to pin Shannon down for two seconds.'

Graham laughed and held up his hands. 'Then I'll leave you to it. Good to see you, Shannon. I'll send you an email. Maybe we can have lunch.'

After he kissed Shannon on both cheeks and left, Kate raised an eyebrow at her. 'Old flame?'

'Graham? No, no. He's married with a couple of children. They were all living over here but it sounds as if he's moved the family back home. Anyway, I have to go soon and we still haven't spoken about why you're suddenly here.' She paused for a moment. 'You didn't only come to see me, did you?'

Kate still didn't know how to describe what was going on. 'No, I came to… It'll take too long to explain now. Can you help me to find a hotel?' She'd feel better once she had somewhere definite to stay. And had called Nina about the costumes. And texted Luke with dinner instructions, and…

Shannon reached over and patted Kate's hand. 'Actually, you're in luck. One of the sales guys got fired yesterday – obviously not lucky for *him*, poor guy – and it was too late to cancel his room for this conference we're holding today and tomorrow. So, there's a spare room at the hotel. I'm going into the office now, but I can text you the hotel address to show a taxi driver.' She plucked her mobile from the tiny bag on her shoulder and sent a text with a few strokes of her thumb. 'That way I can meet up with you later tonight after dinner.' She paused and raised an eyebrow. 'If you're still awake?'

Kate slapped a hand over her yawn. 'That would be great. And maybe we could have breakfast together in the morning?' Kate had no idea yet if she would be able to make the arrangements for the plan that had begun to germinate in her mind. But, as long as she could book the tickets she planned to, she would definitely have the morning to herself.

Shannon leaned over and kissed her. 'I'll call you later.'

At least Kate had a hotel now, and maybe they would have a restaurant or would be able to recommend somewhere local for dinner tonight. She wasn't as brave now as she had been in the old days, when she'd happily wander out for an evening alone and see where the night took her. With or without her shoes.

There were a few hours left of the afternoon yet and, as well as calling Nina about 'dress like a farmer' and checking the Eurostar website, she had a couple of favourite places she wanted to visit before dinner time. She checked her phone messages. There was one from Luke: *Kate, can you call me? I might be late tonight.* If she replied now, it would ruin everything. She might even find herself on a train home to Kent. Nina was already on standby to pick up the kids. Her mobile went back into her bag.

CHAPTER EIGHT

Shannon

What the hell had happened to Kate? Stressing because her kids might have to have chicken nuggets for dinner? And this from the girl who used to count the slice of tomato in her late night dirty kebab as one of her five a day.

The smell of the man next to her on the platform was beginning to get to her, so Shannon shuffled down further. Either Paris was getting a lot more pungent or she was developing a superhuman sense of smell. Was that a pregnancy thing? Or her age? Now she was beside a woman who had quite possibly taken a bath in Chanel that morning. Shannon shuffled further along.

And what was it with the farmer dress-up thing? The old Kate would have laughed at the idea of spending money on a costume rather than sticking on a pair of jeans and a big smile. Was this what Shannon would turn into if she had this baby? She'd seen it before. Perfectly happy, fun, outgoing women who had children and turned kind of *soggy*. Partying less: wimping out at ten p.m. or not coming out altogether. Kate used to be so much *fun*. Once, at a house party she'd organised, she'd locked the front door and refused to let anyone go home before two a.m. One of the guys had spelled out '*Help*' on the window sill in mini donuts. Kate had stood over him with her hands on her hips and made him eat every single one.

The platform was getting more crowded. And smellier. There was also a crooked sales poster screaming at Shannon to be straightened. She'd give it five more minutes and then give up and look for a taxi outside.

Why hadn't she told Kate she was pregnant?

She'd meant to. But saying it out loud would make it kind of real and she wasn't ready for that. No one else knew yet. No one. Well, the man in the pharmacy just now probably had his suspicions, but he didn't count. Before she could tell anyone, she needed to get her own head around it. Moving to another country was one thing, but was she brave enough to move herself into a completely different life?

And why had she made out to Kate that her life was so great? That's how she usually acted towards women who pitied her for not having a husband. The ones who would ask in the first three minutes of meeting if she was married or had children. And then put their heads on one side or wrinkle their noses or even – as had actually happened once – say, 'That's a shame. I'm sure you'd be a really nice mummy.' Something would kick in then, and Shannon would show off about how she could lie in bed late or eat in fancy restaurants on a whim. But she didn't need to do that with Kate. So why had she?

And why had she left it so long since she'd last seen her? It wasn't just the move to Paris. The final year that Shannon had still been in London, they'd barely seen each other. Since Kate had had the children, she never came in to the capital. Shannon had made the trip out to visit her a couple of times, but they'd ended up sitting around the house with the kids, then popping out for dinner at a local restaurant where Kate could hardly stay awake through dessert. There had been no sign of the Kate who would stand on the toilet seat and lean over the top of Shannon's cubicle, jabbering about a cute guy she'd just seen. Or stay up all night talking. Of course, life had to change logistically when you had kids. But did you have to become a completely different person?

The platform had become unbearable. It wasn't just the smell; the heat was oppressive. Shannon headed for the exit, counting at least three pregnant women on the way there. Where the hell were they all coming from? Was it an epidemic?

It wasn't that Shannon disliked kids; it was just that she didn't really know what to do with them. She had nieces and nephews who she absolutely adored – she'd been to see them only a few weeks ago on a trip back to the US – but she enjoyed their company a lot more now they were older and she could have a conversation with them. One of the advantages of working in a busy sales environment was that she rarely had to encounter children. Even those female colleagues who had kids rarely spoke about them in case it hampered their chances for promotion. It was wrong, of course, but it had suited Shannon just fine. Until now.

As she left the station, Shannon gulped down the fresher air. She would walk for a while and cool down before finding a cab. The road was loud and busy: cars revving their impatience; horns blared in anger – Parisian drivers were not known for their patience. On the pavements, business people jostled for space amongst tourists, the former walking a lot faster than the latter. Somehow Shannon got stuck behind an elderly American couple wearing the stock US tourist uniform: checked shorts, slogan T-shirts and sun visors. The pavement was too busy for her to pull out and overtake, so she was stuck behind a couple of embarrassing compatriots. Fabulous.

But even though their snail's pace would normally drive Shannon insane, there was something sweet about the two of them. The man was holding the woman's hand, which was threaded through the crook of his arm, and was pointing out the architecture of the buildings around them. Meanwhile, his wife was nodding and listening and saying, 'That's lovely, my dear.'

Maybe it was the accent which made her homesick, or maybe it was the 'my' that really got to Shannon. Right in the throat, where a huge lump had mysteriously formed. She'd had the same thing when she hugged Kate. A need to feel at home. It was crazy. After her recent trip back home to the U.S., she'd returned to Paris without a backwards glance. This was her home now. For now, at least. The elderly American couple crossed the road and Shannon picked up the pace. She just needed some water. Then she'd be okay.

The first place she saw that would sell bottled water was a bakery. Standing in line, the smell of the bread made her stomach rumble. The sickness seemed to have gone; she hadn't been able to face a croissant at the café with Kate, but maybe she could manage one of those small, soft *pains au sucre* behind the glass counter.

She checked her watch. Before she went into the office, she needed to get to the Louvre and meet up with the sales guys briefly. It was a pointless detour, but she needed to show her face before tonight and make sure everyone was okay. She particularly wanted to check in with Laura. That girl worried her: she clearly wasn't happy. It was none of Shannon's business, but she'd love to bring her over to Paris and show her how much fun she could have if she let herself go a bit. She was only in her early thirties, for Pete's sake. And she was such a worrier. In the last two days, Shannon had had about ten messages from her – she was in full panic mode. One of her major customers was causing problems and she was anxious that she wouldn't make her number for the quarter. All of the sales guys were terrified of Robert; he could be a real hard-ass at times. If only they knew how soft he could be underneath that sharp exterior.

Was she smiling again? That had been happening a lot recently when she thought about Robert. Could pregnancy hormones be changing her? Did it happen that soon? He had been very sweet the night before. Although it was probably due to his ulterior motive: getting her to meet his daughters.

Robert had taken her to dinner last night to their favourite restaurant in Rue Mouffetard. The area had a youthful buzz, which Shannon loved, and there were always far fewer tourists than you'd find in Saint-Michel. Sometimes she and Robert would take a long stroll on a Saturday morning to shop at the market; the brie sold here was the softest and most delicious of any in Paris. Even on a busy evening, the village feel and the quiet, isolated alleyways and cobbled streets made it perfect for clandestine walks. They were unlikely to meet people from work.

Last night, they had walked slowly up the steep hill together, hand in hand like young lovers. Robert had wanted to take a cab, but Shannon had insisted on walking. Her reward at the top was a bowl of unparalleled French onion soup: rich, velvety caramelised onions, strings of Gruyère cheese and one huge toasted crouton. She would have walked three steep hills to get to it. Maybe that had been a craving? She'd managed to explain away her refusal of wine by saying she'd wanted a clear head for today. Pretty soon he was going to get suspicious, though.

Though she hadn't liked him, Shannon had been attracted to Robert from the first time she'd met him. Tall, dark and with enough charisma to float a boat in; hell – she wasn't made of stone. At the beginning, she'd been employed as his PA and there had been comments and blushes and heat. But it had taken a while for anything to happen between them.

One night, they had worked late in the office, just the two of them. Robert had collected pizza from a nearby restaurant and they'd eaten while they worked, sitting at a round conference table in Robert's office. Shannon had been helping Robert put together a detailed strategy plan for his direct boss – the Vice President of International Sales who was based in California. It hadn't taken long for Robert to work out that Shannon had a talent for strategy and customer management, and she was starting to take on more and more responsibility. She enjoyed doing it. Enjoyed being with him. Sitting close to him.

She'd moved the pizza box from the conference table and laid out the printouts of slides from the presentation she'd put together. It was a good piece of work, even if she did say so herself.

Robert obviously agreed. Although he was looking at her, rather than at the pieces of paper. 'Incredible.'

Shannon had smiled with satisfaction. 'You're right. I am.'

He had laughed then. A deep, warm laugh. 'You are very different from other women I know.'

Robert had found a bottle of wine that had been sent to him from their PR firm and they had continued to talk after the plan had been finished, drinking wine from coffee cups.

'What made you come to Europe when you were young? Don't you miss America?'

Shannon sipped her wine – it was a very good Sancerre; she was obviously getting more discerning – and took a moment to consider. There *were* things she missed. And people she missed. But she was better off here. Away. On her own. 'No. I like being in Europe.'

Robert put down his cup of wine and nodded. 'Yes. It's better here.'

Shannon grabbed a plastic document wallet and hit the side of his arm with it. 'Hey! I didn't say that!'

Robert caught the wallet and held it. He looked deep into her eyes. What could he see there? She shivered, but didn't look away. Her heart was pounding. Slowly, he leaned in and kissed her.

She enjoyed the kiss for several moments, then pulled away. 'We shouldn't do this. I have a policy to not get involved with *any* colleagues, let alone my boss.' This was true. For a start, most of her managers in the past had been married. Not that this would have stopped some of them, but it had definitely stopped her.

Even if they'd been single, it was just a complication she didn't need. Keep life straightforward.

Robert nodded, but held her gaze. 'And I have never *got involved* with an employee. Sometimes policies have to be changed.'

The first few months they had dated had been so much fun. Acting as if nothing was happening between them at the office had made it so forbidden and exciting. Of course, it hadn't taken Fabienne long to work out what was going on – their office manager was almost a witch, her intuition was so strong – but no one else in the office knew, even now.

Of course, Shannon had assumed she would be moving on again soon, anyway. She'd been with this company for over a year and this was usually about the time that she started to get itchy feet. It didn't matter about sleeping with your boss if you thought he wouldn't be your boss in a few months' time. As long as it didn't affect any future references. *Shannon is very efficient at time management and French kissing.*

The bakery queue moved forwards and Shannon went with it. She couldn't take her eyes from the tray of *chouquettes* on the top shelf of the display cabinet. The little puff pastries encrusted with sugar were in a perfect formation of sixteen, which was very satisfying to look at. Until the assistant took one. From the very middle. Her phone pinged just as she reached the front of the queue – she must have lost and regained the signal. There were two messages: one from Robert, one from Laura. She paid for her bottle of water and eyed up the tray of *chouquettes*. Too risky? Probably.

Outside again, she listened to the voicemails as she waited in line for a taxi, pressing her mobile hard to her ear to block out the traffic. Laura's first, as she pretty much knew that Robert would just be chasing her up to get to the Louvre on time. Even though she wasn't technically his PA any more, he seemed to need her even more than when she had been. Sometimes she felt more like a wife than a colleague. She shuddered.

Laura's voicemail was just updating Shannon on the customer with the big return – it had been hanging over her head for the last two weeks, the poor girl. There was nothing Shannon could do except sympathise and tell her that they'd deal with it when it happened. Since Shannon had taken on the team coordinator role, the sales guys treated her like their mom – telling her their customer problems so that she could break the news gently to Robert. Not that it did any good; even she couldn't shelter them from his volcanic outbursts. How would they react if they knew that she was sleeping with him? It was hardly professional.

At the end of her message, Laura had made a nonchalant remark that she had already spoken to Paolo and wondered who else had confirmed for the meeting. Laura must have heard the rumour about someone having been fired. Shannon was pretty sure she'd be happy it wasn't Paolo. Bless her.

Shannon had only met Laura's boyfriend once – he had joined them for a drink one time when Shannon and Robert had been at the London office. She hadn't been keen. Laura had been so excited for Shannon to meet James – apparently he was often *very* busy at work – but all he had talked about was himself and his boring job. He'd just landed some celebrity client that he claimed he couldn't talk about. But he had sure used a lot of words *not* talking about them. In his defence, he had been quite attentive to Laura, holding her chair out for her and so on. But there was something that didn't quite work between the two of them. They didn't *fit*.

Laura would fit much better with the lovely Paolo. Shannon had worked with him since she'd started at the company, and he was a total sweetheart. He clearly had a thing for Laura, too. They would be a very cute couple. Should she give things a little nudge? No. She was the last person to be giving out relationship advice, the mess she'd got herself into. Kate used to tell her off all the time for trying to play matchmaker. She just liked to see people *happy*. And she'd made a good job of fixing up Kate and Luke. Hadn't she?

Robert's message was, as expected, pleading with her to make sure she got to the Louvre to meet them after their tour. Anyone would think he wasn't capable of herding a small group of grown professionals out of the gallery and onto a minibus. It wasn't the logistics that were the problem, though. It was the small talk he hated. That's why he ended up talking business all the time; he didn't know what else to talk to people about. Actually, she'd better get a move on to save the team as he'd probably already unofficially started the sales presentations halfway through the Egyptian room. Robert's stony stare would give Tutankhamun a run for his money.

Before she clicked her phone off, she noticed another missed call. This time the caller hadn't left a voicemail. It was a number she didn't have stored in her contacts. An American number. Chicago code.

Please God let it be a misdial.

CHAPTER NINE

Laura

The hotel lobby was large and modern. Apart from the long reception desk, there were small round tables and brightly coloured chairs filled with suits and laptops, and the air was alive with twenty different languages. Laura could see the rest of the team assembled to one side: Gabriella from Germany, André from the French office, Mark from Holland, Sylvie from Spain and Henrik from Sweden. No Paolo yet. She breathed out.

She walked the twenty steps over to them and joined in the 'Hello's and 'How are things?' There were plenty of mumblings about the lack of sales recently, which changed into positive smiles when Robert came over. No point giving him food for thought before tomorrow's presentations.

'Good to see you, everyone!' Tall, slim, dark and very, very smooth. Dressed in a well-cut suit and open-necked shirt, he could have stepped off the cover of a magazine. James had started to wear suits like this in the last couple of years, but his stocky frame didn't carry them off quite as well.

Robert waved a sheaf of papers in the air. 'Shannon will join us at the museum later, once we've finished our tour. She's made sure I know what I'm doing. Are we all here?'

'We are now!' Paolo jogged up, a little out of breath, looking very cool in a linen shirt and jeans. His hair was so dark and his top button wasn't… *Stop it. Just stop it.*

'Great,' Robert held up his papers like a tour guide. 'Let's head!' It was funny to hear Robert use American phrases. He must have picked them up from Shannon.

Laura attached herself to Gabriella and Sylvie. They were speaking in Spanish and she felt guilty that they had to swap to English when she joined them. Paolo was walking with André about five metres in front; she was safe in the short term. But what were the two men laughing at? Was Paolo looking back? Why did she care? *You are a grown woman. Stop acting like a teenager.*

'We are talking about our worries for tomorrow,' Sylvie glanced ahead to ensure Robert was outside of audio range. 'We think it is going to be a tough day. The sales presentations.'

'Not for you, surely, Gabriella?' Laura was surprised. Gabriella was currently the blue-eyed girl of the company. She had just secured a huge retail deal and smashed her target for the quarter. She should be happy. Not that it showed on her face.

Gabriella shrugged, 'I don't think anyone is safe at the moment. Shannon told me Robert has been having big arguments with the US about our numbers. Even his job isn't safe.'

'Hey, who wants to be safe? Safe is boring.' Dropping back to join them, Paolo had appeared at her elbow. How had she not spotted him coming? 'Living on the edge is much more fun. Don't you think, Laura?' He raised an eyebrow at her. He was flirtatious with everyone and she should not be blushing like this. But the way he said her name…

He was still looking at her intently, expecting a reply. Oddly, so was Gabriella. 'Actually, I think safety is underrated.'

The minibus Shannon had booked for them was just a few metres from the front of the hotel. When they got on, Gabriella and Sylvie sat together. Laura dithered; she didn't want to end up next to Paolo. In the end, she had to sit up the front with Robert. He was checking through the paperwork Shannon had given him, so she was free to look out of the window.

The woman on the train had been right: Paris *was* beautiful. Every street they drove along looked like a scene from the kind of black and white photograph you would find on a restaurant wall. A glimpse of the Eiffel Tower in the distance made her gasp: so familiar, yet so new.

The streets were full of people; well-dressed, beautiful people. As they drove around the Arc de Triomphe and up the wide avenue of the Champs-Élysées, Laura wanted to be out there with them, wandering slowly with arms full of paper shopping bags. As they paused in traffic, she caught sight of a woman and her young daughter, just sitting on a bench, eating an ice cream. No cares in the world.

'Your first time in Paris?' Robert broke into her thoughts.

She nodded. 'Yes, I've always wanted to come.' She could hear James' voice in her head: *Paris is such a cliché.* 'How far is it to the Louvre?' Her stomach was full of butterflies. Worry about her order being returned, the argument with James, seeing Paolo again and now having to go to an art gallery: they were not her favourite places.

'Not far. Past the Place de la Concorde and then we're almost there. Do you like art?'

Laura didn't have anything against art. It was the people who liked it who had caused her some issues. 'I don't really know much about it, to be honest.'

Robert lowered his voice. 'I don't know much about it, either. It was Shannon's idea. She loves art galleries. Apparently she dreamed of being an artist when she was a young girl. Studied art at college.' Robert's eyes changed when he talked about Shannon, Laura noticed. He lost a little of his stiffness. He softened.

Shannon had been an art student? That was surprising. Laura had shared halls with a group of art students at university and they had been an airy fairy, unreliable bunch. Particularly Liam. She shuddered at the memory.

The minibus dropped them alongside the pyramid in front of the Louvre and Laura resisted the urge to pretend she was here to solve the Da Vinci code. Inside, the Louvre was huge. Echoed footsteps bounced from the ceiling to the floor and huge staircases swept in front of them; it would be an agoraphobic's worst nightmare. Their tour guide met them and explained that there wasn't time to fully explore the vast galleries but that he would take them to see two of the most famous exhibits: the *Venus de Milo* and the *Mona Lisa*. At least Laura had heard of them. Something to tick off the 'Things to see before you die' list.

But the *Mona Lisa* was a bit of a disappointment. For a start, the canvas was really small; much smaller than Laura had been expecting. Secondly, it was behind a glass case and surrounded by a rope so no one could get anywhere near it. Thirdly, there was a constant flock of tourists obscuring her view. Therefore, she was trying to look at a small painting, from a distance, through glass and other people's hair. She tried in vain to get closer but to no avail. She'd have to just buy the postcard in the gift shop and look at that.

Gabriella and Sylvie were chatting animatedly in Spanish and Laura didn't want to impose herself on them a second time, so she wandered away to look at some of the other portraits in the room. She slipped her mobile out of her pocket and checked her email – still no returns approval request – and then had a quick thumb through Instagram.

Tina had posted a photograph of a passport with its number and security information blurred out. It took Laura a few moments to recognise the name: Tina Hanson. She'd written a comment – *Finally changed my passport to my married name!* – and tagged a few of their friends. Their married friends. Not Laura. Obviously, she couldn't tag the saddo who'd had a boyfriend longer than any of them but just wasn't good enough to actually attain the gold band on her ring finger. Was this some kind of

'Mrs' club now? Only people on at least their first surname change need apply? Did they sit around and discuss married things like... bouquets and... joint accounts and... married bloody sexual positions?

Laura was being unfair. Tina wouldn't have tagged her because she was thoughtful and wouldn't have wanted to rub her (unmarried) nose in it. But Laura still wanted to throw her phone across the room, right through the crowd, right into Mona Lisa's smug – probably married – bloody face. Or cry.

'Not impressed with Mona?' Paolo was behind her. How did he move so soundlessly?

'Art appreciation isn't really my strength.' Laura painted on a smile, pocketed her mobile and turned to face him. 'I was more of a maths and science girl.' She lowered her voice. 'Is it wrong that I wanted her to be about two hundred percent bigger?'

Paolo grinned. 'A lot of people say that – although they are not quite so mathematically specific. I suppose her reputation is so huge, we want her to be big too.' He glanced back at the portrait, 'But what about that smile, eh? I wonder what she is thinking about.'

Laura followed his gaze. 'Probably, *hurry up and finish, Leonardo, my bottom is going numb.*'

Paolo laughed. 'I can see we need to work on your art education. You must come to Italy and I will take you to the Uffizi.'

Damn those butterflies in her stomach. This was not the first time she'd had a man wax lyrical about the Uffizi Gallery. Was it that memory which made her feel so strange or the way that Paolo was now looking at her? *He is just making conversation; he knows you have a boyfriend.* 'You are an art expert then?' Laura tried in vain not to sound remotely flirtatious.

Paolo shrugged. 'Not an expert, just an admirer. I like to find a gallery in every city I visit. You can learn a lot about people from the things they find to be precious.'

Laura narrowed her eyes. Was he feeding her a line? But he wasn't even looking at her now; he was looking at the painting in front of them. Not for the first time, she wondered how someone like him had ended up selling computer hardware for a living; he should have been an artist himself, or a writer, maybe. She could imagine him on a retreat in the middle of nowhere, creating something wonderful. Pen or paintbrush in hand, shirt unbuttoned to the... *Stop it!*

She shook the image from her head. Steer the conversation onto lighter, safer, territory. 'Whereas I like to find a cake shop in every city that I visit: you can tell a lot about people from the dessert that they choose.'

Paolo threw his head back and laughed, drawing a disapproving look from an older gentleman nearby and a different kind of look from the younger woman he was with. Five minutes in his company and Laura felt witty and attractive. How did he do that?

The tour guide called across to them. 'Time to move on, please.' And then Henrik called Paolo over. Paolo winked at her and moved away.

Laura's legs felt a little wobbly as she followed the group. Maybe it was the amount of coffee she'd drunk today. She definitely didn't feel quite herself. And the last thing she wanted was for Paolo to teach her about art; her one experience in that realm – with Liam – hadn't ended well at all.

'Here, ladies and gentlemen, is *Aphrodite of Milos*, better known as the *Venus de Milo*. One of the most famous examples of ancient Greek sculpture, it is believed to depict Aphrodite, the Greek goddess of love and beauty.'

After the disappointment in the size of Mona, Laura was pleased that Venus' proportions didn't disappoint. Despite her lack of arms, she cut a pretty impressive figure. According to the tour guide, she was two hundred and three centimetres tall.

'What do you think of her?' she asked Paolo, who had silently reappeared beside her again.

He nodded and held his chin in mock contemplation. 'I wouldn't leave her lonely.' He winked. 'Although I've heard she's rather *cold*-hearted.'

Laura nudged him. 'Actually, I've heard she's pretty *'armless.'*

Paolo groaned and nudged her back. The hairs on her arms stood to attention. Traitors. And something weird was going on with her breathing.

The expression on Paolo's face changed and he made a small nod to the left of her: Robert was walking towards them. Paolo didn't move his mouth as he whispered, 'Quick, save yourself.' And then slipped away.

'How are things in the UK?' Robert probably wasn't far off two hundred and three centimetres tall himself. Although he did have arms. Which were often folded. He also had the habit of looking at you directly and deeply in the eyes as if he could read what you were thinking. *He doesn't need to know about the Boots nail varnish.* Laura's heart started to race a little. Did he know about the stock return issue?

Robert always did this, brought up work when they were supposedly socialising. Perhaps he had learned it from a Machiavellian Management programme: 1) Get them relaxed 2) Fire off a difficult question 3) Watch them flail around like a tipped-up tortoise. If Shannon had been here, she would have distracted him to give them all a break, but she still hadn't arrived. Laura really wanted to talk to her. And not just about this distribution customer who was threatening to return their order and destroy her sales figures for the quarter. Shannon had become a friend. One who wasn't part of the 'Mrs Club', either.

'Not bad, not bad. Picking up a little.' Laura put a hand on the mobile phone in her pocket. Had they emailed through a returns document yet? *Divert. Distract.* 'What time did you say Shannon was joining us?'

Robert looked at his watch. 'She's going to meet us as we leave here. I'll send her a text and find out whether she's finished where she is.' He smiled, with his mouth but not his eyes, as he took out his phone. 'We'll catch up on those sales figures later, eh?' There was no getting one over on him.

Laura was not a natural saleswoman. She'd originally planned to be an accountant, the same as James, but she'd known at the end of their three-year course that it wasn't for her. She'd loved working with numbers, but the legal documents they'd had to read had made her want to pluck her eyes out after about two pages. The art history girls she'd lived with would laugh and tell her they were taking her out to rescue her from the 'Tyranny of Numbers'.

The life of an art history student was very different from that of an accountancy student. Laura had had classes every day – the maths in particular had been intense – but the girls in her halls had seemed to spend more time in the university bar than they had in a lecture hall. They had persuaded her to come out with them every night and it had been exciting, different, daring. She'd never met people like this at the small comprehensive she'd been to. Liam had been one of the boys on the art history course.

If Laura had known more about art and artists, she might have read something into the fact that Liam's favourite artist was Van Gogh – although in Liam's defence, he had never showed a tendency to remove his body parts. There had been a lot of other warning signs, though. For a start, he'd had a very easy-going relationship with money. If he had money, he would spend it like water on whoever was in the room. If he didn't, he was more than happy to 'borrow' from others or allow them to spend their money on him. Laura's family hadn't been poor growing up, but they hadn't had much to spare, either. She'd been taught to be careful with money, not spend beyond her means. Still, there was something about this boy which had attracted her. He was different. Dangerous. For the first time in her life, she hadn't played it safe. In any sense of the word. A late-night party at one of the boy's houses. Too much cheap wine. A dark room. Deep conversation. Hot breath, whispered words. Instinct over logic. Four hands. Two bodies. And the first and last one-night stand of her life.

The next morning, he'd waved at her across the quad, then continued to chat up the girl he was sitting with. After that, he'd been friendly but uninterested. Laura had been hurt, embarrassed and angry at herself for being so naïve.

When you were at university, there were available men hanging from the trees, so it was only six weeks later that Laura had started seeing James. He was on her course but she'd never really noticed him before. If Liam had been a scatter graph, James was a line of best fit: a smooth, steady progression. Inexperienced and a little old-fashioned, they didn't sleep together until over three months into the relationship – a rare feat in that permissive environment. That's why she'd known for certain it wasn't his when she'd discovered that she was pregnant.

CHAPTER TEN

Kate

Hotels rooms were so wonderfully tidy, so clear of anything except the essentials. There was a walnut desk, a small wardrobe and a pristine bed that Kate would be able to sleep in all night long by herself. No snoring husbands and no midnight visits from wriggling offspring and their soggy, well-loved toys. Kate put her bag down on the bed and went to check out the bathroom. White. Clean. *Empty*. Perfect.

Kate's fantasy self would live in a whole house like this; there would be no overflowing kitchen drawers full of salad servers, pencil sharpeners and tiddlywinks. No walk of fire across the living room over vicious pieces of Lego. No collection of plastic lids stacked up, waiting to be reunited with their missing partner containers.

In a previous life, she'd stayed in hotels all the time, and had been to most of the major cities in Europe for one team meeting or another. Just like that girl on the train. It had been a lot of fun, especially once Shannon had joined the crew. They'd go out dancing all night and still be up for a breakfast meeting. Once, at a nightclub in Antwerp, Kate had whispered, 'We have to go home; I'm so drunk it feels like the floor is moving.' Shannon had held her stomach and laughed for about twenty minutes. How was Kate supposed to have known the place had a tilting dance floor? It didn't matter how drunk they'd been though, no one would ever have realised it the next day. She couldn't do that now.

She needed to text Luke, to let him know that she was here. But what was she going to say? Would she tell him everything straight away? About her plan for tomorrow? She should check the tickets first. Once she had made up her mind that it wasn't a completely insane idea.

It was uncomfortably quiet in here. Kate's heart was racing again. She sat on the edge of the bed and thumbed through her mobile for some music to fill the void and calm her mind. Maybe one of the French impressionists? Like their painter counterparts – Monet, Manet, Renoir – they created a mood and an atmosphere without worrying about the details of the story. She found Erik Satie and lay back on cool sheets, letting the sounds of his *Gnossienne* soothe her. This was what she missed most about playing the piano. The escape. Her fingers tapped out the chord combinations on the mattress. Tim had always teased her when she did that.

Tim. Should she tell Luke about him, too? How she'd bumped into her ex-boyfriend at the hospital that second time, and how he'd suggested that they get a coffee to 'catch up' and talk about 'old times'?

She'd been even more exhausted than usual, that day. Her dad had been in hospital for a week and she'd been there every evening. A coffee had sounded like a really good idea. She had also been intrigued to find out which 'old times' he wanted to talk about. *Do you remember how we lived together and all you wanted to do was hang out in music venues with your mates, playing and getting drunk? Good times.*

He'd pointed at her wedding ring. 'So, you're married?'

Kate had looked at her ring too. 'Yes. With two children.' When they'd first broken up, she'd fantasised about flaunting a perfect family in front of Tim's face one day like an eighties gameshow host: *Just look at what you could have won!* 'You?'

He pulled a 'don't be ridiculous' face. 'No. Living with someone, though. She's a cellist.'

Of course he was dating another musician. Non-musical people didn't exist for Tim. 'Good for you.'

He shrugged. 'What about you? Are you still playing?'

Kate thought of the poor, abandoned piano at home. *Expensive letter rack.* 'Not much. I don't really get the time.'

Tim had shaken his head. 'Then you have to *make* time. I can't believe you're not playing. You were the one who would practise every composition until it was beyond perfect.'

She'd met Tim at Manchester University, where they had both been studying music – and they'd discovered they lived only a few miles from each other back home. But Tim and his saxophone was the only serious relationship he would ever need. If you'd taken the saxophone away from him, he would probably have stopped breathing. Kate had been the same about the piano at one time. They had a passion for performance in common. Or at least, they'd used to.

Kate picked up her paper cup and sipped at the scalding coffee. 'Life gets busy.'

Tim had leaned forwards. 'But playing *is* life, Kate. Listen, I know you're a follow-the-sheet-music kind of girl, but I've started playing at a really great jazz club in Dartford. I know' – he held up a hand at her mocking smile – 'it's hardly bright-lights, big-city, but it's a cool place. You should come.'

She'd shaken her head. There was no way she could fit in a night at a jazz club. Life had already been passing in a blur of home, school run, hospital, school run, home, hospital. Her mum kept saying that she didn't have to come every day, but how could she not? No one had promised them that Dad wouldn't have another heart attack. What if the day she didn't go in had been his last day?

She had been a terrible mother during those weeks of hospital visits. She'd had to give in and let Luke take over every bedtime – much to Thomas' screamed annoyance – because she'd had to dash back to the hospital as soon as he got home. They had barely seen one another. Even when she'd been with the kids, she hadn't had any patience with them: screaming at them for the smallest misdemeanour. And here she was now in Paris, being a terrible mother again.

She sat up and stopped the music on her mobile. Brought up her contacts on the screen.

The phone rang and rang at the other end. Her dad had used to get so cross when she didn't answer her phone. Her parents had never had any comprehension of using voicemail. Wherever they were in the house, or whatever they were doing, one of them would race to reach the telephone before it stopped ringing. Heaven forbid they didn't make it and the person rang off.

'Hello?' came a rather harassed voice on the other end.

'I'm here!' Kate tried to sound enthusiastic rather than nervous.

Nina didn't pick up on her nerves. 'Kate! That was quick. How was your journey?'

'Fine. Easy. No unscheduled trips to the toilet, no arguments about who was sitting where and no painful games of eye spy. It was marvellous.' Kate loved Nina. She was the kind of friend you could tell that you had fantasised about walking out of a play centre and leaving your children behind and she would nod along, rather than threaten to report you to social services.

'Lucky you. We're doing *craft*.'

Kate shuddered. The two of them also shared a common phobia of tissue paper and stick-on googly eyes. Why were children so obsessed with making things? Melissa the Super Mother was regularly posting photographs of her child's latest creations and, to be fair, they were often pretty amazing. Clearly Chloe hadn't done them alone, but still.

'Crikey. Can't you distract him with a rice cake or something?' Nina's youngest child was still at preschool, but this was obviously not one of his days there.

'It's not too bad. I've hidden the glue and glitter, I've just covered a page in double-sided sticky tape and given him a bowl of dried pasta. Anyway, I'd rather talk about you. Have you met up with your friend yet?'

'Yes. She was really shocked. Good shocked.' Kate had been a little shocked by Shannon, too. It had been brilliant to see her – and to remember some of their crazy past – but she hadn't looked her usual vibrant self. To be fair, Kate hadn't seen her in over a year except through Facebook pictures, and everyone knew how much of a lie they were.

'Noah, can you try and keep the felt tip on the paper? Sorry, Kate, I am listening.'

Kate wasn't offended. It was impossible to have a telephone conversation with a small person in the vicinity. Pre-children, Kate had found this immensely irritating, having a third person in every conversation. Never knowing whether to wait for the parent on the other end to finish speaking to their child or whether to just keep talking regardless. Either way, it had always felt like they weren't really listening. Now that she was the parent with the interrupting progeny, she *knew* that they weren't.

'It's fine. It's just a quick question anyway. I've had a text from the school about this "dress like a farmer" day. What are you going to do?'

'Oh, bloody hell, yeah. I think I'm going to pick up a checked shirt in Primark tomorrow. Do you want me to get one for Alice?'

Kate gave a sigh of relief. 'If you could, that would be wonderful. What would I do without you? I really am grateful, Nina. You've been amazing these last few months.' Kate heard the tremor in her own voice. Nina had been a complete rock.

'Hey, it's fine. You've had a tough time. You'd do the same for me. Look, if Luke calls me, what do you want me to say?'

'About what?'

'About what's going on? Does he know where you are?'

Was he going to be surprised that she was in Paris? She'd been suggesting a trip here since Shannon moved, but Luke had always had a reason not to go. He had to travel a lot for his job, just like she used to do. When he wasn't at work, he wanted to be at home: just the four of them. Never mind that Kate was climbing the walls like a caged animal.

'I'm going to text him as soon as I've finished speaking to you. I've had a message from him to say he's going to be late, so I'll tell him to collect the kids from you, if that's still okay? If he asks you anything when he comes, just plead ignorance.'

Nina snorted. 'Well, that's easy enough these days. *Noah, get off the table!* Sorry, Kate, I have to go. I'll definitely pick up the kids and bring them home with me. Will you keep me posted about, you know, everything?'

'Of course. I'll speak to you later.'

As soon as their call ended, Kate started to type a text to Luke. He might not understand. He might think she was crazy. He might not even… She stopped typing. She should think longer about what to write. In the meantime, she needed to check the Eurostar website and see about a return ticket for her, and a ticket for Luke.

The hotel had a pretty fast Wi-Fi connection and it didn't take long to find the tickets she was looking for. The price made her gulp. If she'd got a bargain on her one-way ticket here, they would definitely make their money back on her return journey. And what about Luke's ticket? It was a total extravagance if he refused to come. He could easily get out of it: it was last-minute, he'd have to make arrangements for the kids, it was expensive. But if she bought the ticket… and texted his mum to look after the kids… and told him how much she wanted him there… would he come?

She bought the tickets.

Now she should get out of this room. What was the point of being in this wonderful city and just sitting in a hotel? She checked she had everything she needed in her bag. Alongside broken hairclips and pages of stickers, she found two emergency packets of Haribo in the inner zipped pocket. Of all the things to make her feel a pang of guilt: sweets shaped like fried eggs and diamond rings.

Shannon had said she was going to the Louvre, but its vast echoing halls would be too overwhelming today. No, if Kate was going to find herself, she'd need to go back to the beginning. And she knew just where to start.

CHAPTER ELEVEN

Laura

A work colleague you'd only met a handful of times was probably not the best person to give you advice on your ten-year relationship. Laura's conversation with Paolo about James at the last meeting had been bordering on intimate. The nerves she'd had about seeing him again had only been based around her fears that he would pick up where they'd left off, but now she'd seen him and nothing inappropriate had passed between them, she could relax. That was a relief. Wasn't it?

It was definitely a relief when Shannon turned up to meet them. Robert had spent the rest of their Louvre visit wandering from person to person, making light conversation whilst looking at each of them intently, as if he could read the sales figures which were constantly kicking around their brains. When they emerged from the galleries into the light of the midday sun, they made their way towards the minibus where Shannon was waiting, wearing huge sunglasses and an even bigger grin.

'Laura! So great to see you!' Shannon gave her a huge hug. 'Has Robert been playing nicely?' she asked, without moving her lips from her smile.

'Kind of.' Shannon might be a good ear to listen to her woes, but she still worked very closely with Robert. Best to play it safe.

Shannon leaned in and lowered her voice even more. 'And what about Paolo?' She raised an eyebrow.

Laura felt the heat in her cheeks. What had Shannon said that for? By the time she'd opened her mouth to reply, Shannon was already working her way around the rest of the group, shaking hands and welcoming everyone to Paris, before ushering them back into the minibus.

Hanging back as the others got on meant that Laura could avoid Paolo again and engineer a seat next to Shannon. Robert sat at the back of the minibus, but they were so crowded together on there, that Laura still couldn't talk to Shannon about her customer worries without someone overhearing them. The upside was that Shannon couldn't ask her about Paolo, either. She hoped.

Laura stuck to safe topics instead. 'How come you missed the Louvre tour?'

'I was meeting up with a friend. A total surprise visit. She got the train in from England this morning. We only had time for a quick coffee but she's staying in our hotel, so we can hook up later.'

Now Shannon had pushed her sunglasses onto the top of her head like a headband, Laura could see that she looked a little tired. Sad, even. It must be quite lonely moving to a completely different country on your own. 'Is she a close friend?'

Shannon frowned and thought for a few moments. 'Well, we were *real* close, when I was in England. We worked together in London and we went out a *lot*.' Shannon's intonation was so expressive, Laura could almost see the punctuation marks as she spoke. 'But since I've been here, we haven't spoken very often. She's got a young family and I guess that takes up a lot of her time.' She made the one-childless-woman-to-another face.

Laura knew what that meant. In the last three years, she'd had several friends virtually drown overnight under the tide of motherhood. She missed them. 'Seems like a lot of work, being a mother.'

Shannon nodded thoughtfully. 'Yeah. Plus, she's had a pretty rough ride in other ways this last year.' She didn't go into detail and Laura didn't ask – they were only work colleagues, after all. Well, they were for now. Who knew what these meetings tomorrow would bring?

'Well, feel free to go and meet her during my sales presentation tomorrow.' Laura took a furtive look to see if anyone was listening and lowered her voice. 'And if you could take Robert with you – that would be a real bonus.'

Shannon looked concerned. 'Are you still worrying about that big return from Machon?'

Laura nodded. Why had she agreed to leave the finance department and move over into sales? Making the spreadsheets, creating graphs, writing reports: that had been fun. But trying to persuade customers to take stock of three times as many units as they would ever hope to sell? Not so much. She'd only got this job because the previous sales exec had been snapped up by a rival company, and she'd been persuaded to cover his role while they looked around for a replacement. By a stroke of luck, sales had been good that quarter and she'd met his target purely by taking a few people to lunch and asking them nicely to take a little extra stock. Robert had been so impressed that he'd made her promotion permanent. Now times were a little harder, he had probably started to reassess his previous faith in her.

Shannon patted her hand. 'It'll be okay, honey. And there's no point in worrying about it until it actually happens. I checked the orders again this morning and there's been nothing returned yet. When they do, we'll deal with it.'

Shannon's phone rang and she patted Laura's hand again before picking the phone up and leaning towards the window to speak.

Laura pulled out her own phone to check her email again. Could she be lucky enough to escape? It was a Friday after all; they wouldn't submit a returns request over the weekend.

James had replied to her earlier text: *Glad you're there safely. Sorry about last night – we'll talk when you get back xxx*

She relaxed back into her seat. Maybe she had overreacted. James was actually very kind and thoughtful. He got cross sometimes, but he always apologised, and it probably wasn't the best time to bring up the subject of their future when he'd just got home from a busy day. He liked to wind down in the evenings. For all his foray into expensive tailoring and new-found knowledge of wine, he was actually a pipe and slippers type.

When they'd first got together, Laura's uni friends had teased her about how square James was. The whole time she'd known him at university, he'd been in the library every minute outside of classes, wanting to make sure he secured a first-class degree. He wouldn't even stay in the Students' Union bar past ten p.m. on a weeknight. He had always had such a clear plan of where he was going to go in life. So why was he so reluctant to make a plan with Laura? It didn't add up.

She scrolled back through other messages from James. Some were very sweet: *Hope you're having a good day! x* But there were quite a few apologies too. *Sorry about last night x* and *We'll talk about this when work calms down a bit x* If she kept scrolling back, could she pinpoint the exact moment they had started arguing about marriage and babies?

James didn't know about her past pregnancy. There was no way she could have had the baby. She had only been nineteen, and Liam seemed to have forgotten she even existed. Imagine how he would have reacted to news of a child. She had been terrified: not just terrified of having the baby, but terrified of making the decision *not* to have it. And then going through with that decision. Trying to work out what to do had been the worst week of her life.

In the end, all her indecision had been irrelevant. She'd lost the baby. She'd woken with intense cramps and there had been blood on her sheets. A lot of blood. A miscarriage. Probably about ten weeks, the hospital said. Laura should have been relieved but she had just felt really, really sad. Had her body agreed that she was not ready to be a mother? Had her restless nights and anxious days made the miscarriage happen? The kind nurse had told her it was very common. That one in four pregnancies ended in miscarriage, and most of those were in the first trimester. That it didn't mean she wouldn't be able to have a perfectly successful pregnancy next time. But was that true? At the time, Laura hadn't thought about it too deeply, but a couple of years ago, she'd done some research and read on a hospital website that one in a hundred women have recurrent miscarriages. It was small odds, but that one in a hundred had to be someone. What if it was her? And how would she know for sure until she tried again?

Shannon was still on her phone. She mouthed 'sorry' at Laura and turned back to the window. Laura looked past her to the busy roads outside. Off down a side street, she saw a man and a woman strolling along, holding hands. They were both beautiful: she wore a long white dress and trailed a loose bouquet, he was in a shirt and trousers and… there was a photographer following them. Another bloody wedding! Was the whole planet getting hitched except her?

Circumstances had made it easy for her to keep her secret. They'd had some important accountancy exams going on at the time, so James had been at the library even more than usual. He'd believed her story that she wanted to study alone in her room: had even approved of it. And when she'd been reticent about their relationship also moving to the bedroom, he had been such a gentleman, had never pushed for anything. Gradually, they'd come together and the sex had always been nice, kind of comforting, safe. James was much more suitable for Laura than Liam would have been. Sensible. Dependable. Safe.

Laura turned back in her seat to see Paolo looking at her from across the aisle. Quickly, she looked back at her phone screen and pushed down the butterflies. *Sensible. Dependable. Safe.*

For no other reason than to avoid Paolo's gaze, she checked through her apps: email, WhatsApp, Instagram. There were another two property links from her mother on WhatsApp – why had Laura ever shown her how to use it? – and a message from Tina.

Hi lovely. I know you're away with work but I have some news. I would have waited until you were back but Phil can't keep his mouth shut and I wanted you to hear it from me.

There was a scan picture with the heading: BABY HANSON: TWELVE WEEKS AND COUNTING.

Tears pricked the back of Laura's eyes and her throat tightened. What an awful, selfish cow she was. She should be happy for her friend. She *was* happy for her. It was just…

Shannon ended her call, dropped her mobile back into her bag and turned around in her seat so that she could speak to everyone. 'Okay guys, I'm planning to take you all back to the hotel so that you can have a few hours to yourselves before dinner. Lunch is paid for at the hotel if you want it, but we have the minibus for the day if anyone wants to be dropped somewhere else?'

Paolo raised a hand. 'Can you drop me at the Rodin Museum? It's not too far.'

'Of course,' Shannon winked at him. 'Not had enough sculpture for one day, eh? A man after my own heart. Anyone else got a destination in mind?'

A couple of the others requested shopping areas or tourist attractions. It might be a good time for Laura to go back to her room and take a nap; she hadn't slept very well last night. Once she'd composed herself, she'd write a long and enthusiastic message to Tina, promising to laugh at her when she got fat and her feet swelled up. And saying how happy she was for her.

But Paolo leaned across the aisle towards her. 'Come to the museum with me; you'll love it.'

Her heart raced a little. Be on her own with him? That didn't seem like a good idea. What if he took up where they'd left off last time? It didn't matter, because he wasn't her type. James was the kind of man she should be with. *Sensible. Dependable. Safe.* But how could she say no without seeming rude? Blame it on work. 'I really should finish a few things on my presentation for tomorrow.'

But Paolo wasn't put off so easily. 'We'll only go for an hour. Then I will get you get back to your laptop so you can slave away before dinner.' He put his hand on his heart. *Do not look at his well-defined chest under that tight-fitting shirt.* 'Promesso.'

Shannon turned back and grabbed Laura's arm. 'Oh, you *must* go! The Rodin Museum is wonderful. The sculpture garden is amazing. *The Gates of Hell. The Thinker.*' She paused and raised an eyebrow. '*The Kiss.*'

Paolo winked at Shannon. 'I will leave you to persuade her.'

When he turned around, Laura took the pen that Shannon was holding, wrote on her map from the Louvre and held it up to show her. *Save me!*

Shannon smiled. Took the pen back and wrote underneath: *I am.*

Before Laura had time to think of another excuse, they were pulling up near the Rodin museum and Paolo had taken her hand and pulled her off the bus.

'See you later!' There was a definite twinkle in Shannon's eye as she waved goodbye.

CHAPTER TWELVE

Shannon

They said things turned up in threes. First, the sales team. Then Kate. Then another damn email from Adam.

The European head office for Sentek Inc. was in an old hotel which had been converted into medium-sized offices. Sentek were on the second floor. There were only six people who worked from here: Robert, Shannon, Frans the financial director, Jacques in marketing, André, who was with the sales guys at the hotel, and Fabienne, who managed the office day-to-day. Right now, only Fabienne was there.

'*Bonjour*, Robert. *Bonjour*, Shannon. *Café?*'

'*Oui.* Yes please.' Shannon tried to speak French as often as she could, but working in US company, she ended up swapping between the two so frequently it ended up a kind of Franglais. Add into the mix the difference between US English and UK English – when she'd lived in London, it had been difficult enough to remember what a lift and a brollie were – and it made for some interesting conversations. Fabienne disappeared to the communal kitchen they shared with the other company on this floor; she regarded instant coffee as the work of the devil, so she'd be a while.

Shannon slid behind her desk. Clearing it of paperwork each night before going home was a personal ritual, but Fabienne had sliced open her mail and left it in a neat pile, waiting to be inspected. She flicked through it: just advertising or invitations to product launches. Everything important came by email these days. Like the ones Adam kept sending? Hopefully not.

'It's Veronique's birthday next weekend.' Robert was standing in front of her, leaning forward with his hands on the desk.

Shannon continued flicking but not looking. She knew about the extravaganza that Robert's ex-wife had planned for their eldest daughter's birthday. He had complained often enough about his half of the costs. Which usually started a rant about how expensive children were in general. Very, apparently. 'You already told me that. That's nice for her.'

'Her twentieth. It's an important birthday here. *The* important birthday.'

Shannon sighed and looked up at him. 'I know, Robert. You've said. Repeatedly.'

He nodded, but didn't take his eyes off her. 'You still haven't told me if you are coming.'

Why was he so intent on introducing her to his family? They'd only been dating a year; that was still early, right? A year was nothing. It had taken her a year to decide to cut bangs in. There was no point meeting the family unless you were planning to be together for a long time. She put a hand on her stomach. Or unless you had no choice.

'I don't think that it would be the best time for me to meet her. It's her night. She doesn't want her dad's latest girlfriend turning up.' This was a pretty reasonable excuse. Surely a twenty-year-old didn't want her party full of forty-somethings? Shannon remembered being twenty; forty would have seemed ancient.

Robert looked as if he'd been slapped. 'You are not my "latest girlfriend". You make me sound like a... what's the word you use? A player! You make me sound like a player. You are my girlfriend, Shannon. My partner. We are something important.'

Was she? Were they? Would he be so keen if he knew that she was carrying a baby? Robert, whose two grown-up daughters, according to him, were 'much better company' now they were grown as they had been 'horrifying' as babies? More than once, she and Robert had had to move to a restaurant table on the other side of the room – and once to an entirely different restaurant across the street – because there were babies in the vicinity.

Shannon massaged the space between her eyes. 'Robert, can we not talk about this here?'

He threw his hands up in the air. 'When *can* we talk about it? You *never* want to talk about it.' He leaned in close. She could smell his expensive cologne and the freshness of his shirt. Did she want to kiss him or push him away? 'I love you, Shannon. I want you to be part of my life – my whole life. And that includes my girls.'

Fabienne walked back in with their coffee. Robert took his with a nod of thanks and stalked off back to his desk. He was the only one with a separate office. Sometimes it was a real blessing.

'*Merci,* Fabienne.' Shannon took the steaming cup.

Fabienne stayed where she was. She had the easy elegance Shannon envied in French women: a well-cut suit, stylish hair, discreet make-up. 'Are you okay?'

Not her, too? 'I'm fine.'

Fabienne tilted her head to one side and crossed her arms. 'You look pale. Have you eaten today?'

Shannon crossed her fingers under the desk. 'Of course. I just had a huge croissant and now I'm having this, look.' She held her coffee cup and took a large sip. Damn, that was hot. And bitter.

Fabienne screwed up her eyes and looked Shannon up and down. 'Are you pregnant?'

Shannon nearly spat the coffee across the desk. She swallowed, scalding her throat. 'What?' she gasped.

Fabienne nodded knowingly. She was only five years older than Shannon but she had three children and a husband, so that made her a lot older in adulting years. 'You are late in the mornings. You are pale. You eat 'orrible dry biscuits.' She nodded at Shannon's midriff. 'You keep touching your stomach.'

Shannon whipped her traitorous hand from her belly and placed it flat on the desk, pushing herself up straight. 'I don't know what you're…' She breathed out and folded back into her chair. She wasn't fooling Fabienne. 'Please don't tell Robert.'

Fabienne looked triumphant. 'I knew it! Why does Robert not know?'

Shannon shook her head. 'I still don't know what I'm going to do.'

Fabienne was Catholic. Not going through with a pregnancy would not cross her mind. She had also worked for Robert a lot longer than Shannon had. 'What do you mean?'

Shannon put her mug down and placed her hands on her face. 'I just don't know if…'

Robert's office door banged open and he marched over to her desk. 'Fabienne. Can you give us a few moments? Maybe take an extra break.'

Fabienne didn't need asking twice. She took her coat from the peg, mouthed '*Bonne chance*' at Shannon and left.

Robert started to pace the floor. 'I just do not understand. Why do you not want to meet them?'

Shannon sighed. This again. Maybe she should have a handout printed that she could give to him each time he brought this up? 'I'm just not the maternal type, Robert. I've told you that. I've never wanted to have a child.' Her hand started to slip toward her stomach again. She clenched her fist. She was going to have to keep an eye on that.

He threw his arms in the air in that passionate way that she loved. Most of the time. 'They are adults! I am not asking you to be their mother. Just meet them. I could understand if they were small children. Believe me, even I am happy to leave those years behind me, but they are young women now. And…' he stopped pacing and looked at her. 'It's important to me.'

Shannon just wanted to lay her face down on the desk and close her eyes. This was all too much. She had been very careful to make sure that she was *never* in this situation. No kids. No ties. No fuss. And now this man, this man who she had stupidly fallen in love with, was trying to make her meet his children without knowing she was growing another one as they spoke.

But he had said it again. He was 'happy to leave' the baby years behind. What the hell was she going to do? Thank God Kate was here. She could speak to her tonight.

The door opened and Frans and Jacques appeared, back from their lunch meeting. They stopped and looked at them. *'Pardon.'* Jacques looked from Robert to Shannon and then back again. 'Shall we come back later?'

'No, no.' Shannon got up and took her coat from the peg. 'I need to go to the hotel and make sure everything is set up for the meeting tomorrow.'

Robert threw his hands up again and walked back to his office.

Without sitting down again, Shannon leaned across her desk and clicked on her email inbox to check there was nothing pressing. Advert. Advert. Meeting date change. Forecast request. Adam Towers. Again.

At what point was he going to wise up to the fact that she did not want to hear from him? They'd had a clear agreement. No relationship. No contact. No strings. He was in the US. She was in France. There was a rather large ocean between them, and that was just fine by her.

There was no point reading this one. She'd made the mistake of reading the first two he'd sent and they were both just a variation on a theme: *We need to talk.* Why should she make herself feel bad by reading this one? If she ignored him long enough, he would get the idea and stop sending them, surely?

She dragged the email into a folder she'd made for that purpose, giving it the heading News rather than Adam, because she didn't want his name staring at her accusingly from the sidebar. If only she could turn back time so that she'd never have slept with him. A few hours of mediocre passion and it had had repercussions for her whole life. God, she'd been stupid.

Jacques held up a coffee cup in her direction to ask if she wanted a drink and she shook her head. She still had the one that Fabienne had made, but it tasted funny so she didn't fancy another one. Maybe she'd bought different coffee beans?

Plus, she needed to get out of here before Robert appeared out of his office for a third round.

CHAPTER THIRTEEN

Kate

Saint Julien le Pauvre is one of the oldest churches in Paris. In a city that is home to the grand Notre Dame Cathedral, the outside of the church is so simple, you could easily walk past it without a backwards glance. Inside, the high gothic arches and cool stone columns often play host to performances and concerts, and this was how Kate knew it. There was a poster advertising a Chopin concert that very evening: nocturnes, waltzes, études, polonaises, scherzos, mazurkas. In front of the altar was a Steinway concert grand piano. Kate stood very still and just looked around. It was just as she had remembered. Simple and beautiful.

A tour guide was speaking to a small group of tourists towards the back of the nave, but Kate didn't need one of those. She found a chair at the side of the church and sat down. Closed her eyes.

She and Luke had not got around to visiting this place on honeymoon, so it was the first time she'd been here since she'd been a music student, living in a cold apartment in Montparnasse, with a bonking couple next door and the constant sounds of cars going past. What had she imagined her life would be by this point? Award-winning pianist? Able to actually do something approaching stylish with her hair? Had she even envisaged herself with children when she was twenty-one? If she had, would she have known that she would be making such a half-arsed job of it right now?

Her parents had always seemed to know what they were doing. She'd ask them a question and get an answer. It might not always have been the answer that she wanted, but they'd always been very definite about it. ('Dad, can I go to see a band in London and stay at my boyfriend's house afterwards?' 'Over my dead body.') They'd carried their parenting responsibilities with confidence. How had they *known*?

Opening her eyes, Kate realised she had been joined by an older lady, looking upwards at a man who was probably her husband. They were English.

'You go on and follow the tour. I need to rest my legs. I'll be all right here.'

'Okay, if you're sure.' Her husband wandered off back towards the guide Kate had seen when she came in. He was pointing out the iconostasis – the wall of icons and religious paintings – which separated the nave from the sanctuary.

Kate smiled at the old lady. 'It is a beautiful place; you might want to take a look around once you've had a rest.'

'Oh, you're English too!' Repositioning herself so that she was angled towards Kate, the woman seemed pleased to find someone to talk to. 'Are you on holiday?'

Was this a holiday? 'Sort of, I'm visiting a friend. She's at work at the moment.'

'We're visiting our granddaughter.' The old lady smiled again. 'She's studying here for a year, part of her degree. She's got classes today so she's written us out an itinerary of what to do; she's a thoughtful girl.'

Kate had done something similar for her own parents when they had come to visit. 'She sounds like a great girl. I hope my kids will do something like that for me one day.'

'I'm sure they will, lovey. How many children do you have?'

Kate could see them clearly in her mind as she answered. She felt a pang. She was beginning to really miss them. 'Two. A six-year-old girl and a four-year-old boy.'

'How lovely. I bet they keep you busy?'

Kate nodded. Busy was one word for it. 'Stressed' was another. So was 'breakdown'.

'Has your husband got them today?'

Husband? Children? These were the questions that strangers always asked. What must it be like for single parents? Or women like Shannon who didn't want kids? Or who couldn't? Kate shook her head. 'They're both at school. My friend is collecting them. He'll pick them up from her later, though.'

'Well, that's an improvement over my day. He' – she motioned in the direction of her husband who was studying his guidebook – 'wouldn't have known how to change a nappy to save his life. Dads are a lot more involved these days, aren't they?'

Luke *was* involved. When he was home.

The woman was clearly enjoying reminiscing. 'I remember when mine were young. Some days I didn't know whether I'd make it to six p.m. when my husband came home.'

This was new. Usually when you spoke to someone whose children were all grown up they would tell you how lucky you were, how they wished they could go back in time. Kate let out a long breath. 'I must admit, it's more difficult than I thought it would be.'

The woman nodded her head. 'Of course it is; no one tells you about the sheer monotony of it all, do they? Feeding, changing, washing, cleaning, playing.' She leaned in conspiratorially and lowered her voice, 'The playing was the part I found most difficult. Kids' games are so boring.'

Kate laughed. She'd thought she was the only one who hated playing hide-and-seek or make-believe games. Luke was brilliant at playing with the kids. When he was left alone with them for the day, she would often come home to an encampment built from dining chairs and blankets. Even though it bored her to tears, she would try her best to play when he wasn't there. Once, she'd been doing her best 'take off' noise during a game of spaceships and Thomas had sighed deeply, 'I wish my Daddy was home.'

'Still, they have a way of making it all worthwhile, don't they?' The lady patted Kate's leg.

From nowhere, Kate started to cry.

'Oh, my dear. Whatever is the matter?'

She couldn't stop crying. Her throat was tight. And her nose was snotty. She tried to wipe it with the back of her hand and rummage around in her bag for a tissue. Which of course she didn't have. Only good mothers were prepared with emergency tissues.

The old lady was clearly one of the good ones. She produced a pristine packet of Kleenex Balsam. 'Come on, dear. Nothing can be that bad. What is it?'

What was it? It was the not knowing that was the worst part of this. She had a loving, if slightly thoughtless, husband. Two healthy, happy children. They were financially stable, had a comfortable home and there were moments when the four of them were together and Kate felt like the luckiest woman alive. But other times…

'I don't know. I really don't know. The thing is, I… kind of… ran away. This morning. I just left without telling my husband and came out here, to Paris.' Where had that come from? She didn't normally confide in complete strangers like this. She looked at the old lady through her dripping eyelashes. Waiting to be told what a terrible mother she was. Instead, the woman patted her on the back.

'Good for you, dear. Good for you. Sometimes it does them good to realise what it's like when you're not there. Taking you for granted, is he?'

Kate felt terribly disloyal. Luke was a good husband. A good dad. But he was at work so much and she couldn't make him see how difficult it was for her when he missed bedtime. Or spent a Saturday in the corporate box with a client. Or slipped off to the pub on a Friday night. 'I don't think he means to.'

'Of course he doesn't, but they just don't understand what it's like, do they?'

Kate sniffed and dabbed at her nose. 'I think I'm just tired.'

'Of course you are. It's worse for you mums today. All those clubs you take the children to. And making sure they eat their five-a-day. And providing all these educational toys.' She nodded, wisely. 'My youngest daughter has two little ones and she is just the same. Always driving them here, there and everywhere. Having those, what does she call them?' she clicked her fingers together. 'Playdates! That's the word. What the heck is one of those, I asked her. Apparently it involves sitting in someone else's house watching the children playing together whilst you think about the million other things you need to be getting done.'

Kate smiled a watery smile. She had spent some painful play-dates at Melissa's house, apologising for the fact that her children wouldn't eat any of Melissa's healthy snacks and pretending that she had no idea why they kept asking for crisps because they *never* had those at home.

'I wonder at the lot of you. When I had my children, they were just expected to get on and play with each other whilst I got on with my jobs. I wasn't taking them to, what does she call it?' She clicked her fingers again. 'Sensory play! That's it. Lying on a blanket playing with bits of tin foil and glowing bouncy balls apparently. My lot got some upturned saucepans and wooden spoons at home and they were happy for hours.'

Kate had had this conversation with her own mother. *You do too much*, she always said. But when Kate compared herself to Melissa and some of the other mums at the school, she felt like she didn't do anywhere near enough. The latest thing was swimming lessons. But the thought of taking them to the pool, getting them changed, getting them dry again… It had just felt overwhelming.

The old lady must have read her thoughts. 'What about your mum? Isn't she around to help?'

Her mum. Kate really should call her and check she was okay. She wouldn't tell her she was in Paris. It would only worry her. 'She used to but we… er… my dad. He passed away and I don't like to… to…' She started to cry again.

'Oh you poor love.' The old lady put her arms around Kate. 'You're having a right old time of it. Is your mum not coping very well?'

Kate sniffed. 'She's great. She's doing really well. Keeping herself busy, seeing her friends. I just don't like to, you know, worry her. Or ask her to have the kids or anything. She has enough to deal with.'

Two weeks after her dad's first heart attack, Kate and her mum had been on their way home from afternoon visiting time when they'd received 'that' call from the hospital, asking them to come back as soon as they could. They drove back to the hospital in silence: a unique occurrence. When they got to the door of the ICU, the staff wouldn't let them in. Something was happening and they told them they had to wait. They knew this wasn't good. Not good at all.

The other relatives waiting in the corridor did their best not to look at them as they wrapped their arms around each other. Distracted for a few moments from their own grief, guiltily grateful that it wasn't them, the other people turned away or pretended to be studying the curling posters on the noticeboard. Kate's mum had been so strong: 'Whatever happens, we'll get through this. Nothing will change. We'll be okay.' Whatever fear had been piercing her own heart, her first instinct had been to protect her daughter: even in her early forties, Kate was still her child and that was what mums do, wasn't it?

Kate's mobile started to ring. She found it in her bag. *Luke.* She pressed the 'cancel call' button.

The old lady moved her arm but gently rubbed Kate's back. It felt so nice. 'Have you actually asked your mum?'

Kate frowned. 'What do you mean?'

She kept rubbing. 'Maybe she would like to be asked to have the children. If my daughter was struggling, I'd want her to come to me. I'm sure your mum feels the same.'

'But she's on her own. She's just lost my dad and...'

'And she'd probably like nothing more than to feel that you still need her. That her grandchildren want to spend time with her. That she still has an important part of her life to lead. I can see you mean well, love, but let your mum decide whether she can help you out or not. For her sake as well as yours. Oh, my husband's back, must have changed his mind about the tour. You take care of yourself. And think about what I said.' She squeezed Kate's hand and left with a wave.

Kate stayed where she was for a while longer, reluctant to leave this place behind. She watched as a tall, slim man sat down at the Steinway and arranged some sheet music. Would he play something?

Kate didn't usually open up to strangers like that. It was as if the old lady had been sent – like a fairy godmother – to speak to her. She made a lot of sense. Was she right about Kate's mum? Should she speak to her about helping out with the kids again if she was ready? And what about Luke?

She listened to the lengthy voicemail he'd left when she'd rejected his last call. 'Hi, love. Your ringtone sounds funny. Hope you're having a good day. Listen I, er... I know I said about getting a takeaway tonight but I'd forgotten, there's a leaving do. One of the finance guys. Really should go and stick my head in at the pub. Shouldn't be a late one. But you might want to go ahead and eat with the kids. Maybe we can get a takeaway tomorrow? Sorry. Love you.'

Every muscle in Kate's body was tight. Her shoulders were up to her ears. Yes, she did bloody mind, and it wasn't the retracted offer of sodding chicken korma that was giving her the urge to throw her mobile across Saint Julien le Pauvre's floor.

It was just expected. That she would be there to feed the kids, bath them, put them to bed. There was no possible chance in the entire universe that she might have plans. That she might want to do something other than sing sodding 'Wind the pissing bloody Bobbin Up', wrestle two slippery eels around a bath tub and then lie down in a dark room barking 'Go to sleep' every four minutes until they gave in.

Yes, she was a stay-at-home mum. But did that mean she had to stay at home every sodding night?

She punched a message into her phone with an aggressive forefinger. *I am not home. You need to collect the children from Nina by six p.m.* And then she turned the phone off.

Then she turned it back on again. Because you never knew when an emergency might happen.

Into the hushed silence, the strains of Chopin's Nocturnes reached out to her as the pianist began to play *Serenity and Dream*. Kate closed her eyes again. The haunting melody washed over her like cool water, its familiar notes in this place bringing something she had not had in a long time. Peace.

The pianist stopped playing and she ached for him to begin again. He leafed through his sheet music. As he began *Fantasie Dreams of Love*, she took a deep breath and her chest expanded. Its romance filled her. Did she remember how it felt to fall in love? Hopeful, vulnerable, excited.

A man leaned in front of her. 'Hello again.'

It took a moment to realise that he was the man who Shannon had spoken to in the café earlier. Dressed in casual clothes now, he looked very different than before. Younger, maybe. 'Hi, sorry, I didn't recognise you straight away. Graham? Is that right?'

He nodded. 'I'm finished for the day so I thought I'd lose the suit. I'm here to buy some concert tickets for next month – schmoozing an important client who loves classical music. How come you're on your own?'

'Shannon had to go back to work. Turns out when you surprise people they still have normal life to attend to. She has a business dinner to go to later.'

Without missing a beat, Graham said, 'That's a shame. I'll be going out to eat later if you want to come with me?'

Kate panicked. What should she say? She didn't even know this man; would it be appropriate for her to go to dinner with him? Worse, did he think she was hinting at him to invite her to dinner?

Graham must have seen the fear in her face. 'It's fine if you want some time alone, just a thought.'

Now she was really embarrassed. Anyway, he was married, it's not like there was anything naughty going to happen. 'Sorry, I was just surprised. What time were you planning to eat?'

He shrugged. 'Around eight?' He took a card from his pocket and started to write on it. 'There's a really nice restaurant not far from here. I'll write it down for you, with my number. I'll meet you there at eight o'clock unless you text me to say otherwise.'

Kate took the card from him. This wasn't part of her plan. She had thought she'd be sitting with Shannon tonight, telling her all her woes. Instead, she would be eating with a man she'd only just met, in what sounded like a rather expensive restaurant. She should just say no. 'Okay, thanks.'

'Hopefully see you later.' Graham nodded and left.

Kate felt the hot prickle of nerves on her skin. What had she just agreed to? Maybe she should text Shannon and see what she thought? She knew this man. This could be perfectly normal and Kate was completely overthinking it. Or Luke. Should she ask Luke? She shook her head. No. She didn't need to ask his permission. If Luke could go out whenever he wanted with whoever he wanted, then why the hell couldn't she?

And it wasn't as if this was the first time recently she had been out with a man without telling him.

CHAPTER FOURTEEN

Shannon

Between the office and the hotel, Shannon had had two more calls from the US. The code was from Chicago. It had to be Adam. But why the hell was he so desperate to get hold of her?

The company used this hotel for a lot of off-site meetings, so the staff here knew her well. The sales team plus Robert and herself made eight people; there should be plenty of space in one of the smaller conference rooms. Still, it was important to check everything they might want was there. Water, snacks, paper, pens, projector, screen. It was good of the corporate hospitality team to let her have the room this afternoon. This way she could be certain that everything was ready for tomorrow. Ordered to perfection. If only the rest of her life was so easy to organise.

The meeting room was light and airy with windows on two sides. Sadly, the furniture was functional rather than beautiful, but she'd asked for the desks to be laid out in a rectangle so that they could at least all see each other. The blinds would need to be closed tomorrow, otherwise it'd be too bright to read the projector screen. At least the green décor was nice and peaceful; those poor sales managers were going to need every ounce of help they could get to counteract the stress of presenting their sales figures to Robert. The soft side she saw to him was rarely in evidence in a meeting room; if things didn't go his way, he was intransigent and cold. She'd been a witness to him terminating more than one contract and he had been icy. Her stomach lurched. This time, it wasn't morning sickness.

Just keep busy. Working her way around the rectangle of desks, she laid a pad of hotel branded paper and a pen in front of each seat. Then she did the same rotation with water glasses. Symmetry and order was so soothing. Despite the amount of work necessary to organise a sales conference – the hotel rooms, the food, the entertainment, the equipment – it was one of the most satisfying parts of her work. Maybe she should change to a career in hospitality. Could you do that with a baby strapped to you?

Shannon stood back and frowned. She'd laid out too many places. The sales manager from Belgium wasn't going to be there – that's why she had been able to give Kate his room. Though she'd told the others that he couldn't make it, he was one of the ones she'd seen fired. It was a tough time for the business. It was a tough time all round. That's why she needed to be make sure everything went smoothly; those sales guys didn't need Robert in a bad mood before they started. She could live without it, too.

It had been lovely to see Kate. Just seeing her face had made Shannon want to tell her absolutely everything, so they could thrash it all out together. That's what they would have done in the old days. Got a bottle of wine – or two – and sorted out whatever was bothering them. Any date who hadn't called back was a loser, any woman who had been rude was a bitch, any boss who had passed them over for a raise was an absolute imbecile. One time there had been a particularly unpleasant manager who'd made a point of singling out Kate when he was in a bad mood. Shannon had put a sign on his phallus of a sports car which read: *For Sale – £250 for cash. Ask for Jack.* By the time he'd got back from lunch, he'd had a queue of about twelve people waiting to see him, some of whom were really angry because they'd waited over half an hour. She'd had Kate's back and Kate had had hers. Always.

She walked around the table again, putting a hotel branded paper coaster under each glass, which she turned upside down.

It was all Shannon's fault they had lost touch. She was the single one with no childcare to arrange, so she should have made more effort. Gone down to visit Kate more often. Been a better friend.

It wasn't even the first time she'd let this happen. When other friends of hers had had children, they'd got busy with their own lives. They'd got new friends. Friends with babies. Then they'd sat around and talked about baby things and went to places that babies liked. Shannon had had nothing to bring to the party, so it had been easier to just fade away, leave them to it. But this was Kate. Her lovely, funny friend. She should have tried harder.

Air conditioning. Must check it was functioning properly. There had been one conference when the room had got so hot, one of the young men from the US office had almost passed out. That had done wonders for Robert's fierce reputation. She turned the dial until it clicked and heard the fans start to whirr. It was fine.

Standing at one end of the table, she tapped her fingernails on its top and looked around. Everything in the room was exactly as it should be. Now she needed to find something else to do with herself. Walking slowly around the table, she straightened the pens and pencils so that they were exactly parallel to the notepads. This was ridiculous. Why couldn't she just relax?

It was those damn emails from Adam. And the missed phone calls. Why was he doing this *now*? They'd had a deal. Shannon would stay out of his life and he would stay out of hers. It was better for everybody that way. He was on a different continent, for goodness' sake. How difficult would it be for him to just forget about her? She had done her damned hardest to forget about him.

And then there was Robert's Veronique. Turning twenty. Having a huge party to celebrate. Why couldn't she just do what Shannon had done on her twenty-first and dance on the counter in a bar surrounded by work colleagues she had only recently met? Although, Veronique may want to avoid sleeping with the barman. From hazy memory, that particular encounter had not been the best way for Shannon to start her metaphorical adulthood. She'd definitely wanted to be as far away from her relatives as she could possibly be, though – surely Robert's daughter must be having this family party under protest? And she certainly wouldn't want Shannon there. What would Robert introduce her as? His colleague? Sexual liaison? Girlfriend? Partner? How excruciating. Worse still, she'd have to do the whole thing sober.

Shannon slid down onto one of the chairs, put her elbows on the table and let her face fall into her hands. The baby. At some point she was going to need to give this some serious consideration. There was her job, for a start. Would she be able to hold onto any kind of career if she had this child? Right now, her hours were pretty unsociable, because of the time difference to the US head office. And it wasn't as if she had family around the corner to help. There must be French nurseries she could use in the daytime, but she was out in the evening with clients quite frequently too. She could just picture the look on a CEO's face if she rocked up to an evening reception in high heels and a baby carrier thingy. She'd mixed business and pleasure for the last year, but business and babies was a whole other thing.

And what was Robert going to say when she told him? This had never been part of their plan. They hadn't even *had* a plan. According to Fabienne, Robert had dated a *lot* of women after he split from his wife. None of them had lasted more than a few dates. When Shannon and Robert got together, it had not been supposed to be anything serious. Shannon didn't tend to stay in a job – sometimes not even in a country – for more than two or three years. She wasn't looking for a serious relationship. A partner. A *future*. She had assumed Robert felt the same. But now, here he was, piling on the pressure for her to meet his family.

Marie, from the hotel hospitality team, popped her head in the door. 'Hi, Shannon. Everything okay?'

Shannon sat up and pulled on a smile. 'Perfect as always. The room is big enough. Plenty of sockets for laptop cables. Thanks for laying out the tables and letting me in to get organised today.'

Marie waved her hand. '*De rien*. I'll make sure you have coffee and a selection of tea in the morning. Anything else?'

'Some pastries would be great. Maybe some cookies?' Preferably dry, ginger ones.

'Of course.' Marie nodded her head and left.

Shannon unzipped a bag and slid out her laptop. Might as well get some work done here if she wasn't going to head back to the office yet. She already had their Wi-Fi code, so she could clear her email inbox at least. With her finger on the touchpad, she hovered the mouse over the 'News' folder she'd used for Adam's emails. Should she just read them? Get it over with, like pulling off a band-aid? No. She had enough to think about right now.

Like Kate; there was definitely something up with her. This surprise visit for a start, but also the way she looked. Harassed, uncomfortable, ill-at-ease.

She clicked on the 'Kate' folder in her email. There were lots of long, chatty messages from when Shannon had first moved to Paris, but for the last three months there had been nothing. The last email she'd sent had been a short statement about her dad. It was a generic message, probably BCC'd to a ton of people. *Apologies if you haven't heard from me in the last couple of months but…*

No one is ever ready to lose a parent; you never think it's going to happen. Shannon knew how close Kate was with her parents and what a massive blow her father's death would have been to her. She'd called her several times after hearing the news, but they'd only managed to speak briefly; Kate was organising the funeral and juggling the kids and trying to find some time in the middle of it to grieve. To mourn her father. Her beloved dad.

Of course, Shannon had offered to fly over and help, however she could: funeral arrangements, cooking meals – even childcare. But Kate had declined. *Thanks, but there's nothing you can do. Honestly.* Obviously, she just wanted to be home with her family. It was understandable. That's one of the reasons Shannon had made the trip back to the US to see her own family. Who knew how long she'd have them? Losing a loved one was hard. And painful.

Family. Did it get more important as you got older? It had been a real surprise to Shannon when Kate had given up work completely to stay at home and raise a family. She had been so good at her job: so organised, so professional. It must have been a big change to swap the spreadsheets and invoices for diapers and pacifiers. Financially, it made a lot of sense; Luke's job paid a lot more than Kate's, and his career was doing well, but she hadn't even considered going part-time. Or even a career change. Surely that would have been the perfect time to do something with her musical talent – giving music lessons, or even following her dream to become a professional pianist? Clearly, she'd wanted to be a full-time mom more. But, if the startled rabbit face she'd had earlier was anything to go by, she wasn't enjoying it so much.

Maybe that's what happened when you had children. Once you were in, there was no getting out. You got trapped and could never, ever leave. Your choices were limited, your options reduced. You lost the one thing that was important over everything else. The thing that was the best part of being, and staying, single: freedom.

For the last eighteen years, Shannon had made the most of her freedom. She'd lived in three different states and two other countries. Thriving on change and new beginnings. Of course, there had been friends, and boyfriends, along the way, but no one to keep her in one place for too long.

Until Robert.

And the baby inside her.

And the nagging worry about why Adam kept trying to contact her.

She shut her laptop lid. Her brain was in knots. She needed to talk to someone and get all this noise out of her head.

Kate would help. Hopefully their old ability to thrash out a problem would work just as well on mineral water.

CHAPTER FIFTEEN

Laura

'"Housed in a stunning eighteenth-century mansion, the Musée Rodin is a Paris must-see. Famously the sculptor leased the property from the French government in return for the gift of all of his work upon his death."'

Paolo put a hand on the top of Laura's guidebook and gently pushed it down outside her line of vision. When she gasped, he smiled.

When he'd suggested a museum, she hadn't expected to be greeted by such verdant grounds. The gardens themselves were beautiful, and Rodin's famous sculptures were displayed to perfection. Not expecting to recognise any of the sculptures – having barely recognised Rodin's name – she was pleased to turn right around a hedge and meet *The Thinker*.

'He looks like I feel today.' Paolo nodded at the muscular, naked man, bent over with his fist pressed to his forehead. His self-esteem was clearly very good. *The Thinker* was also a looker.

'Really? A lot on your mind?' Was her tone flirtatious? She'd gotten over her shock at seeing Tina's scan picture, but it had left her feeling a little odd. Reckless, even. She was never able to speak normally around Paolo as it was. Her tongue actually felt bigger than usual in her mouth. Which wasn't even biologically possible.

'Yes,' he looked at her intently. 'Many things.'

The main house contained a lot of the collection, but it was crowded with tourists so, after shuffling around a few of the rooms, the two of them wandered out into the gardens behind and found a bench at the other end of a large rectangular pool, looking back at the house. The late afternoon sun was warm and Laura felt sleepy; she'd had an early start this morning and, between her argument with James and worry about the sales presentation, she'd probably only had about five hours' sleep last night. How nice would it be to just lay her head on Paolo's shoulder and…

She sat up straight.

Paolo stretched his legs out in front of him, crossed at the ankle. 'I think this might be my last sales meeting.'

She knew exactly how he felt. Hopefully, they were both overreacting. Having to find a new job might just send her over the edge right now. Being the only childless and unmarried one of her friends she could just about cope with. The unemployed one, not so much. 'Don't be silly, it can't be that bad. And they can't fire all of us.'

Paolo shook his head. 'Oh, it *is* that bad. But that's not what I mean.' He pulled in his legs and turned to face her. 'This was supposed to be a temporary job. I was going to make some money and then use it to travel. Asia. Africa. All over. My original plans were… changed. Somehow, I have stayed. But I still have the dream. I want to see more of the world. And I think that it is time.'

Laura didn't know what to say. She felt a crushing disappointment which was ridiculous in the circumstances. And her tongue felt even bigger. A silence stretched between them. It wasn't actually uncomfortable, but it was full. She should say something. Anything. But her lips stubbornly refused to open.

Eventually, Paolo leaned back and stretched his arms across the top of the bench. Maybe it was the emotion of the moment, but Laura wanted to giggle. She hadn't had a boy pull the 'arms across the back of the chair' move since Jacob Jenkins had taken her to see a film in Year Eleven, and all his mates had followed them to the cinema and sat two rows behind. At least Paolo was unlikely to attempt to slip his arm forwards and down her top in the fervent hope of making contact with a female nipple. Teenage boys were not the most subtle breed.

'So, Laura, how are things with you and your boyfriend?'

That knocked the suppressed giggles into touch. Older boys obviously weren't hot on subtlety, either. 'Fine. Fine. Everything is going well.'

Paolo never used James' name. Did he not remember it? Laura leaned forwards with her arms crossed. She wasn't in the mood to discuss her almost-living-together boyfriend right now. Particularly not with Paolo. He wouldn't understand.

Paolo studied her and raised an eyebrow. 'Really? Has he proposed yet?'

Laura shifted in her seat. 'No, not yet. But, you know, things are moving in the right direction.' She crossed the fingers of her right hand which was hidden in her left armpit and looked across the lake towards the house.

Paolo leaned forwards and turned his head so that he could look her in the face. 'You're lying, I can tell.'

This was becoming irritating. There was an attraction between them, she wasn't denying that. And, if she had not been with James, maybe she would have been interested in him. But that didn't give him the right to act like he was the font of all knowledge. He didn't know James and he didn't really know her.

Laura turned back to face him, narrowed her eyes and sat up straighter, in a manner which she hoped was firm. 'You don't know what the situation is. I was upset when I spoke to you last time, I probably gave the wrong idea. Anyway, I'm focused on my career at the moment.'

This was a lie. It was the same lie her mother used when her friends asked if Laura and James were getting married. *She's a career woman.* Laura wished she did have a career that she cared about. It drove her crazy, listening to the judgement levelled at the 'career woman' who 'decides' to wait until her late thirties to have a baby. Why was no one blaming the commitment-phobic men who run five miles in the other direction at the thought of sharing space in their wardrobe, let alone a life of nappies and Friday nights indoors? For women who wanted children, it wasn't their choice of career which stood in their way, it was their ability to find a willy attached to a suitable man.

Paolo was nodding his head. 'Okay. Let's assume you are telling the truth and are passionate about the printing needs of the population. Why does that stop you getting married? Babies, yes, I understand that takes some thinking and juggling around your careers. But marriage? Why does your boyfriend not ask you to marry him?'

Laura folded her arms. 'There's no point in discussing this with you. You don't even know James.'

Paolo threw his head back and laughed. 'Oh, but I think I do.' He put his hands out in front of him as if he was weighing out two different options. He raised his left palm. 'He loves you, but he needs more time.' Then he lowered it and raised the right. 'He loves you, but life is busy right now. You are the one for him, but there are things he needs to do before he settles down.' He paused and raised an eyebrow. 'Am I close?'

It was a fifty-fifty split between wanting to slap him and bursting into tears. Laura didn't trust her voice, so turned away from him. Feeling traitorous tears at the corners of her eyes, she tried to focus on one of the windows of the house until the urge to cry, or be violent, went away.

Paolo put his hand back onto his knee and his knuckle grazed the outside of her thigh.

Laura couldn't explain the feelings that went through her body at that moment. Her chest was so angry it felt as if it might burst into flame. And yet, at the exact same moment, her leg appeared to be melting and the rest of her body wanted to follow. Fight or flight?

Her heart thumping, she took a deep breath. She didn't dare to look at him. 'You don't know him. Some people just need more time. They don't rush into things.' And they don't put their hands anywhere near the leg of a girl who already has a boyfriend.

Paolo held his hands up. 'You're right, I don't. But this is not a new story, Laura, and it never ends well. How long have you been together?'

Like a stroppy schoolgirl, she muttered, 'Twelve years.'

Paolo shook his head slowly. 'If he doesn't know by now, he never will.'

Laura's head whipped around so fast, she almost heard the air move. 'I'm not sure what you call this in Italy, but in England we call it sticking your nose into other people's business and we don't consider it a good thing to do.'

Paolo held his hands up in submission. 'You're right, it is none of my business.' He used that look again, the one that felt as if it drove into her. He seemed about to say something else and then changed his mind. Getting up from the bench, he held out a hand and pulled her up. 'I am sorry, Laura. Please forget I said anything, blame this Italian nose for being too big.' He tapped his nose and winked at her.

But she couldn't forget. Because deep down, part of her knew he was right.

CHAPTER SIXTEEN

Kate

The café Kate was looking for was still there; at least, she thought it was the same one. It had the same bottle-green awning, the same wicker chairs, the same worn mahogany tables. She was almost knocked sideways by a sudden memory of sitting there with her dad. There was a picture at home, from the days before digital cameras, when people had actually printed photographs and kept them in albums. Her dad with a glass in his hand and an arm around Kate. She was beaming while he looked serious. Her dad hadn't often smiled in photographs. She and her mum had always teased him about it. He'd get cross with them, 'But I *am* smiling on the inside.'

A waiter in a black waistcoat nodded at her and motioned towards a small table outside with two chairs.

Why had she said she would go out to dinner with Graham? When was she going to learn how to say no? That's why her diary was so ridiculously full: kids' clubs and playdates and various special events. Whenever someone invited her to something and she didn't want to go to, she would flail around, trying to think of a reason for not being able to make it. Luke would look at her incredulously, 'Just say that you don't want to.' Obviously, this was impossible. Instead, she'd say: 'Sure, I'd love to come out to a Cub Scout fundraiser on Saturday night. I have to take the kids to karate in the morning, then a birthday party in the afternoon and I have got to go food shopping and do three loads of washing, but I'm sure I'll be able to get there by eight.'

Kate slipped into a seat and looked at the menu, although she already knew what she was going to order: the same thing she'd eaten when she'd come here with her parents. *Croque monsieur* and a glass of red wine.

Her dad hadn't wanted to come to Paris; he'd had that unexplainable dislike of the French that some people of his generation seemed to have. But Kate had been out there for the third year of a Modern Languages and Music degree, and so he'd come. Her mum had been so pleased: 'I'd never have got him here.' It was probably true: Kate had seen the same sort of power already with her daughter and Luke – Alice was the only one who could get Luke on the dance floor at parties. Fathers and daughters – it was a known phenomenon.

'Bonjour Madame. Que désirez-vous boire?'

Madame. In her student days, she'd been *mademoiselle.* Another change. *'Oui. Un verre de vin rouge, s'il vous plaît.'*

He nodded. *'Et pour manger?'*

She knew this without looking. *'Un croque monsieur, s'il vous plaît.'*

He nodded again and took the menu. *'Parfait.'*

They'd had a lovely day when they'd come here. Her parents had come to Paris to visit her and she'd taken them to the Musée d'Orsay – her favourite art gallery in Paris – a converted railway station, with impossibly high ceilings and the old station clock at one end. They'd spent some time in the impressionist galleries – her mum loved a bit of Monet – before coming to this café for lunch. Her dad had raved about the *croque monsieur*; he'd always been a sandwich kind of a man. Given the choice, he'd have put pretty much any foodstuff between two slices of bread to make a sandwich. Obviously, he wasn't often given the choice. With a wife and a daughter, the poor man rarely had a choice about anything. When Kate had still lived at home, her dad would come downstairs ready to go out and be met by the two women in his life shaking their heads at him. He'd sigh, turn around and go back upstairs to change.

The waiter arrived with a glass of wine and a small bowl of crisps. She smiled at him. *'Merci.'*

As she sipped at her wine, Kate tried to imagine her dad sitting here, next to her. But she had the same problem she'd been having since he'd died. She couldn't remember him; not even what he looked like. When she tried to grasp at memories, they would slip away like a child in a crowd. She would have glimpses of him in her mind: telling a joke in a kitchen at someone's house; sitting in a Little Chef, just the two of them, on the way home from university; holding Thomas a couple of hours after he was born. Even those snapshots had only been uncovered recently. She would take each one out slowly and carefully, feeling them painfully into existence, having to hold her breath before she could even touch the corners of them, letting her breath out again slowly, carefully, as long as she could bear it, before covering them up again.

The waiter was back with her sandwich. Even the smell of it reminded her of her dad. After his first taste of a *croque monsieur* here, it had become one of his specialties. You could be always be sure to find a block of Gruyère cheese and a jar of Dijon mustard in her parents' fridge.

People said that grief got easier with time but that was misleading. It was true that hours could pass without Kate thinking about him; sometimes even a whole day or more. But grief was just hiding, biding its time. When she least expected it, it jumped on her, punched her in the stomach, closed her throat, snatched her breath. Coming from nowhere, she was never prepared. How do you explain to the lady on the checkout that you suddenly can't speak, or to your young child that you don't know why the jigsaw puzzle is making Mummy cry?

She took a bite of the sandwich.

She had called Tim to tell him about her dad. She'd still had his number stored. Maybe it had been speaking to him on the phone that had done it. Maybe it had been the fact he was so kind and seemed so upset about her dad. Maybe it had been because she was feeling weak, and tired, and like she just didn't want to be grown up about this any more. But when he'd suggested they meet for a drink, she'd accepted.

She hadn't exactly lied to Luke.

They'd had so much to organise after her dad's death. Funeral arrangements came with an awful lot of questions to answer. As an only child, it had been down to Kate and her mum to make all the decisions. They'd actually laughed almost hysterically, imagining what her dad would have said. 'Three thousand quid? Just stick me in a cardboard box and put me out with the recycling!'

She'd been here, there and everywhere that week. Printers for the order of service, florists for the wreaths, caterers to book the sandwich platters. It had been easy to slip out for an hour in the late afternoon on a Saturday.

'I thought you weren't coming.' Tim had stood up and kissed her on the cheek. He was still wearing that ridiculous necklace.

'Sorry. I've had a lot of running around to do.'

'Yeah.' Tim ran a hand through his hair. 'Sorry about your dad. He was a nice bloke.'

He might not have said that if he'd heard what her dad had wanted to do to him after they'd split up. 'Thanks.'

Tim had bought her a glass of wine and they'd shared a few memories about her dad. Then Tim had brought the jazz club up again.

'I know you probably don't feel like it at the moment. But, if you need a night out, you should come to that club I mentioned. You'd love it.'

Would she? 'I'm not sure it's my kind of thing.'

He looked like he'd been waiting for her to say exactly that. 'But it is! They have a brilliant pianist and she's really cool about other musicians getting up to play. You could get up on stage again.'

Get up on stage? Could she even still play a complete piece from memory? There was no point getting into that with Tim, though. His life had a constant soundtrack; hers barely had background music. She'd made some vague noises about not feeling up to a night out at the moment, which he'd had to accept. She really hadn't intended to set foot in the jazz club he was so keen on. Especially not without telling Luke. She still wasn't sure why she'd changed her mind.

Kate drained her wine glass and looked around for the waiter to order another. As she did, she saw a face which looked familiar. Pensive, but familiar. It wasn't until the girl was almost next to her table that she placed her. Kate smiled and waved. 'Hi! Laura, wasn't it? We met on the train. Are you okay?'

CHAPTER SEVENTEEN

Laura

Was she okay? It was hard to say. Laura's legs were wobbly. Her brain was fuzzy. And her stomach had been performing somersaults for the last two hours. 'I'm not actually sure.'

The Rodin Museum didn't close until quarter to six, but Laura had made the excuse that she needed to leave early to check through her presentation. Then she'd made another excuse about wanting to clear her head with a walk along the Seine, and had refused Paolo's offer to come with her. Using Google maps, her walk towards the Seine had taken her past some cafés. As she'd passed one of them, she'd seen a kind of familiar face. And a waving hand.

'Hi! Laura, wasn't it? We met on the train. Are you okay?'

It was the lady from the train. The one with the baby photos. Kate.

Kate pulled out a chair. 'Why don't you sit down and have a drink with me? What would you like? Wine? Beer? Coffee?'

Laura sank down on the chair and rubbed her forehead. 'Which one will give me psychic powers? I could do with that right now.'

Kate pretended to consider the idea. 'You could try absinthe? I think that can be hallucinatory. But it might be a little early in the day. Red wine to start?'

It was a little early in the day for Laura to be drinking anything alcoholic. James didn't really approve of her drinking too much. But what the hell, she couldn't feel any more disorientated. And red wine was likely to be maximum twelve percent proof. That would be okay if she only had one glass. 'Yes, please.'

Kate motioned to the waiter and he came to take their order. '*Deux vins rouge, s'il vous plaît.*' Laura watched her with envy. She clearly had her life together. Married. A couple of kids. Managing to pop over to Paris to visit an old friend. Speaking French. If only Laura could get herself to that point. What was the trick?

Kate turned back to face her. 'Do you want to talk about it?'

Did she? What was there to talk about? Maybe she did. 'I'm not really sure where to start.'

The waiter brought their wine and Kate chinked her glass onto Laura's. 'How about the beginning?'

Laura sighed. Where even *was* the beginning? What was it she actually wanted to happen? Was she asking for too much? Too needy? Too demanding? 'Did your husband want to have children? Or did you have to persuade him into it?'

Kate looked surprised. 'Where did that come from? Er, yes, he did. We both did.'

Her sudden questions must have sounded really rude. Poor Kate didn't know what was going around Laura's head. 'Sorry. I'm sorry. It's just…' She paused. 'Okay. This is the basics. I have been with my boyfriend for a long time. Everything is fine. He's a nice guy. We're happy. But…' How could she phrase it without sounding pathetic? *He doesn't want to commit to me? He's not sure he wants to be with me? I am pathetic and desperate and…*

'But?' Kate prompted.

'But he doesn't want to make plans. To talk about the future. Marriage. Children. The usual stuff. And I'm thirty-two.'

She could see Kate trying to stifle a smile. Maybe thirty-two didn't sound very old to her. 'And you want all these things. Marriage, children and so on?'

'Yes. I do. I mean, I don't necessarily want them right *now*. But I want to know that we are planning for them. That we have an idea when we are going to have them. I can't bear this "let's see how life goes" mentality.' In fact, if James used that phrase one more time there was a seventy-five percent chance his life wouldn't be going anywhere. Permanently.

Kate sipped her wine and nodded slowly. 'I get that. And has he said why he doesn't want to make plans? Does *he* definitely want children?'

That made Laura stop and think. Did he? He'd never actually said that he *didn't*. But then, he had never really talked about wanting them, either. How had she never posed this question? 'I think he does.'

Kate looked at her over the top of her wine glass. 'It might be an idea to ask.'

Of course some people didn't want to have children. Laura's aunt and uncle hadn't had children, and they had a very nice life spending half the year in England and half in the Canaries. But *most* people did the marriage and babies thing, didn't they? 'I'm pretty sure he would have told me by now if he didn't want kids.' Either that or he was complete sadomasochist who liked to have the same row on a loop with his girlfriend.

Kate gave a small shrug. 'What if he doesn't want to tell you he doesn't want children? What if he's afraid to lose you?'

Laura frowned. Was that possible? 'I don't think so. He's not usually afraid to say what he thinks about anything.'

'I'm sure you're right. But if not… Is it more important to you to be with someone who wants children, or to be with him? Do you love him enough to sacrifice having children if he doesn't want them?'

Laura picked up her own glass and took a large gulp. She shivered. That was strong. She took another gulp. 'And was it really important to you? I mean, if that's okay to ask? How did *you* know that you wanted to have children?'

Kate screwed up her face. 'Gosh. That's the second time I've been asked that today. I guess it just felt like the right time.'

Everyone Laura asked said that. It was exasperating. What did that actually *mean*? What was the right time? The right age? Thirty? Thirty-three? Older? Why couldn't someone give her a definite number? 'I see.'

Kate sighed. 'The thing is, you can't always plan these things too precisely. Babies don't always come on demand'

Laura felt an icy finger down her spine. She knew that first-hand. Babies could come uninvited. And they could go the same way. 'Isn't that why you should have a plan? You need to give yourself the best chance. Ovulation kits, temperature charts and so on?'

Kate looked horrified. 'Oh my word, Laura. You don't start off with all that. It might become necessary for some people, but at the beginning you just cross your fingers and, you know, have a bit of fun.'

Fun? Laura didn't feel like she'd had much fun lately. James had worked a lot of late hours and when he was home he just wanted to relax or get an early night. Of sleep. He didn't want to see other people at the weekends or make plans to go away or anything. When they did spend any time together, it didn't take long before the conversation deteriorated into marriages and babies and tears and storming off to bed. No fun whatsoever. 'I just want him to tell me yes or no. He just continually puts off talking about it. All I seem to do is moan. His refusal to discuss it properly is making me into the kind of girlfriend I never wanted to be.'

Kate laughed. 'I'm sorry. It's just I said a very similar thing to my kids a couple of weeks ago. I was dragging them around the supermarket and they kept picking stuff up or running around so that all I was doing was yelling at them and saying, "I was going to be such a cool mum and you're both ruining it!"'

Laura laughed. She twirled her wine glass in her fingers and stared into the dark red liquid. 'There's something else. Or rather...' She might as well tell this woman. It wasn't like she was ever going to see her again. 'There might be... some*one* else.' She looked up at Kate. Was she shocked? She didn't look it.

'I see. And is he – this someone else – is he here, in Paris?'

Laura nodded. Although saying it out loud made her feel silly. It wasn't as if anything had happened. 'I'm not having an affair or anything. I just feel... attracted to someone.'

'And does he feel the same way?'

She gave a tiny nod this time. 'I think so.'

Kate looked at her intently and then motioned to the waiter. *'Pommes frites, s'il vous plaît.'* She turned back to Laura. 'We need chips for this.'

It may have been the chips or the wine, but Laura found herself spilling it all out. Kate didn't interrupt once. Just sipped her wine and offered Laura the basket of chips whenever she took a breath. It felt good to get it all out. When she finished, she felt about ten percent lighter.

'Okay.' Kate put the basket down and leaned forwards. 'So, you love James, but you are attracted to Paolo?'

Laura nodded. 'Yes.'

'And you want to have children with James, but you don't know if he wants the same thing.'

This time she was less definite. 'Yes, I think so.'

Kate narrowed her eyes. 'You think you want children, or you think you want them with James?'

Laura took a deep breath. 'I do want children and... I do love James.'

Kate shook her head. 'You didn't answer my question.'

Laura rubbed her temples. The wine was beginning to fur her thinking. 'I'm thirty-two. If I break up with James, it would take me months to get over him and then I would have to meet someone else and then wait for the relationship to get serious and then…' She looked up at Kate, surprised at the sound of tears at the back of her throat. 'I just don't have time.'

Kate laughed. Not unkindly, but it was a laugh all the same. 'I know thirty-two feels old, but it really isn't. I don't know James and I don't presume to tell you what to do with your relationship. But let me tell you something that I know *is* true. Having a baby is hard work. *Really* hard work. And you need to be with someone who is as on board with it as you are. Otherwise you don't stand a chance. Not a chance.'

It sounded as if Kate had a catch in her voice too. Was there something in this French wine? 'But, if I have feelings for someone else. For Paolo. That must mean I don't love James. Doesn't it?'

Kate shook her head. 'No. Of course it doesn't mean that. It just means you are attracted to Paolo. It has nothing to do with James.'

Was that true? Did it mean nothing? Should she just ignore these feelings and carry on with Plan A? Was this… attraction to Paolo just confusing her? Or maybe it was her old lurking fear that was muddying the waters… Whilst she was talking this all out with Kate, she might as well get everything off her chest. She took a very deep breath. 'I had a miscarriage. Thirteen years ago. I was nineteen. I'm worried I can't have a baby at all.'

She didn't look up. Just attempted another slug from her wine glass, which was empty.

'Oh, love,' Kate reached over and put her hand on Laura's. 'That must have been awful for you. But that doesn't mean you can't have a baby. It is incredibly common to lose a baby in the early stages of pregnancy. Especially your first one. Surely they told you that?'

They had told her that, but it still didn't stop her feeling like this. 'But you should have a baby before you're thirty, shouldn't you? There are risks and everything.'

Kate topped up Laura's wine glass and then her own. When had they got a whole bottle? 'There are risks in any pregnancy. But you're taking a much bigger risk on your happiness by rushing into parenthood if you, or the other person, are not ready. And some men' – she shrugged – 'are never ready.'

Laura's stomach flipped. This was her deepest fear. That she would wait and wait until it was too late. 'But how do you know?'

Kate settled herself in her seat as if she was about to tell a story. 'I lived with a guy for nine years. Perfectly nice, fun to be around, bought me nice gifts for my birthday. I thought I was set; he was my future.' She stopped and shook her head slowly.

Laura leaned forwards. 'What happened?'

'Tim was a musician and he had big dreams. He was going to be in a hugely successful jazz combo, get discovered and signed by a major record label. The only problem was, everything else in his life was on hold until that happened. He went from job to job because he left every time they wouldn't give him time off for a last-minute gig. Which meant he couldn't get a mortgage or a loan for a decent car. And marriage? Children? Answer was always the same. *Someday*.'

Laura felt sick. 'What did you do?'

Kate took a long sip of her wine, put it back down on the table and placed a hand each side of the glass. 'I got to the point of no return and gave him an ultimatum. We made a plan for the future and stuck to it, or we were over.'

Laura could barely get the words out. 'And what did he say?'

'He came home one day with a gigantic bunch of flowers.'

Laura leaned forwards. 'And?'

'And… told me that he was moving back to his mother's.' Kate's face was expressionless for a moment. Then she started to laugh. 'It took me a very long time to find that funny.'

Laura smiled weakly. She didn't have a long time to wait. She needed to know now. Maybe fancying Paolo meant nothing. Maybe he was just a distraction. She should focus on James. James was her boyfriend. She'd go back to the hotel now and call him. It was after five p.m. He might even be on the way home.

CHAPTER EIGHTEEN

Shannon

As Shannon approached the Jardin du Luxembourg, the warm smell from a crêpe stall made her feel hungry for the second time that day; maybe this time she could risk being able to eat something. She queued with the tourists for a *crêpe au jambon et fromage* and a *café au lait* and then walked into the gardens to wait for Kate.

The Jardin du Luxembourg was one of Shannon's favourite places in Paris. The green manicured lawns and hedges dotted with sculptures of literary figures and explosions of flowers were both formal and beautiful. Tall and vibrant with orange, brown and red leaves, the trees whispered in the breeze. Her pace slowed and her shoulders began to relax. *Just breathe.*

She had arranged to meet Kate by the pond. As she approached, the air was alive with the chatter of small children using long poles to push miniature sailboats across the huge expanse of water. Shannon watched as a chubby-legged toddler waddled towards the edge before being caught by his mother. The mother swept him up into her arms and buried her face into his delighted, wriggling body. Walking a little further round, Shannon found a spare chair near to another young mother with a pram and a young girl. Watching her rock the pram whilst calling to her other child not to go too far, made Shannon's stomach flip over.

Where had all these mothers and babies appeared from lately? She'd never noticed them before.

She felt Kate's hand on her shoulder. 'You'll spoil your dinner, eating this late.'

Kate's eyelids were suspiciously droopy. Shannon had seen that expression many times before. 'I think you've already spoiled yours. Liquid lunch, was it?'

When Kate laughed, she looked more like herself. 'I was just leaving a café when you called. Bumped into a girl who was on my train this morning. We *might* have had a couple of glasses.'

'Good for you.' Shannon was jealous. She'd kill for a glass of wine right now. The smell of this takeaway coffee was turning her stomach and she'd only managed a few bites of the crêpe. Her eyes were obviously bigger than her belly. Although that might be about to change. She stood to join Kate and threw them both into a bin.

Kate looked horrified. 'I was only joking! You should have finished that.'

Shannon linked her arm into hers. 'I'd had enough. Come on, let's walk back towards the hotel.'

Kate squeezed her hand and they started to walk out of the gardens. 'This is a nice surprise. I wasn't expecting to hear from you until later. I thought you had things to do at the office.'

Shannon shrugged. The last place on earth she wanted to be right now was in the office with a prowling Robert. With any luck, he would be too busy tonight and tomorrow to bring up the subject of his daughter's party again. 'I got everything done, so I thought we could catch up.' She walked a few more steps before taking a deep breath. 'Actually, there's something I wanted to tell you. Something I didn't mention earlier.'

'Oh?' Kate looked sideways at her and raised an eyebrow. 'That sounds intriguing. What exciting information would merit an impromptu meeting in the park?'

'I'm pregnant.'

Kate tripped and righted herself. The shock on her face was almost comic. Standing still, she took Shannon's arm and stared at her. 'I'm sorry I… I mean, I'm not sorry you're pregnant, I'm just sorry that I… or am I… I mean, are you pleased?'

Shannon took Kate's hand and linked it through her arm again, gently tugging her into walking. 'Not especially, no.'

Kate swallowed hard. She glanced at Shannon and they continued to walk in silence for few moments. She was clearly trying to choose her words carefully. Finally, she said, 'Well, that sobered me right up.'

Shannon laughed and felt her whole body relax. Kate was definitely the right person to talk to about this. 'Shall we sit and have a drink before we go back to the hotel?' Robert might be checking into the hotel by now and she didn't want to run the risk of bumping into him yet.

Once they were sitting outside a café with a drink, and Shannon had filled Kate in on the details of how pregnant she thought she was, she told her the thing that was bothering her the most. 'Look at me, Kate. How can I have a baby? I love my job, my life, as it is. I'm not mother material. I'm just not made for it.'

Kate frowned. 'What do you mean? What's "mother material"?'

How could she put this? 'You know. Changing diapers and mashing up food and…' She trailed off at the look on Kate's face.

Kate pursed her lips together. 'You mean you don't want to turn into someone like me?'

Damn. That had been tactless. Although a little bit true. 'No, I don't mean that. You wanted children. It's different.'

Kate sat back in her chair and sipped at her drink. Eventually, she spoke. 'So, you definitely don't want a child? I mean, I'm not saying you *should* want one. God knows, I know how much of a commitment it is. But you need to be sure.' She paused. 'Okay, I'm just going to say this. It might be your last chance.'

Shannon had thought of this, of course she had. Approaching forty and single, it was thrust down your throat by everyone and everything. 'It's not as simple as that.'

'You mean Robert?' Kate looked surprised. 'I mean, of course it would be wonderful if he wants to be a part of this, but surely you can do this on your own if you need to?'

Shannon shrugged. 'I don't know if I can.'

Kate leaned forward. 'If you don't want to have a child, Shannon, that is completely your choice. But to say you *can't* do it… I don't understand. I've never heard you say you couldn't do something before. Never.' She paused, then a smile curled at the edges of her mouth. 'Do you remember when you tried to save my life?'

Save her life? Was she joking? When had she… Suddenly, Shannon remembered. 'Your cardigan arrest!'

Now Kate was laughing, 'I pushed up the sleeves of my cardigan and my arms were so blue, I was convinced I was dying!'

'And you'd drunk so much the night before – well, we were both horribly hungover – that we thought it was alcohol poisoning.'

'I was screaming and running around…'

'And I made you sit down and loosen all your clothes while the receptionist – what was her name? – while she called for an ambulance.'

Kate's shoulders had started to shake. 'I really thought I was a goner.'

Shannon had known she had to stay calm but when Kate had taken off her cardigan, her entire arms really had been mottled and blue. 'It was the tears that did it. I was rubbing your arms to try and get your circulation back and the blue…'

'… started to come off!'

'Your new cardigan!'

'The bloody dye had come out of it! Must have been the cold sweat of my hangover.'

Maybe it was the stress, maybe it was the joy of being here with her dear friend, but Shannon laughed hysterically at the memory of calling 999 and explaining why they didn't need the ambulance after all. The call handler was probably still telling the story of the crazy Yank and her buddy Smurfette.

Kate joined in. But when they had finished laughing, she reached forwards and took Shannon's hands. 'What is this really all about?'

Shannon took a deep breath. If she wasn't honest about her feelings, there was no point to this conversation. 'I don't think I have that *thing*. The maternal thing. I don't think I would love a baby enough, and…' Her voice caught. Was she going to cry? 'A baby needs love.'

Shannon didn't do crying. It wasn't that she was tough – she was actually a pretty soft touch – it was just that she didn't cry. It didn't happen. But right now, she did have a strange burning sensation at the back of her throat.

'How can you say that?' Kate put her drink down. 'You are one of the most loving people I know. You always greet everyone with a hug – whether they want it or not – and you were the person I needed when I didn't know what to do about Tim.'

It was true. They had sat up until five a.m. going through the whole thing. To Shannon, it had been straightforward: Tim had been a Peter Pan loser. She'd had to couch it to Kate a bit more gently than that, of course. In the end, Kate had agreed to give Tim an ultimatum, and he'd made the decision for her.

But this wasn't about caring for your mates. This was life-changing. 'Yes, I love my friends, of course I do. But a baby? That's different.'

Kate took her hand again. 'Of course, it's different. The love you have for your baby is overwhelming. It's like being in love with someone times about a thousand. You become besotted by them. Enslaved by them. Every tiny movement becomes the most important thing in the world.' Kate paused. Her lip was wobbling. She regained control. 'You don't have to worry about loving your baby, Shannon. There is a lot you might have to consider, but loving them? That will hit you between the eyes.'

A single tear made its way down Shannon's cheek. 'I don't think I am made like that, Kate. In fact, I know that I'm not.'

'What do you mean? You can't possibly know.' Kate's phoned dinged. She screwed up her face. 'Bugger. Sorry, I have to just check this. In case it's something to do with the kids.'

This was what it was like. Once you had a child, your whole life revolved around them. You couldn't even have a conversation in peace. Shannon watched Kate's shoulders get higher and higher towards her ears as she read the text. Was everything okay? It didn't look it. She waited for her to finish reading before asking, 'What is it? What's happened?'

Kate shook her head. 'It's nothing important. Let's get back to you and the baby.'

No way could she ignore the fact that her friend looked unhappy and go back to talking about herself. 'That can wait for a moment; you look agitated. What was the text about?'

Kate sighed. 'It was just that woman again – Melissa. She's looking for volunteers to man stalls at the school fete.'

She must be lying. The look on Kate's face was more akin to being told that Luke had lost the house at a poker game. 'Why would that stress you out?'

Kate closed her eyes and then opened them again. 'Because the school fete is bedlam. Sugar-fuelled kids clutching sticky twenty pences and running from stall to stall to win as much plastic crap as they can. It's bad enough fighting my way around as a customer and trying to ensure Alice doesn't see the Teddy Tombola stall.' She grimaced.

'So, don't volunteer.'

Kate held out her hands. 'But how can I say no?'

There must be something here that Shannon wasn't getting. 'You just open your mouth and say it. No.'

Kate appeared to consider it. 'But what excuse will I make?'

Why was Kate playing dumb suddenly? 'Why do you need an excuse? Just say you don't want to do it.'

Kate looked into the middle distance, eyes darting around as if she was formulating a strategy. 'Maybe I could say that I have to take my mum out that day?'

Was she seriously trying to concoct a plan rather than just ignoring this request? 'Or you could just say no.'

'I mean, if I apologise and explain that she needs me for something…'

Shannon was going to stage an intervention in a minute. 'Hello? Are you listening to me? Just say no!'

'You don't understand. Everyone will think I don't care about the fete.'

'But you don't.'

'I know. But I can't show that. I mean, it's an important event. Parents are *supposed* to get involved.'

'Why is it so important?'

'It raises money for the school.'

Well, that was easily fixed. 'So, give them some money. Put it in an envelope. Write on the front, "*Money in lieu of standing behind a table for three hours.*"'

Kate rolled her eyes. 'Oh, if only I could do that.' She picked up her glass and drained her drink. 'Let's just forget that for now. It's really not important. Let me quickly go to the toilet and we'll get back to talking about you.' She paused and leaned across to Shannon, squeezed her hand. 'I've missed this, Shan. I've missed you.'

Another damn lump rose up in Shannon's throat. It was an epidemic. She put her hand over Kate's. 'I've missed you, too.'

While Kate was gone, Shannon checked her own messages. Then wished she hadn't: there was one from Adam.

Why are you not picking up your phone? I need to speak to you urgently. Faye knows everything. Including your work address. Please call me.

This time, Shannon's sickness had nothing to do with pregnancy hormones. What the hell was he thinking, telling Faye? And why give her Shannon's *address*? How dare he! Thank God Faye was on another continent… But that wasn't the point. There was absolutely no reason for him to have done that, especially without warning Shannon or asking her permission or… How the hell had it happened? What did Faye know? Shannon needed to call him, but she was scared that Faye might answer and she wasn't brave enough to risk that.

Kate slid back into her seat. 'So, where were we?'

Shannon looked at her watch. 'Actually, I really need to get back to the hotel and get ready for this damn dinner cruise this evening. But I feel better for just telling you and getting it off my chest. We can chew it over later. Are you just going to eat at the hotel tonight? God, I wish we could just have dinner together.' She motioned to the waiter that they wanted to pay their bill. It was difficult to make normal conversation when her heart felt as if it might beat itself out of her chest. Why the hell had Adam told Faye?

Kate picked up her cup to drink the last of her coffee. 'Me too. But actually, I forgot to tell you about the other person I bumped into. Was Paris always so small? That guy from earlier – Graham. He invited me to meet him for dinner.'

Shannon felt an uneasiness. Dinner with Graham? 'Really? Are you going to go?'

Kate shrugged. 'I said yes because it felt rude not to. Plus, I don't really want to go out for dinner on my own. Lunch on my own was weird enough. Do you think I should cancel?'

Shannon knew that Kate had eaten dinner out on her own in the past. When you worked in field sales, there were plenty of overnight stays in the back of beyond ready to meet a customer bright and early the next morning. It seemed a bit strange that she didn't feel able to do it any longer. Plus, Shannon wasn't sure Graham was the best choice of dinner partner. 'Okay, but don't drink too much.'

Kate rolled her eyes. 'All right, Mum. I promise to be good.'

Kate was joking, but the word *Mum* made Shannon's stomach flip again. *Just stay calm.* Get through the dinner cruise with the sales team tonight, sort out the meetings for tomorrow, and then there would be time to sit down and have a big think. At least Adam was over four thousand miles away. Her wrath towards him could wait until at least tomorrow.

CHAPTER NINETEEN

Kate

After the text she sent from Saint Julien le Pauvre, telling Luke she wouldn't be home to collect the kids, he had called fourteen times, left four text messages and three voicemails. Kate had ignored them all.

She took her time dressing for dinner. She'd packed a floral dress and pumps which were unlikely to set the Paris fashion paparazzi on her tail but would have to do. Languishing in the shower without small people throwing themselves at the door or Luke shouting up to ask if she'd seen his credit card was a luxury. As were the clean towels, bathrobe and slippers – all brilliant white, without a trace of grubby fingers or nose wipings.

After the shower, she wrapped her hair in a towel and sat at the dressing table to do her make-up. She even had time to do her nails. There were two nail polishes in her make-up bag: she chose the one that wasn't psychedelic pink with Barbie's face on the front. In the mirror, she saw a regular woman. Not a wife, a mum or a daughter. Just Kate. Just her.

Once she was ready to go, she sent Luke a long text message. *The* text message. The one that outlined the plan. Gave the Eurostar ticket information. And asked him to come.

… Meet me tomorrow. No kids. The Eiffel Tower. two p.m. Your ticket is booked.

*

The restaurant was crowded and full of young, attractive people. A few years ago, Kate would have been one of those people in the huge group at the bar, laughing and joking and not at all aware of anyone other than the friends around her. Now she just wanted to scuttle to the table before anyone had the chance to point at her and say, '*Who* let *you* in here?'

Graham seemed to know the waiters and got a table in the corner with the merest nod of his head. It was a little quieter there, and mercifully darker, so she didn't feel so exposed. There was nothing wrong with her having dinner with someone. They were just two married people having a night out and there was nothing 'date-like' about it at all. But she did feel guilty. Like the night out with Tim, she just pushed those feelings down.

Graham passed her the wine list and she passed it back. 'Can you choose? I hate choosing wine, never really know what to pick.'

Graham laughed. 'What kind of wine do you like?'

Well, that was a silly question. 'The kind with alcohol in.'

He laughed again; clearly, she was very funny this evening. 'Red or white?'

By now, Kate had picked up the menu and was flicking through it. It felt a long time since the *croque monsieur et frites*. 'I think I'm going to have steak, so it'd better be red. Have you eaten here before?'

'Yes.' He closed his menu and laid it down on the table. 'I'm a creature of habit, I'm afraid. I keep coming back to the same spots.'

'With a different woman each time?' As soon as the words were out of her mouth, Kate wanted to shove them back in. What kind of question was that? It sounded like an accusation or a flirtation. *Move the conversation on quickly, before he has a chance to reply.* 'Do you travel anywhere else for your work, or just Paris?'

'Just Paris really. Let's not talk about work though – too boring. Let's talk about you.'

He was either mocking her or he actually was flirting – 1980s style. The longer they were here, the more uncomfortable she was feeling. What was wrong with her? Couldn't she just have dinner without overthinking every single comment? Why did she have the feeling that she should have told Luke she was doing this? Especially when she hadn't felt the need to tell him when she went out with Tim.

When she'd told Tim that she wouldn't go to the jazz bar with him, she'd meant it. Jazz had always been more his thing: making his own path through the chords, comping, experimenting. He always used to tease her about sticking to the sheet music: *See past the dots, babe.*

But when he'd asked her again, he'd caught her on a particularly bad day. The children had been fighting relentlessly over an old toy they hadn't looked at in months, and in the time it had taken to snatch up the toy, berate their behaviour and separate them, she had burnt the mushroom frigging frittata for their dinner. Then Luke had called, whilst she was scraping the frigging frittata into the bin, to say he would be late home. Tim's text – *There's a pianist at the jazz club tomorrow night. You have to come!* – had arrived when she was staring into a cup of tea and fantasising about contracting a non-fatal illness which would necessitate a week's stay in hospital.

Although she hadn't exactly mentioned Tim, she *had* asked Luke along. 'I'm meeting some friends to listen to a pianist. Do you want to come?'

He'd shaken his head. 'Not my kind of thing. You go, I'll babysit the kids.' Firstly, she had been angry at the word 'babysit' when he was talking about looking after his own children. Secondly, her whole life consisted of doing things that were 'not her kind of thing.' Did he think she enjoyed drinking foul coffee in stinky play centres or cramming into a hot, sweaty viewing gallery at the gymnastics club whilst Alice had her lessons? It was this irritation that had prevented her from mentioning Tim. Plus, Tim *was* just a friend nowadays. It wasn't like anything was happening between them.

And nothing was happening tonight either. So, there was no need to tell Luke, was there? She smiled at Graham. 'Not much to say, really. I lead a rather dull existence. Does your wife work?'

He shook his head. 'No.'

She waited for him to say something else, but he didn't. There was a lull in the conversation so Kate studied the menu. She already knew what she was going to order, but had no idea what else to do. She had become socially inept. Was it because he was a man? Because, if it was, that was totally nonsensical.

The guilt wasn't going away. Would she have felt comfortable with Luke going out for dinner with a woman he had only just met? She knew the answer to this, but didn't feel good about it. But there was nothing to be ashamed of, was there? Luke wouldn't want to go out to dinner with some woman, because he hated making small talk. The thought of it just being him and someone, of either sex, that he didn't know would probably be his idea of hell. Whereas Kate had always liked meeting new people; she found it fun to chat about irrelevant and unimportant things with someone new. Which meant that it was less important if she had dinner with a stranger, for the purposes of idle chit-chat and company, than if Luke did. Because if Luke did it, it would mean he was making a huge effort and therefore it would mean something. Whereas this meant nothing. Didn't it? *Brain, stop. Just stop.*

Graham spoke and pulled her out of the downward spiral. 'I'm going to have the duck, I think.' He topped up her wine. 'You're a slow drinker.'

'I'm trying to pace myself. You don't want me dancing on the table with my knickers on my head before they even serve the dessert.'

'Don't I?' There it was again. Was he flirting? Did it matter?

Graham excused himself and went to the toilet. Kate gulped down some of her wine and looked around. Who was she trying to kid? If this man was planning on anything untoward there were a hundred women in this place alone who were more enticing than she was. Had she forgotten that she'd put on over two stone since having children, and that many nights of broken sleep had done nothing for the youthful glow of her skin? She needed to get over herself and enjoy tonight for what it was – dinner with someone who may turn out to be interesting company. He wasn't trying to chat her up and she wasn't cheating on Luke by being here. It was just dinner.

Graham appeared back at the table and Kate decided to kick her personality up into first gear.

'Where's the best place you've been to?' This was hardly witty banter but at least she was trying.

The meal went pretty well after that. They chatted, drank, ate, drank, chatted some more, drank. The more wine she drank, the more she wanted. She didn't feel drunk, just bubbly and funny. Oh yes, she felt incredibly funny.

And then they were dancing.

Whilst they were eating or drinking or talking, the mood in the restaurant had changed. There was only a tiny dance floor, in front of the bar, and when she'd arrived, she hadn't recognised it as a dance floor at all. But now, here they were, dancing.

Kate had always loved dancing, but never got the chance to do it nowadays. She was too old to go to a nightclub. She'd tried with some friends a couple of years ago, but they'd all felt unbelievably sad in both senses of the word. Of course, there were nightclubs aimed at people their age but, in reality, over-thirties nightclubs were actually full of over-fifties and, much as they didn't want to be out with people young enough to be their daughters, they didn't want to spend the night with people who could be their mothers, either. And family parties weren't the same any more, since the children. Luke, always on the lookout for an excuse not to go or to leave early, would start saying how tired the children looked as soon as they arrived. Kate couldn't get up and dance for fear of what the children would get up to in the meantime – and having them on the dance floor was just a liability. Thomas was just at the right height to be knocked out as soon as someone started off the twirling and kicking of 'Uptown Girl'.

Now, here she was, jiggling on the spot with a man she'd only met a few hours previously. Dancing with a man was, in itself, a surreal activity. She hadn't managed to get Luke on the dance floor since their wedding. He wasn't a bad dancer, but he seemed to consider dancing in public to be a form of torture. When they'd first been dating, he could be persuaded to join her for a couple of slow songs. Now they'd been married for nearly nine years, the 'conversation' consisted of her looking at him hopefully and him saying, 'No.'

The combination of nervousness at finding herself dancing with a stranger and realising, now she was standing up, that she was indeed drunk, meant that her technique was more than a little off. She was doing the 'mum dance'. Maybe it was due to having spent the first eighteen months of both children's lives with them permanently on her hip. That awkward pose must have lasting consequences for your stance. And your dance stance.

Graham, on the other hand, seemed to be a pretty smooth mover. And that was when Kate began to mistrust his motives: a man who volunteered to dance that enthusiastically was probably either gay or looking to get laid.

Stupidly, she didn't take this as her cue to leave.

CHAPTER TWENTY

Laura

After the brightness of the early evening, the inside of the restaurant cruiser seemed dim. Laura had been expecting touristy plastic-ness, but the interior of the boat looked very much like an exclusive restaurant. They didn't always eat somewhere so nice – had Shannon booked it to make them feel good before the meeting tomorrow? What did she know that they didn't?

The hors d'oeuvres had been fantastic – even James wouldn't have found fault. He considered himself a bit of a gastronome these days: long gone were their student days of Beanfeast from a packet. That wasn't the only thing that had changed – his dress sense had had a major overhaul, too. The girls in his office who looked so surprised at the two of them being an item, might not be so surprised if they'd seen the cardigan he was wearing when he'd first asked her out at a student night in the town nightclub.

Gabriella waved at Laura from across the room and pointed to the seat next to hers. Laura's heart sank. She'd hoped to sit next to Shannon, but she was still at the entrance of the boat, chatting with the maître d'. It wasn't that Laura didn't like Gabriella, but she never felt entirely at ease around her. Was it because Gabriella was so tall and blonde and certain? And beautiful?

And where was Paolo? He was standing a short distance from the other end of the table, recounting something hilarious by the look on Henrik's face. Shannon joined them, and Paolo made a grand show of taking her hand and bowing before her. Shannon pulled her hand away and gave him a playful shove. Gabriella caught the direction of Laura's gaze.

'Paolo is his usual self today, I see.' Her icy tone confirmed that this wasn't meant as a compliment.

Laura poured herself a glass of wine from the bottle on the table. The effects of her drinking with Kate earlier had worn off so she should be safe to drink some more. 'What do you mean?'

Gabriella held out her own glass for a top-up and then swirled the wine around it with authority before bringing it to her nose. 'Oh, you know, chatting to everyone, making sure that he is the centre of attention. Getting his ego massaged?'

His ego? Paolo? Laura sneaked another look. Paolo was flushed and animated and the guys around him were hanging on his every word. He wore a fresh linen shirt with the top button undone. The pale blue was bright against his tanned throat. His Adam's apple moving in time to the gesticulation of his hands and… My God, she needed to stop thinking like this. She coughed. 'He's just telling a joke, I think.'

'He's good at that.' Gabriella ran her finger around the rim of her glass. 'I know that you two *get on well*, but just be careful with him.'

Gabriella knew that Laura wasn't single, so what was with this rather patronising advice? 'I don't know what you mean. We're just colleagues. I have a boyfriend, you know.'

Gabriella nodded, sipped her wine and then fixed her blue eyes on Laura. 'That's what I mean.'

Sylvie joined them and filled them in on what she'd gleaned from Shannon about the agenda for tomorrow. As she was talking, Laura glanced over at Paolo again and he looked up and winked. Still smiling and joking with those around him, he didn't seem remotely affected by the conversation they'd had this afternoon.

Laura had spent the two hours between returning to the hotel and going to dinner brewing on it. Was he right about James? Should she even have spoken to him about it? Why was her heart beating so quickly every time she thought about their conversation?

When she'd got back to the hotel earlier, in a desperate attempt to get some perspective, she'd called James from her room. Miraculously, he'd answered. 'Hey you – how's it going?'

There was something reassuring about just hearing his voice. 'Fine. Fine. Can you talk?'

There was a lot of traffic noise in the background and the reception wasn't great. 'Er, well, I'm just in a cab at the moment so I have about ten minutes?'

She'd taken a deep breath, opened her mouth and then words which she had absolutely not planned to say came out of it. Maybe it was the wine. Or the chips. 'James, I know I've talked about this a lot, but I need an answer. An honest answer. Are you ever going to want marriage and children? With me?'

'What? Oh… crikey, Laura, you can't seriously want to have this conversation over the telephone?'

A coldness had washed over her and made her voice a thousand times calmer than she felt. 'On the phone, on the sun loungers at the beach, at home in bed. You never give me an answer. You're *too busy to talk about it* or *life is too hectic right now* or *we're too young to be talking about this*. It's the same conversation, James, over and over and over and I don't think I can keep having it.' She knew she was being ridiculous. What kind of loon gives their boyfriend an ultimatum over the telephone? The probability of getting the answer she wanted was infinitesimally small. How many times did you have to throw the dice before you got a six? And what if you'd begun to suspect that you'd rather throw a three or a four? Or a seven?

Whatever James liked to say about her overactive imagination, there was definitely an irritated tone to his voice. 'Laura,

I don't know what is going on over there, but this is just a little bit ridiculous. I love you, but this is not the way I want us to be. Look, I'm at my destination and I need to pay the cab driver. I can't talk now, but we will talk about this, I promise. It's all good, Lau, it's all good. Take care.'

Now Gabriella was looking at her expectantly. What had she missed? 'Sorry, I didn't catch that, what did you say?'

'I asked if you were trying to lip read.' Gabriella nodded in Paolo's direction.

Laura hadn't even realised she was still staring at him. She hoped fervently he hadn't noticed. 'I wasn't… I just…'

'Ignore Gaby.' Sylvie patted Laura's hand. She was equally as stunning as Gabriella with her thick dark hair and olive skin, but didn't wear her beauty in such a hostile way. 'You do whatever you want to do, Laura.'

'But I wasn't… I mean, I'm not…'

Gabriella held up her hands. 'I'm not the bad guy, here. I'm just trying to make sure you don't get hurt.'

What was this with everyone suddenly having such a great regard for Laura's welfare these days? She didn't dare look at Paolo again, but was pretty sure he would be enjoying himself in the middle of the group at the other end of the table. How she wished she were down there with them, rather than here with the Voice of Doom.

Gabriella leaned forwards, conspiratorially. 'Some of us have worked together a long time. We have seen the other side to people.'

'Stop it, Gabriella.' Sylvie finished her wine and pulled on her arm. 'Come on, let's go and dance before the food arrives. You too, Laura.'

Laura shook her head. 'I'll finish my drink first. Go on, I'll see you up there.'

Doing her utmost to resist looking at Paolo, Laura stared out of the window of the boat. Outside, she could see the cathedral of

Notre Dame slowly drifting past; she'd try and visit it before she went home. Before coming to Paris, she'd assumed that the Eiffel Tower would be the monument to see, but there was something about this melancholy cathedral which was surprisingly attractive. Lost in her thoughts, she didn't notice Paolo sit down beside her until he spoke.

'Beautiful.' She jumped and turned to see his mock-innocent expression. 'Notre Dame, I mean. It is beautiful.'

Feeling Gabriella's eyes drilling into the back of her head, Laura shifted in her seat and tried to look disinterested. 'Yes. It is.'

He put his hand lightly on her shoulder. She almost melted. 'Look, I wanted to apologise again for this afternoon. I had no right to say anything.' If he mentioned again about not wanting to see her hurt, she would start looking for some kind of sign on her head. Without meaning to, she glanced in Gabriella's direction; yep, she wasn't imagining those eye-lasers.

Paolo caught the direction of her glance. He removed his hand and sat back in his chair. 'What has Gabriella been saying?' He rubbed his chin in a way which made Laura wish she'd paid more attention to a body language article she'd seen in the paper last week. Did rubbing your chin mean you were nervous or guilty? Or both? 'I suppose you know we had a bit of a thing last year?' Laura tried not to show the shock on her face. 'It was nothing. I mean, it was *something*, but *nothing*. I'm not particularly proud of my behaviour but, there you are, you can't take it back.' He looked above Laura's head and she realised that Gabriella was now standing behind her. Were these people trained by the SAS? 'Hi, Gabriella.'

'Paolo.' She nodded coolly.

'Anyway, I'll go back to Robert and the others and start rounding them up; I assume we'll be sitting down to eat shortly. Maybe we can speak later, Laura?' Paolo looked to be about to put a hand on her shoulder again, but then thought better of it. He nodded at Gabriella, who picked up her wine glass and raised it at him, and then returned to his seat.

'Interesting conversation?' Gabriella raised a perfectly groomed eyebrow.

Laura was still reeling with the news that Paolo and Gabriella had had a 'bit of a thing'. Her face was hot. Jealousy? Embarrassment? 'Not as interesting as the one I'd like to have with you.'

Gabriella smiled. Laura knew it wasn't going to take much of a sales pitch to get her to talk. Gabriella picked up her wine glass and nodded in the direction of the dance floor.

As soon as they were out of earshot, she began to talk. 'I don't normally date men I work with. We all know what a terrible idea that is.'

She paused as if she wanted Laura to agree with her, but Laura wanted to work out what she was agreeing with first. 'And?'

'And then I met Paolo. He was very persuasive. Very charming.' She paused again and glanced over in his direction. Laura couldn't help but look too. When she turned back to Gabriella, she was looking at her intently. 'Very Paolo.'

Laura wasn't sure she wanted to hear this.

CHAPTER TWENTY-ONE

Shannon

Desserts were being served. Crème brûlée: how predictable. Shannon had planned to book a more modern restaurant, but Robert had wanted to come here. At least the sales guys all seemed happy. When Robert played bad cop, Shannon was needed to be the good one. It was great to see people enjoying themselves, particularly when she was the one who had arranged everything. The food had been decent. The tables were well dressed. The music was good but not too loud. *And relax.*

Robert was deep in conversation with André and Mark. Were they talking business? She had given Robert strict instructions that tonight was purely social. With their offices spread across Europe, nights like tonight were vital in making them feel like a real team. It was those kinds of soft skills that Robert needed Shannon for. She leaned closer to where he was sitting. Ah, no. They were just talking about soccer. That was allowed. Robert looked up and winked at her before putting both hands behind his head and miming throwing the ball onto the pitch. The other two laughed. Boys.

How were the girls doing? Laura was talking to Gabriella. And they were glancing in Paolo's direction. That didn't look good for him. Gabriella was really good fun – and an excellent saleswoman – but she was most definitely not a fan of Paolo's. Not since they'd broken up. That was why you shouldn't get involved with people you work with. *Don't screw the crew.* That had been Shannon's mantra. Until Robert.

Shannon glanced back at him. The men had been joined by a young woman she didn't recognise, although there was something familiar about her. And she was a very attractive young woman. Robert had his back to Shannon, but the rest of the sales guys looked like love-sick puppies. What was it about long blonde hair that turned grown men to mush? It wasn't even this woman's natural hair colour. Shannon shook the uncharitable thought from her head. What was she? Jealous?

Robert was leaning back in his chair and speaking up at the young blonde woman. Who was listening intently. Shannon loved him, but he wasn't *that* interesting. What was going on? She glanced back at Laura; she should go and join her conversation with Gabriella, make sure that history wasn't being rewritten. Shannon liked Laura a lot. She was a little naïve, but that just made Shannon want to look out for her. She liked Gabriella too, but Gabriella was more than capable of looking out for herself.

Now this young blonde attractive woman was throwing back her head and laughing. What *were* they talking about? And why was Robert glancing around to look at Shannon? Was that guilt on his face?

Shannon snapped her face away. It was burning. When did it get so hot in here? She pulled at the top of her shirt as she walked over to Laura and put her hand on the back of her chair. 'Everything okay, ladies?'

Laura scratched behind her ear. She didn't look particularly comfortable. 'Er… yeah… Dinner was great. We're just… um… chatting.'

Gabriella looked far more satisfied. 'Yes. I am just giving Laura some *information.*'

Shannon could guess what kind of information Gabriella was imparting. She needed to split these two up. But as she opened her mouth, there was a hand on her shoulder.

It was Robert. And the girl. 'Shannon, can I have you for just a moment?'

Shannon followed Robert – and the girl – back to the bar area. This involved them negotiating their way across a dance floor filled with older couples dancing in pairs. Shannon marvelled at people like that, who had kept a relationship going for decades. Of course, there was no guarantee that these people weren't on their second, or even third, marriage. Maybe serial monogamy was the key to happiness. It had worked for her so far.

When they reached the bar, Robert turned and smiled nervously. The young woman stood by his side. 'This is Veronique. She would like to meet you. She is my daughter.'

To say Shannon felt angry was a colossal understatement. A rage of which she hadn't known she was capable burned in her stomach. But she was a professional. On the surface, she mustn't show a thing. Not yet.

Shannon smiled and held out her hand. 'Nice to meet you, Veronique.'

Of course, this was Robert's daughter. She'd seen pictures of both his daughters but – made up for a night out – Veronique looked older than Shannon remembered. Still, the family resemblance was clear. Long limbed, easy smile, dark brown eyes. Right now, both sets of eyes were looking at her intently. One was curious, the other anxious. He should be bloody anxious. She was going to unleash hell on him later.

'Please, call me Vero. I've wanted to meet you for a long time. My father has spoken about you a great deal.' Her English was perfect. As was her young skin. She made Shannon feel old. How could Robert be the father of this fully-grown adult? Shannon stopped herself from placing her hand on her stomach again.

'Well, I hope I don't disappoint you.' Shannon had meant this to be a flippant comment, but something caught in her throat as she said it aloud. What was that all about?

The coward formerly known as Robert backed away. 'I'll go and look after everyone. You girls get to know each other.'

Girls? Patronising crapbag. He was going to pay for that later, too. She smiled at Vero again. 'I had no idea you were coming.'

Vero flicked her hair from her shoulder. She really was stunning. No wonder Robert was so proud of her. 'It's a coincidence. I'm here with some friends.'

Shannon knew a lie when she smelled one. She looked around her. 'How nice. Where are they?'

'Over the back somewhere. Are you having a nice evening?'

The girl had lovely manners, too. Clearly very well brought-up. 'Yes, thank you. Although, you know, these work things.'

What a dumb thing to say. What would this young woman know about work social events?

But Vero nodded politely. 'Papa used to moan about them all the time. He doesn't moan so much now that you are there.'

Shannon smiled. 'Yes, well. I am very good at organising.'

Vero looked at her intently. 'You are very good at managing my father. And making him happy.'

Shannon felt a rush of pleasure. She squashed it down. 'Well, he's pretty easy to please.'

Vero shook her head. 'We both know that's not true. You should have seen him when we were young. My sister and I used to hide from him when he was raging about our untidiness or noise. He definitely prefers us a lot more now we are older and can behave ourselves in restaurants.' She raised an eyebrow and smiled. 'And he also seems very happy since he met you. He talks about you a lot, you know.'

Shannon was still angry with Robert. Whatever this girl said wasn't about to get him out of hot water. 'I guess we spend a lot of time together.'

This time Vero nodded. 'I know. That's why we wanted to meet you. My sister and I. We've been wondering if we might get a stepmother sometime soon.'

Shannon felt her crème brûlée bidding to make a reappearance. *Marriage?* She laughed nervously. 'Oh, I think you're safe for a while.'

Vero shrugged. 'I've never seen him like this before. He's clearly in love with you. And, well, we'd like to get to know you. We'd like you to feel like part of the family.'

The 'F' word. The one Shannon had worked so hard to distance herself from. And here was this young and beautiful daughter of Robert's, offering her just that. On his behalf. Had he even known that was what she was going to say? And if he had, why the hell was he using his daughter to run his errands for him? Did he think Shannon would just cave into a pool of gratefulness because he was making a space for her in his life?

This wasn't her. She didn't do the family thing. She was a single. A unit. A Shannon.

Except now, she really did need to consider someone else. Even if that someone else was a tiny foetus. This time, the crème brûlée really did feel like it might reappear. 'I'm sorry. Excuse me, I just need to…'

She almost pushed the maître d' from behind his podium in her rush to get outside. The cool city air soothed her burning face, and the urge to vomit subsided a little. She laid her cheek against the steel handrail. That felt good.

Notre Dame moved slowly past as the boat made its way back up the Seine, its gothic façade looming out into the darkness. Shannon could imagine, but not see, the gargoyles on the roof – her angry face probably bore some similarities.

She had been determined not to speak to Robert about any of this tonight. She wanted to wait until the sales people had gone home and they could talk about it sensibly and like adults. And now he was trying to force her hand, make her become something she wasn't sure she ever wanted to be. Well, he had no idea what was coming. When she told him about the baby – *if* she told him about the baby – was he going to change his mind? Vero's version of his fatherhood didn't paint a picture of a man who was gaga over small people. And, on top of that, did Shannon really want to be with someone who was clearly so used to getting his own way that he would ignore her clear instructions that she did not want to meet his daughter and just invite her along anyway?

Inside her bag, her mobile dinged. Then again. Then a third time. It must have located a signal now she'd come up from the inside of the boat. She popped open her clutch bag and checked the screen of her mobile. Three missed calls. From America. Adam.

There was a voicemail, too. And a text message.

The text message felt like the safest option right now. But it wasn't.

Shannon. You MUST call me. Did you get my emails? Faye is IN PARIS. I need to explain. Just call me!

CHAPTER TWENTY-TWO

Kate

The dance floor was getting crowded, so Graham suggested they go back to their table. Kate started to relax. She was actually having a really nice time. It had been so long since she'd done this. Just a woman, out for dinner. No time to be home. No early morning alarm call tomorrow. Nothing and no one to worry about, except herself.

But then he had to go and ruin it.

The wine was flowing, the night was warm and they had been laughing about something. Then he leaned in towards her – she thought he was going to whisper something – and tried to kiss her.

It had been a long time since someone smelling of expensive aftershave had tried to kiss Kate. The kisses she shared with Luke were more the brief, perfunctory I'm-leaving-for-work kind of kisses or almost-as-brief precursors to let's-try-and-have-sex-before-we-fall-asleep. Kissing a stranger was different. For a moment, she felt that long-ago excitement which rises up from your stomach as you feel the magnetism between you and someone you hardly know yet.

Then she came back to herself. A married woman with two young children, sitting opposite a married man who also had his own children. What was she thinking? More importantly, what was *he* thinking? What kind of woman did he assume she was?

Slutty? Desperate? Which would feel worse? 'What the hell are you doing?'

He smiled again, but this time there was something rather sleazy about it. He wasn't actually as attractive as she'd first thought. 'I was hoping to kiss you.'

He could have pretended he'd fallen forwards in his chair; that his hands were full and he was squashing a gnat that had landed on her lip; that he had seen her choke on an olive stone and was preparing to give mouth-to-mouth. However implausible the excuse, she would have happily swallowed it (the excuse, not the imaginary olive stone) and they could have continued to have a nice evening. But he wasn't letting it go.

She picked up a napkin from the table and twisted it. 'I'd rather you didn't.'

He laughed. 'Don't go all coy on me. We both know where this has been heading all evening.' He picked up the bottle of wine and started to refill her glass.

Kate had told him she was married and he knew that she knew that *he* was married; why would she have thought the evening was heading anywhere? 'But I'm married.' If in doubt, state the obvious.

He looked at her shrewdly, 'I thought you and your husband were having a break? You said you'd come out here without telling him?'

That sobered Kate up like a wet fish around the face. A break? She had not left Luke. She was merely… Well, what was she doing exactly? She shook her head; whatever it was was none of Graham's business. 'You have a wife, too. And children.'

He shrugged. 'What difference does that make? My wife doesn't need to know about these kinds of things.'

These kinds of things? Obviously, this was a regular occurrence. Suddenly, Kate felt very old, very vulnerable and very, very stupid. She looked at the man sitting opposite, the one she'd thought was outgoing and exciting. She pictured the man at home looking after their children, not as spontaneous or as outgoing, but warm, funny and trustworthy. The idea that Luke would ever sit opposite a strange woman in a restaurant and try to kiss her was unthinkable. And that was one of the reasons she loved him so much. If she'd been wearing a pair of ruby slippers, she'd have clicked the heels together right there and then. As it was, she had to resort to more commonplace solutions. She picked up her bag and started to look for her purse. 'I'm going back to my hotel.'

When women in the movies leave a man sitting at a restaurant table, they manage to do it immediately and with style. They throw a sheaf of notes onto the table, 'That should cover my share of the bill,' turn on their heel and, with a flick of their hair, they are gone. In her still slightly drunken state, Kate was trying to stand up whilst rummaging in her bag to find her purse. This meant leafing through sweet wrappers, bits of Lego and old supermarket receipts. It was less Greta Garbo and more Getta Life-o.

'Hey, slow down.' Graham put his hand on her wrist. 'This is no big deal. We're just two lonely people having a bit of fun together.'

'I'm not a lonely person!' Kate could feel the tears climbing up her throat. Damn her inability to keep her emotions in check. 'I chose to be here alone! I don't need you to keep me company or, or, or… whatever it was you had planned.'

'Okay, okay.' He held both hands in the air. 'I got it wrong, I misread the signals. You don't need to react like this.' He tried to catch her eye but she was having none of it. 'And stop rooting around in that bag.' He had started to sound irritated. 'I told you I would pay for dinner.'

'I don't want you to pay for my dinner. I want to pay for my own dinner.' Her voice cracked. This was why she hadn't been able to join the debating soc at university: as soon as she felt strongly about something, the waterworks went on. 'I just want to leave.'

'Then I'll pay the bill and see you back to your hotel. I'm not a monster, you know. I'm just an ordinary guy.'

She looked at him. Was he an ordinary guy? Was it normal for married men to behave like this? Surely not.

Once she was in a taxi on the way back to the hotel, Kate had to fight an overwhelming urge to call Luke. Vulnerable and lonely, her need for him was overwhelming. But he was probably in bed by now and so were the children: it would be selfish to wake them all up. Even more selfish than leaving them all for a weekend without warning. What had she been thinking? She was so, so stupid. What had she done?

A text message would be better. If he was awake, he'd reply, and if he was asleep, it wouldn't wake him. Once Luke was asleep, you could send a marching band past his bed and he wouldn't wake up. Kate was normally the one lying awake, remembering everything she'd forgotten to do that day. Or thinking about Tim.

It had become like an addiction. For some of the mums she knew, it was a crafty cigarette once the kids were asleep. For others, a night out on the town, or a bottle of wine. For Kate, it was Tim.

Being with him was so exciting yet so familiar. Like finding a favourite pair of sexy shoes that you thought you'd lost and then slipping them on. Tim was like a pair of black patent kitten heels. Luke had become a pair of slippers.

She'd felt guilty at first. Especially when Luke seemed so pleased that she was starting to go out again. Since her dad had died, she hadn't had the energy or the desire. But going out with Tim was so easy. And there was nothing romantic between them, so there was nothing to actually feel guilty about. It wasn't like she was having an affair.

Maybe she could call her mum now? It had been so nice to talk to that older lady at the church earlier. Maybe she'd been right. Maybe Kate's mum didn't need to be protected from Kate's troubles.

But Kate hadn't told her mum that she was coming to Paris alone, and she didn't want to worry her. Her mum was a real worrier, almost had a PhD in it. Except in a real crisis. Like Dad's heart attack; then she'd come into her own. But Kate couldn't call her at this time of night from Paris, alone in a taxi, and expect her not to panic.

Could she call Tim? He would undoubtedly be up, and probably out, at this time on a Friday night. It had been two weeks since that night at his house, and they hadn't contacted each other since. Would it be weird to call him now?

She took her phone from her bag. She had a message.

Bloody Melissa.

Last-minute thought about the bake sale. Wouldn't it be fun if we all dressed up in matching aprons and baker's hats?

Deep down inside Kate, something snapped. She was tired, embarrassed, lonely and feeling really, really stupid. Somehow, Melissa's message stirred that cocktail of emotions into something much darker and angrier. And swearier.

Dear Melissa. She was typing so hard it was amazing she didn't put her thumb through the screen. *I am not wearing a pissing baker's hat because I am not, amazingly, a bloody baker. I have had it up to my shitting eyeballs with your cocking bake sale and, if I'm honest, with you and your shitting, cocking perfect bloody mother act. If you come anywhere near me with a pissing matching apron I will literally shove it up your…*

Shit. She'd pressed send. She hadn't meant to. She'd just been venting. *Bugger. Bugger. Bug…*

The phone rang in her hand. Was it Melissa? *Shit. Shit. Shi…*

It was Shannon. 'Hey, just checking in on you. I'm in the hotel bar when you're done.'

Thank God. Shannon would help her to work all this out. 'I'm on my way. I'll be there as soon as I can.'

CHAPTER TWENTY-THREE

Laura

Anyone sane – whether they've had a drink or not – takes one look at the two hundred-plus steps up to Sacré-Coeur in Montmartre and opts to take the funicular. The prospect of riding up to the top almost improved Laura's mood after the conversation she'd had with Gabriella. Almost.

She had been tempted to return to the hotel with Shannon when the dinner cruise had ended, but Shannon had disappeared shortly after dessert. Then Henrik from Sweden had persuaded them all that they should go to Place du Tertre in Montmartre. André had been disgusted with them – it was a tourist trap, he said, and he could think of a hundred better places to take them other than there. But Henrik had been adamant that he wanted to go and have his portrait painted for his girlfriend. Clearly, someone had been hitting the cognac too hard after dinner.

Considering how late it was, the funicular was busy. Laura had successfully stayed away from Paolo since the boat but, as they shuffled in to the carriage, he ended up right beside her. Despite the warm and sticky evening, and the amount of bodies in a small space, Paolo looked cool and calm. And he smelled fresh. Laura's heart beat harder. She needed to make sure there was no contact. *Don't look. Don't listen. Don't smell.*

But his smile was difficult to blank out. Particularly when it was directed right at her. 'Where have you been hiding?'

Hiding? She wasn't the one with anything to hide. If anything, she had been *too* honest with him. 'Nowhere. I've just been talking to *Gabriella*.'

She watched him for a reaction to her emphasis on Gabriella's name, but he just nodded. Then wrinkled his nose. 'I don't think she's my biggest fan.'

Laura had been an absolute fool. Gabriella had told her in detail – slightly too graphic detail, in places – about her relationship with Paolo the previous summer. The intensity, the passion, the burnout. 'And when it was over,' she'd said with glittering eyes, 'nothing.'

'Nothing?' Laura wasn't sure what she'd meant. The more Gabriella had got into her story, the stronger her German accent had become.

'Nothing.' Gabriella repeated. 'It was as if nothing had even happened between us. He treated me as if I was just another colleague. Someone he barely knew. Not someone he had shared…'

Laura interrupted to avoid any more over-sharing of the physical details. 'Yes, yes, I see what you mean now.'

Gabriella finished her glass of wine and nodded in Paolo's direction. 'Look at him. He knows how he looks, how people are attracted to him, and he enjoys it. That's what he is doing to you.'

Laura blushed. She was an idiot. But she didn't want Gabriella to know that. 'No, no. It's nothing like that. I'm just having some… issues with my boyfriend and he's been talking to me about it. There's nothing between us.'

Gabriella wouldn't have had to be a behavioural expert to know that Laura wasn't telling the whole truth. Her face was hot, she was swallowing hard and she had no idea what to do with her hands as they fluttered between her neck and her lap. Gabriella narrowed her eyes. 'Let me guess. He thinks you should leave him?'

Laura was sipping at her wine and nearly gagged. Wasn't that exactly what Paolo had said? 'Actually, it was about settling down. My boyfriend and I, we've been together quite a long time, and…' Laura didn't finish.

Gabriella had a smirk on her face and was nodding along. When Laura stopped mid-sentence, she leaned forwards. 'Paolo wouldn't understand a man who could be in a relationship for that long. Not his style at all. In and out quickly, that's more his thing.'

Quickly? Laura had contemplated throwing away a very long-term relationship because she was attracted to someone she knew nothing much about. What an idiot.

And now he was dismissing poor Gabriella on the basis that she was not his 'biggest fan.' Laura shuffled away from him and faced forwards. 'Sorry, I need to face the same direction as the driver. Otherwise I get travel sickness.'

Paolo smiled. 'But there isn't a driver.' He leaned towards her and lowered his voice as she tried not to breathe in the scent of him. 'Exciting, huh?'

Place du Tertre was indeed the tourist trap that André had described. James would have hated it. After a few cobbled streets, they entered an open square surrounded by restaurants. Along each side, facing out towards the restaurants, were portrait painters and silhouette artists. There was such a lively atmosphere that Laura couldn't help but like it. Henrik had found someone to draw his caricature, and the others watched and laughed as the artist captured his large nose and lively eyebrows so well.

Paolo was behind her and he leaned in towards her ear. 'Do you enjoy this kind of art more than the Louvre?'

Laura had been fascinated by watching the different artists at work. The caricaturist drawing Henrik swept his thick black pen across the large white page with flamboyant confidence. A portrait painter to her left was slower and more methodical; there was something mathematical about the way he divided up the paper before he began – it was mesmerising. But Paolo knew a lot about art and André had been totally dismissive of this place. Was he mocking her?

She didn't look at him as she replied. 'It's nice to watch people at work.'

She walked away from the group towards a souvenir stall and began to flick through postcards of artists' impressions of Paris.

Paolo followed her. 'Okay, this is getting weird. Why do you keep ignoring me? Why are you being so strange?'

How could she explain without making it sound like she was disappointed in him? Maybe it would be better to flip it the other way? Just say it. 'Gabriella seems to think that you like me.'

He nodded. 'I do like you, Laura.'

Laura felt her cheeks grow warm. It was the way he said her name. 'But you know I have a boyfriend.'

Paolo smiled. 'I know. That's why I haven't said anything. I also assumed it was quite clear how I felt.'

His eyes glinted as he looked at her. Laura was aware of another pair of eyes on them: Gabriella's. Gabriella had been right about him. What kind of man made a move on a woman in a serious relationship? Laura had thought he was helping her, listening to her, giving her impartial advice. Was that just part of his usual patter? Was he *seducing* her?

She lowered her voice. 'I didn't know you'd had a relationship with Gabriella.'

Paolo sighed and scratched the back of his head. 'Ah, that. I don't know what she's said, but we didn't have a relationship. Not really. It was more of a fling. It wasn't important.'

Laura stiffened. 'It was important to her.'

She had been here before. A man who was 'in and out' of a woman's life and didn't have any idea of the devastation they might leave behind. What had she been thinking?

Paolo wrinkled his nose again. 'I didn't behave particularly well towards her. I am not proud of myself. Honestly? I never really had feelings for her. Not like with you.'

Laura had no idea whether the bubbling heat in her stomach was anger, disappointment or… lust? What was wrong with her?

She felt a hand on her back and turned to see André. 'Henrik has his terrible picture and we're going to head back towards the hotel. There's a bar around the corner which I know. It has a lot more class than this place.'

Laura and Paolo joined the rest of the group. Her head was going to explode. She needed to talk to someone calm. Someone who knew Paolo and Gabriella. Someone who had her own life in order and could teach Laura how to do the same. She needed to find Shannon.

CHAPTER TWENTY-FOUR

Shannon

Shannon was so pleased to see Kate's friendly, sensible… Was that an angry face?

'What happened?'

Kate slumped down onto the opposite chair. 'Get me another drink and I'll tell you.'

The hotel bar was emptying out and it didn't take long for Shannon to get drinks for them both. When Kate recounted what had happened with Graham, Shannon put her hands up to her face. She'd had a bad feeling about Graham, but hadn't thought he'd actually try it on. *Damn sleazebag.* 'Oh, Kate, I am so sorry. I can't believe he did that.'

Kate shrugged. 'It's okay. I feel stupid more than anything. Completely misread the signals. Out of touch, I guess?' Kate smiled, but her eyes weren't happy.

What was wrong with her friend? It had felt like old times, talking together this afternoon, so why wasn't Kate opening up now? Was there something serious? Shannon should ask her. Be there for her.

But Kate beat her to it. 'Have you spoken to Robert yet?'

Shannon's heart plummeted further into her stomach. Speaking to Robert was the last thing she wanted to do, but she wasn't going to be able to put it off much longer. Springing his daughter on her like that had made her so mad. How could she bring up a baby with someone who just wouldn't take no for an answer? How could she trust him? 'Nope.'

Kate took a large gulp of her wine. She already looked pretty drunk; maybe Shannon should tell her to slow down. Although maybe she just seemed drunk because Shannon was stone-cold sober. 'Why don't you just get it over with? Thinking about it will be a whole lot worse that just telling him. Rip off that plaster. Sorry, *band-aid*.'

Shannon smiled and nudged her. 'I know what a plaster is. I'm practically American and English bilingual.'

'You do need to tell him, though. I mean, if you are planning on having the baby? He might notice.'

Shannon took a deep breath, as a memory of Adam's face flashed across her mind. 'There are a few things he and I need to talk about. But I'm not sure I can do it.'

Kate frowned. 'Tell Robert?'

Shannon shook her head and took another breath. 'Have the baby.' Once she'd said it out loud, Shannon held her breath. Kate was a good friend, but she was also a mother. Would she be shocked? Angry?

Kate put her wine down on the table and gave Shannon her full attention, speaking slowly. 'Okay. I can understand that. This wasn't planned. You have never said you wanted children. But when you told me about it earlier, you seemed…'

Shannon raised an eyebrow. 'Happy?'

'Well, yes, happy.' Kate put her head on one side. 'How *do* you feel about it?'

Shannon sipped at her mineral water. How was she feeling? Shannon tried to focus her thoughts so that she was only thinking about the baby, nothing else. 'Terrified.'

'Of having a baby?'

It wasn't exactly that. Although she was terrified. It was… 'Of making the wrong decision.'

Kate nodded slowly. 'It's a toughie all right.'

There was so much that Shannon wanted to ask her, but she didn't know if Kate would be honest. If she *could* be honest. What mother would admit she wished she hadn't had kids? But this was Kate. If Shannon could ask anyone, it would be her.

'Don't answer this if you don't want to. Do you ever regret having kids?'

Kate sat back in her seat and took a long time to answer. Had Shannon offended her? Crossed a line that all women with children knew you shouldn't cross? She should take it back. Quickly. 'Don't answer that, I'm sorry, I…'

But Kate held up a finger. 'Yes. Some days I do regret it.'

Shannon didn't breathe. Was this what was wrong with Kate? She was unhappy? Regretful? What should Shannon say? But Kate shook her head, sat up straight and clapped her hands. 'You need to make a list. Three lists.'

Shannon wanted to ask Kate more about her regret, but she had compressed her lips into a straight line and didn't look like she wanted to elaborate. It was probably best to follow her lead for now. If she wanted to talk, they had all night. 'I don't have paper.'

Kate waved a dismissive hand. 'Get a napkin. The barman will have a pen. Flash him your pearly whites. If that doesn't work, bend over and show him your cleavage.' Her eyes glittered. Amusement? Or tears?

Shannon had a pen in her bag. She retrieved a napkin from a nearby table. 'What am I supposed to be writing down?'

'All the people involved in this. Three headings. You. The father.' She paused. 'The baby.'

Shannon flushed, but she did as she'd been told. 'Okay. Done. What now?'

'Now you need to work out what each of you wants. What do you want, first?'

That was the Million Dollar Question. 'Can I leave me until the end?'

Kate considered this. 'It's against normal procedure, but I guess so. What does Robert want?'

This one was almost as difficult. What did he want? Shannon knew how he liked his eggs. What he liked in bed. 'Robert... Well, he seems to want me. And for me to meet his daughters. That's all he talks about at the moment.'

Kate nodded her approval. 'Well, that's positive, isn't it? He's a family man. And he wants you to be a part of it.'

Shannon wasn't sure whether this was positive or not. But Kate was on a roll. 'Now, what about the baby?'

The baby? The baby. *Her* baby. 'I guess it just wants to be born.'

Shannon had meant this to be funny, but it didn't come out like that. In fact, her voice wobbled and she had to swallow hard to stop her chin from doing the same.

Kate came around the table and put an arm around her. At the same moment, Laura appeared, looking flustered and nervous.

'Hi. Sorry, I didn't mean to interrupt. I can come back later?'

Shannon pulled her work face back on. 'Hey! Nice to see you – not interrupting anything at all. This is my friend from England...'

'Kate.' Laura grinned. 'What a coincidence!'

Shannon looked from one to the other. 'Do you guys know each other?'

Kate was grinning too. 'We were train buddies this morning.'

'And don't forget the wine you made me drink this afternoon.' Laura rolled her eyes.

'Jeez – you guys have seen more of each other than I have. Where are the others?'

'I left them in a bar around the corner. It's livelier than here. But I wasn't in the mood. Can I have a chat to you about something?'

At least this would rescue her from the baby conversation. 'Sure. Can we talk here, or is it something private?'

'Here's fine.' Laura smiled at Kate. 'Kate knows some of it anyway. I wanted to ask you something about Paolo.'

This was much more fun than trying to sort Shannon's own life out. 'Of course.'

Laura pulled over a chair and sat down. She fiddled with her fingers as she spoke. 'The thing is, Paolo and I, we... get on well.'

Shannon smiled. Boy talk was a very welcome distraction from worrying about Adam and the baby. Paolo was a sweetheart, and he could be just what Laura needed. This girl was way too serious for someone in their early thirties, and her English boyfriend seemed about as much fun as a check-up at the gynaecologist. 'I'd kinda noticed that. Good for you. He's a great guy. You'd have a real good time with him.'

Laura had picked up a napkin and was starting to twist it. 'Yes, well, that's kind of the problem. I'm at the stage when I'm looking to settle down and, from what I've been told, Paolo is hardly settling-down material.'

Shannon would bet her bottom dollar who had been telling her that.

'Gabriella, I presume? Listen, I have a lot of time for Gabriella, but I wouldn't necessarily believe anything she tells you about Paolo. She's got a tendency to be quite... dramatic. And I think she and Paolo got their wires crossed. Get his side of the story before you make your mind up about him.'

Laura stopped twisting and looked up. 'She was pretty convincing. And she said that he wasn't the relationship type.'

Shannon leaned forward and took the napkin from Laura's hand so she couldn't start the irritating twisting again. 'Look. Paolo's girlfriend split up with him. Now, what was her name? No, can't remember. Anyway, she was like me: didn't want children.

Paolo loved her, but he couldn't give up on the idea of a family. Italians are all about their big families.'

Laura stared at her. 'So he finished the relationship?'

Shannon nodded. 'He was really cut up about it, acted mad for a while. Went through quite a few women. One of whom was…'

'…Gabriella.' Laura finished for her.

Shannon nodded again. 'Gabriella. Although, in Paolo's defence, she did slightly throw herself at him. It didn't last long, but it was a bit messy and, if she's still bad-mouthing him to you, she is obviously still mad about it. He swore to me that he would never ever get involved with anyone he worked with again, and he hasn't.' She paused. 'Until now, of course.'

Laura sat back in her chair. 'Oh.'

Shannon smiled at Kate. It was weird, thinking the two of them were the voices of reason here. How often had Kate had to talk her down and away from some unsuitable guy?

Kate smiled back at her and then turned to Laura. 'Is it the baby thing?'

Shannon stopped smiling. Why was Kate talking to Laura about *babies*? Was she drunk and getting confused which conversation she was in?

But Laura was nodding. 'I know you just said Paolo was a family man, Shannon. But what if it doesn't work out between us? What if it turns out to be a fling and then I have finished with James? And even if it did work out, we would need to be together for at least twelve months before we thought about settling down, and then you have to plan a wedding, and then try and get…'

Shannon had thought that she was the one with the crazy, hormone-addled brain. Was Laura going loopy too? 'Whoa, whoa, whoa, lady. You're only just over thirty. Where's this crazy talk coming from?' Shannon raised an eyebrow at Kate. Did she have a clue what Laura was getting so worked up about?

Kate did seem to know. 'I think you need to put the baby thoughts to one side. Firstly, you need to decide if you want to stay with your boyfriend. What was his name?'

Laura's chin dropped onto her chest and she raised mournful eyes towards Kate. 'James.'

'Hold up.' Shannon needed to find out what the heck they were talking about. 'What baby thing? Have I missed something?'

Kate looked at Laura, who nodded her permission. Since when did these two have shared secrets?

Kate leaned forwards and lowered her voice. 'When we met at the café earlier, Laura said she feels she should be thinking about starting a family. I was trying to tell her that she should only have a baby when she is really, really ready. It's a big thing. And she definitely needs to be with the right man.'

Shannon gulped. That wasn't quite the same advice Kate had given her. Admittedly, Laura was almost a decade younger than Shannon, but still. Was Kate just trying to make Shannon feel better?

'But how do I know? How do I know if liking Paolo means I don't love James any more, or if it's just an attraction and means nothing?' Laura was back to napkin twisting. Where had she got another one from?

Shannon shrugged, reached out and rubbed Laura's arm. 'Well, only you can answer that, honey.'

Kate held out the pen Shannon had used. 'What about making a list? Pros and cons for each of them.'

Shannon snatched it from her. 'What is it with you and the lists, woman? You didn't used to be this organised. Save yourself, Laura!'

Laura smiled. 'I'm going to head back to my room and raid the minibar. If there's a problem chocolate can't solve, I haven't met it. Thanks, ladies. I'll see you in the morning.'

The idea of raiding the minibar appealed to Shannon, too. So did going to bed and forgetting about everything. She definitely wasn't in the mood to continue discussing the baby. But she couldn't leave Kate just sitting here, either. She'd been a rotten friend to Kate this last year and it was time to step up. Find out what was bothering her. After that, she could work out the method she was going to use to kill Robert slowly. And then Adam.

CHAPTER TWENTY-FIVE

Kate

Kate liked Laura, but she was glad when she left to go to her room. Kate needed to get to the bottom of this baby business with Shannon.

'So, back to you.'

But Shannon shook her head. 'To be honest, I'm real tired of talking about it. I need to wait until this weekend is over and I have some head space.' She sipped at her water. 'Let's talk about you, now. What's with this trip all of a sudden? Be honest.'

Kate sat back in her chair and rubbed her temples. She wanted to talk to Shannon about this – it was one of the reasons that she'd come here – but now her brain felt muddied with guilt and worry and too much Châteauneuf du Pape. Another sip wouldn't hurt. Where should she start?

'I've been meeting up with Tim.'

Shannon looked startled. 'Your ex, Tim?'

Who else would she be talking about? 'Yes, my ex-boyfriend, Tim.'

Now Shannon looked cross. 'The ex-boyfriend who you were dating for eight years and who still didn't know whether he could make arrangements more than two weeks in advance in case he got an offer of a gig in some shitty bar?'

Kate took another glug of wine. 'Yeah. That one.'

'Are you actually insane?' Shannon tapped her temple with her forefinger.

Kate sighed. 'Nothing happened between us. It was just friends going out, listening to music.' So why did she feel so guilty about it?

Shannon leaned back in her chair. 'So, Luke knew all about it?'

'No.' And that was why she felt guilty.

Shannon started to shake her head. 'You are crazy, Kate. Luke is such a nice guy. You've been so happy with him. You've got the kids. What's happened? Is there a problem between you?'

Where should she start? Shannon was right – Luke was a great guy. But that wasn't the problem. How could she make Shannon understand how she was feeling?

'The thing is, some days it's just hard work being a mum. No individual task is difficult – getting them dressed, making meals, keeping them busy – but the whole thing is *relentless*. You asked me earlier if I ever regret having kids and the honest answer is, yes, there are moments when I do. I sort socks into pairs to the backdrop of the third episode of Paw Patrol and think of all the other things I could be doing if I didn't have the children. I mean, some days a trip out to the freezer in the garage feels like a mini-holiday.'

Kate pulled a face and Shannon laughed gently. 'Is it always like that? I mean, aren't they at school during the day?'

Kate sighed. 'No, it's not always like that. Usually the feeling passes and I feel okay again, but lately I just feel overwhelmed all the time. These last few months, I've just felt… lost.'

That was the best way Kate could describe it. She looked in a mirror or heard herself speak and didn't even recognise herself. She'd lost interest in going out or inviting people over. Didn't really care what she wore or whether she'd brushed her hair. She even found herself boring. How had it happened?

Shannon leaned forward and rubbed her arm. 'But you've had a tough time this year, honey. Losing your dad and all.'

Kate shook her head. She was grieving for her dad, yes. But this had been going on for longer than that. 'You asked me about Luke, and he is part of the problem. I love him and he's a great dad, but he just doesn't understand what it's like for me. It's not just looking after the kids, that bit's okay. It's all the other stuff.'

She hadn't expected Shannon to understand the baby stuff, but this was about relationships, feelings. Shannon was usually good at this, but right now she looked like she didn't understand a word Kate was saying. 'What other stuff?'

Kate flailed around for examples. 'Taking the kids to parties, buying a gift for the party, remembering the dates for school events, buying costumes, helping them write out twenty-eight Christmas cards, scheduling play dates…' As Kate reeled off the list, she could feel her chest get tighter and tighter. Each of these things sounded tiny, pathetic and easily achievable. Put together, they stretched out like the Andes. Insurmountable.

Shannon frowned and sipped at her water. 'But do you *have* to do all these things?'

This was like talking to Luke. How could she make Shannon understand? 'Yes. If I don't do them, no one will. That's what I'm trying to say. Luke doesn't even think they are important.'

When she had told him that they had to sign the children up for swimming lessons, he had suggested that they start taking them at weekends for a 'bit of a splash about'. When she'd found out about a dressing-up day at the last minute – and he had picked up a couple of costumes from the supermarket on his way home from work – he had thought she was mad sitting up until three a.m. to make home-made ones instead, after seeing a photograph on Melissa's Facebook at eleven p.m. He had been in bed at two a.m. when she had cried and wished she could have called her mum. But she couldn't keep doing that. It wasn't fair on her mum. She had enough to deal with.

Shannon put her head on one side. 'And *are* they important?'

For the love of God… 'Yes!'

Shannon put her head on the other side. 'Why?'

Kate screwed her hands up tightly. She could feel the wave coming up over her shoulders. 'Why? Why? Well, because, because the kids want to do these things.'

'They want to write twenty-eight Christmas cards?'

'Well, no, maybe not that one.' Kate had spent three hours at the table with Alice that night. By the end of it, Alice had been in tears because Kate had yelled at her that it was the last possible day they had to get them done. The last three, Kate had written herself, and it had taken several attempts to accurately forge Alice's handwriting.

Shannon nodded. 'And the birthday presents. Why don't you just stick five pounds in a card?'

Kate was shocked. 'Because that shows no thought at all.'

Shannon picked up her glass of water and raised it at Kate as if she had won this argument. 'Exactly! That's my point, nut-job. Less thinking, less hassle. And probably less plastic shit in the environment.'

Clearly, Kate hadn't managed to convey the magnitude of the problem to Shannon. 'But what would the birthday child's mum think?'

Shannon frowned again. 'What mum?'

'The mum of the child. She would think I didn't care.' Kate could just imagine the boxes and boxes of brightly wrapped gifts on the present table and her sending Alice in with a measly envelope. And what if the envelope got lost because someone thought she'd just brought a card, and then they would think she hadn't bothered to send a gift at all. And then Alice might never get invited to another party again.

This wine was giving her heartburn.

Shannon shrugged. 'And she's a friend of yours, this imaginary mum?'

Friends? Well, Nina was her friend, but Nina wouldn't care what she brought. In fact, Nina wouldn't be insane enough to host a children's party in the first place. 'Well, no. Not especially. I'm not really friends with many of the mums; I just see them in the playground at drop off and pick up.'

'So why the hell do you care what they think? Next? What other inane tasks are you doing which are time-consuming yet irrelevant?'

Before Kate could answer, a tall, dark attractive man entered the bar behind Shannon and strode over to their table. He held out a hand to Kate. 'Hi. I'm Robert. You must be Kate.'

Wow. So this was Shannon's boyfriend. He was a very good-looking man. That baby was inheriting some pretty good genes on both sides. Kate shook his hand. 'I am, yes. It's nice to meet you.'

He smiled and turned to Shannon, who was staring straight ahead, her mouth tight. 'May I speak to you for a few moments?'

Shannon still didn't look at him. 'I'm with my friend right now. I will speak to you tomorrow.'

Kate had seen that face before. It was scary. It was Shannon's 'take no crap' face and there was no debating with it. Not if you wanted to escape alive.

Robert had obviously seen it before too, as he nodded agreement. 'I'll be around for a while tonight; I'm going to get a drink and sit at the bar. Maybe we can speak once you're finished here.' He smiled goodbye to Kate and backed away. Kate almost felt sorry for him.

Once he was out of earshot, she leaned towards Shannon. 'Don't you think you should…'

But Shannon cut her off with a cough as she sat up straighter in her chair. 'I think a lot of this is your own fault.'

Had she heard her correctly? Shannon was supposed to be her friend. She was a plain speaker, but she was also supportive. Kate must have misunderstood. 'Pardon?'

Shannon was tapping on the table. 'I'm not saying it's easy, being the one at home. But I think you're bringing a lot of this on yourself.'

Kate felt the hackles rise at the back of her neck. This was not what she had been expecting. 'On myself?'

Shannon nodded. 'You care way too much about what other people are thinking.'

Kate clenched and unclenched her fists under the table, pressing her nails into her palms. 'Really?'

'Yes. All these other mothers who aren't even your friends and who probably don't actually give a shit if your kid has the right costume or if you've baked an amazing cake for the bake sale. And it's not Luke's fault, either.' She raised her mineral water to Kate. 'You did this to yourself.'

Kate felt as if her face was on fire. Shannon had absolutely no idea what she was talking about. How dare she! 'You don't understand. You don't have children.'

Shannon shrugged. 'Maybe not, but I can see how much you've changed. And not entirely in a good way.'

Instinctively, Kate put her hands to her waist. She knew she wasn't as trim as she used to be. But that had nothing to do with this.

But Shannon was shaking her head. 'I'm not talking about looks. You are beautiful. I'm talking about your personality. Your outlook. Your general demeanour. Where has your fun gone?'

Fun? Kate couldn't even remember what fun was. The word 'fun' was followed by other words these days. Fun Factory. Fun Palace. Funfair. None of which were Kate's idea of a good time. It was very easy for Shannon to sit there and go on about 'fun' when her life was exciting and different and she had the freedom to do what she wanted, when she wanted. Just wait and see how much fun she had once the baby was here and she had to juggle her life the way Kate had to. Kate felt the roar start in the back of her chest. She couldn't stop it.

'You just wait until you have this baby. It is *nothing* like you're expecting.'

Shannon raised an eyebrow. 'I'm not intending for it to take over my life, though.'

'Ha!' That had come out a lot louder than Kate had intended. 'That's what everyone says. You have no idea what it's going to be like. No bloody idea whatsoever.' Kate was drunker than she realised. Her tongue was going and she couldn't stop it. 'It's so easy for you to judge! To sit there telling me what I am doing wrong with my life! I know I am in a mess, I know. But you can't tell me how to fix it, can you? Can you?'

Tears were rolling down her face. Where had they come from?

Shannon took her hand. 'Kate, I'm sorry, I…'

But Kate felt a fool. A stupid fool. For the second time that evening. She pulled her hand away from Shannon's. 'I'm going to my room.'

'No. Don't go, please, I need to…'

But Kate was on her feet. She swayed slightly as she scooped her room key from the table. 'I'll see you tomorrow.'

CHAPTER TWENTY-SIX

Shannon

Robert had one of the most expressive faces Shannon had ever known. If something was on Robert's mind, it was on his face. A grin or a scowl; she couldn't decide which was more attractive.

Right now, his mind must be pretty mixed up, though, because she couldn't read his face at all. Except that it seemed determined. 'We need to talk.'

Shannon was trying to disentangle her blazer from the back of her chair so that she could follow Kate. She had completely spoken out of turn. The look on Kate's face! What a terrible friend. It wasn't her place to tell Kate what she should and shouldn't feel. Trying to fix her problem, telling her what to do when all Kate had wanted was for someone to listen to her. Who did Shannon think she was? A man? 'Not now, Robert. I need to speak to Kate.'

He caught her by the arm and scowled. 'Yes, Shannon, now. You have been avoiding me all day. It's ridiculous; we're not children.'

Shannon froze. Looked down at his hand around her forearm and then back at him. He let go.

'*Désolé*. I'm sorry. I just really want to talk to you. I can't bear this.' He ran his fingers through his hair.

Shannon rubbed her arm. He hadn't hurt her, but how dare he think he could grab her like that? 'I have not been avoiding you.

I'm not sure if you've noticed, but we have the entire European team to look after. We are supposed to be working.' She didn't have time for this conversation. Kate was probably in her room by now, alone and upset. And it was Shannon's fault. She needed to go to her right away.

'And tomorrow we will be with the sales team all day. It is late now. They are all asleep, or will be soon. Let's go to your room and talk. Or mine?' Last night after their row and tonight in the hotel would be the longest they had slept separately for months. Apart from Shannon's recent trip home to the US, that was. She hadn't invited him to come with her then.

It had felt a little lonely, waking up without him this morning, although it had helped not to have to conceal her nausea. It would be the most natural thing in the world now to take his hand, go back to the same room and curl up together. There was no one from Sentek around so, as long as they set an early alarm, they would probably get away with it.

But Shannon was tired. Really tired. She didn't want to blame the unborn child for her fatigue – poor little guy or girl was getting a rough enough deal as it was – but it was most unlike her to feel like this. Normally an event like this would make her energised, running on adrenaline and black coffee. She couldn't even blame alcohol, as she hadn't touched a drop since her first suspicions that her sickness might be womb-related. 'Robert, I am honestly just too exhausted for this right now. I'll speak to you tomorrow night, when the others are on their planes home. *Bonne nuit.*'

She headed out of the bar in the direction of the elevators. What room number was Kate again? As soon as she got this sorted out with Kate, she would also need to call Adam. Hopefully, she could persuade him to contact Faye and tell her to stay away. That there was nothing to be gained from her confronting Shannon. In fact, that she might end up even more hurt. At the same time,

Shannon would bawl him out for giving Faye her work address. What the hell had he been thinking? Much as she had promised herself she would never speak to him again, it needed to be done. And soon. What time would it be in Chicago right now?

Robert was following her. Why was he not getting the message? 'Shannon. I can't go to bed until we have spoken about this. I don't understand…'

His intensity was something that had drawn her to him in the beginning. Shannon herself was pretty straightforward – what you saw was what you got. This Parisian man with his tempestuous outbursts and dramatic pronouncements had been exciting and different. Right now, though, she could do without it. She stopped and closed her eyes. 'Robert. I can't do this.'

He threw his hands in the air. 'What is so difficult? I love you. You love me. We are in a relationship. I have a daughter. She has a birthday.'

For the love of God, why wouldn't he shut up about this for one minute? A wave of frustration rose in her chest, her fists clenched by her side. 'I do not appreciate being trapped, Robert. Springing your daughter on me like…'

His eyes widened. 'But I didn't! I didn't! It was a… a… what's the damn word? Coincidence!'

Shannon crossed her arms and looked at him. Did he think she was a total fool? 'Yeah, because Parisians often go for dinner on those tourist boats. Especially twenty-year-old girls. I hear they just can't get enough of the frogs' legs.' She turned and stalked out of the bar. Faster this time.

It was Robert's fault that she had spoken to Kate like that. Seeing him had wound her up so much that she'd snapped. At the wrong person. *Get to Kate. Fix it.*

Why was he *still* following? Usually he found her sarcasm humorous. Not today. His voice was getting louder. 'So now I am a liar, too?'

She was about to snap again. He really needed to back off now. 'Come on, Robert. Don't be an idiot. You hassle me all day to meet your daughter and then, as if by magic, she appears.'

Robert put his fingers to his scalp and started to pull his hair at the roots so that it stood in dark peaks from his scalp. His voice got even louder. 'You gave me no choice! Vero was out nearby and suggested she came to the boat to say hello. What was I supposed to say? "No, Veronique, you can't meet my girlfriend even though I have been dating her for a year." How would that have looked? She's my daughter, Shannon.'

One of the many things that Shannon would not accept from a man was being shouted at. Especially in public. They were outside the elevators by now and there was no one around, but the principle was the same. She loved this man, but right now she wanted to be as far away from him as possible. She had a million things to say and she had to put them in the right order. Now was not the right time. Kate, and Adam, were more urgent. Robert was going to have to wait. She lowered her voice. 'I am *not* talking about this now.'

She turned towards the elevator and pressed the call button, still with no idea which floor Kate was on. In the safety of her own room, she would call Kate's mobile. If she didn't answer, she would contact reception. The room was on the group booking she'd made in her name for the sales delegates, so they would let her know the number.

But Robert was too riled to recognise the signs that he should stop badgering her. He continued to pull at his hair, but at least had the decency to lower the volume of his voice. 'You always say this! "Not now, Robert. Later, Robert. I am not in the mood, Robert." The party is next weekend. Why not right now?'

Shannon whipped around. She had tried to warn him. Had asked him to wait until tomorrow. She had wanted to do this calmly, sensitively. But now he was going to get it.

Her hands clenched either side of her body and she took a step towards him, her voice low but angry. 'Why not now? Well, let me think. Maybe because we are in a hotel lobby and anyone could walk in at any moment. Maybe because we have sales people here from across Europe who are – incidentally – absolutely crapping themselves about presenting their sales figures to you tomorrow. Or maybe – just maybe – it's because I am pregnant and I am absolutely freaking devastated about it!'

Robert froze. His fingers an inch above his head, holding his hair. His face drained of colour. '*Enceinte*? Pregnant?'

In contrast, Shannon's face was aflame. 'Yes. Pregnant. With a baby. What do you think about that, "Papa"?'

The lift door opened. Shannon turned and walked inside. They looked at each other as the doors closed. Robert didn't move to follow her.

CHAPTER TWENTY-SEVEN

Laura

Laura found some hotel headed paper on the dressing table in her room and drew a line straight down the middle. What was it Kate had said? When in doubt, make a list.

James.

CON: Commitment-phobic. Workaholic. Doesn't even want to practise baby making, let alone make one for real.

PRO: Been together a long time. Makes me laugh. Invited me to live with him.

Paolo.

CON: Possibly a player. Lives in another country.

PRO: Likes to travel. Apparently wants children. Says my name a lot. Makes me laugh as well, but also makes my legs melt.

There must be an algebraic formula that would help her to decide, but she just didn't seem to be able to work it out. Paolo to the power of ten minus James squared? That was just stupid.

The conversation with Shannon had thrown everything up into the air again. Although Gabriella's story of her and Paolo's affair – recounted in all its lurid detail – had disappointed Laura, on another level she'd been relieved. If Paolo was just looking for a fling with a colleague, he was definitely not the man for her and she could go back to James and carry on as normal. Bored and unhappy.

Chucking the pencil down onto the page, she lay down on the bed, facing the ceiling. It was all so confusing. She would trust Shannon over Gabriella any day of the week, but Shannon was different from Laura. Shannon had talked about how fun Paolo was. It was okay for Shannon to prioritise fun – she didn't want to get married and have a baby. Laura had a different wish list.

Gabriella's version of events had really hit a nerve. She'd admitted that their fling had only lasted a few weeks, but she'd said that he couldn't get enough of her until she'd started to refer to their affair as a *relationship*. Sounded like Paolo knew what he was talking about when he'd told Laura that James wouldn't suddenly want to settle down.

So, why hadn't this turned her off him? Why did her heart rate appear to double whenever he came near her? She could feel him getting closer and closer and, unless she stopped it, something was definitely going to happen. Should she feign a headache and claim an early night? But she didn't want to. She wanted to go back out to the bar and speak to him. What did that mean?

Rifling through the minibar, she found wine and a packet of pistachios and took them back to the bed. James always warned against eating from the minibar. When they stayed in a hotel he would buy water and snacks beforehand; much more economical. Right now, she didn't give a stuff. She needed them.

Be logical. Logic was her friend. It had never let her down. Paolo was very good-looking, and it was flattering to have someone good-looking paying you attention. Appearing beside you, looking at you intently, brushing his leg against yours… *Be logical!* That didn't mean she was actually attracted to him. Although her heart, stomach and… other parts might beg to differ.

To be fair to James, he was also quite good-looking. He got more than his fair share of attention from other women and Laura had never been concerned that he might take them up on it. He was dependable. Solid. *Safe*.

The problem was, he paid *Laura* very little attention, either. She knew where she was with James, but it wasn't somewhere she actually wanted to be. She shook her head. This was not helping.

She got up from the bed again and went to the bathroom to wash the pistachio salt from her fingers. She stared at herself in the mirror. How had a girl like her got herself in a pickle like this?

It was crazy. James was her *boyfriend*. Paolo was just some guy she knew from work who – in his own words – would most likely not even be working for the company by the end of tomorrow. Was he just looking for the last notch on his bedpost before he went?

But, if something happened between them, and then he did leave, then no one would ever know what happened.

But she would know.

The girl looking back at her from the mirror was not the sort of girl who could just sleep with someone and forget about it. She would love to claim to be a modern, empowered woman, but she still actually needed to have feelings for someone before she could even think about taking her pants off in front of them.

Did she have feelings for Paolo?

If she did have feelings for him, then she might be about to get hurt. Unless he had genuine feelings for her, too?

Her brain was going around and around in circles. No, more like hexagons: every moment going at this from a different angle.

She walked back to the dressing table and drained her glass of wine. It was all a moot point, anyway. She'd never cheated on anyone in her life and was not likely to start now. While she was going out with James, she couldn't even contemplate doing something with another man. It was not who she was. She was nothing if not faithful.

And she was being unfair to James. He was a good boyfriend. He took her to nice restaurants and bought her thoughtful gifts. They were a good match, liked the same films and music, and knew each other's families and friends, even if he didn't much like spending time with hers. He never came home late without explanation and he still made her laugh. Sometimes.

And he'd been more than happy for her to move in with him. Although, had he? When she'd suggested it was crazy to be commuting back and forth from her parents' all the time, he had just told her she was free to stay. On the day she'd moved into his flat though, he'd even put a flower at the side of her bed and cleared a space in his wardrobe and emptied a drawer for her.

A space in his wardrobe.

A drawer.

She knew she had to call and tell him it was over.

CHAPTER TWENTY-EIGHT

Kate

Kate banged at the lift button. How long was this bloody thing going to take? She punched the button again. And again.

She had been so wrong to come here. Wrong about Shannon. She hadn't understood at all. All very well for her and her 'you brought this on yourself, Kate' and 'you need to say no, Kate'.

The lift opened. She got in and started the ascent.

Shannon had no idea what it was like when you became a mum. You just had to do all that stuff, didn't you? You had to put them first all the time. That was how it worked. And if you were a stay-at-home parent, that *was* your work. Your job.

Kate made it to her room. She slid the key card in and out of the slot. Red. Bugger. Bloody things never worked first time. In and out again. Red. She wanted to roar. In. Out. Green! Finally!

What would the kids be doing now? Luke would probably have let them fall asleep on the sofa or climb into bed with him or made a bloody tent in the living room. That's why they bloody loved him so much. He was 'fun daddy'. She was the one who would have to get them back in a routine when he went back to work on Monday. Who would have to listen to 'but Daddy let us…' on repeat. She banged open the minibar. Sodding Toblerone. How predictable. There was a mini tub of Pringles which probably cost more than crack cocaine, but this was an emergency.

And goodness knows how many sweets he'd have let them have this evening. He'd probably taken them via the supermarket on their way home and brought them back dragging a bag of pick and mix which was twice their body weight. Kate tried to restrict them to a few sweets each day but Luke would have let them scoff the lot. They would probably be running around into the small hours, jacked up on sugar.

This trip had been insanity. She should never have done it. What the hell was Luke going to think when he got that message? … *Meet me tomorrow. No kids. The Eiffel Tower. two p.m. Your ticket is booked.* Her face burned with embarrassment. He must think that she'd bumped her head. And when he didn't turn up, where was that going to leave her? Standing at the Eiffel Tower like a loser, for a start. And Shannon had let her down, too. Kate had been expecting a friendly ear, someone on her side. That's not what she had got.

She popped the top of the Pringles tub and took three, pushing them into her mouth and swallowing without even tasting them. She wanted the wine from the minibar too, but that probably wasn't a good idea in her present mood. She would have coffee instead.

She tried to fill the kettle from the tap in the bathroom basin but she couldn't fit it under. This was ridiculous. How the hell else was she supposed to get water? She pushed, even though she knew it wasn't going to go. She pushed again, harder. Then she pulled it out and began bashing it against the basin. *Stupid, stupid kettle. Stupid. Stupid…* She began to cry.

She sat down on the bed. Shannon was completely right. What had become of her? What did it matter if the children stayed up late? What was she trying to prove? And to whom?

She looked at herself in the mirror. A few more wrinkles and her hair was a bit thinner, but she was essentially the same person. Still Kate.

She had to find Shannon.

*

When Kate came back to the bar, it was emptying out. Shannon had gone. She felt a rush of disappointment. *Don't let the sun go down on your anger.* That's what her dad used to say. Looks like she wouldn't have a choice this time.

She was about to turn around and go back to reception to ask for Shannon's room number, when she saw it. In the centre of the bar was a beautiful white baby grand. The kind of piano she had dreamed of having in her perfect white house with the perfect white carpets and the perfect clean children. Hadn't really worked out like that. She brushed her hands down the front of the piano and touched the keys gently.

'*Savez-vous jouer?*'

'Sorry?' She looked up at the waiter who was clearing a table nearby.

'*Pardon.* Do you play? You can play if you like?' He motioned towards the piano with a towel.

Kate smiled. 'I did. It's been a while. I might be a bit rusty. I mean, out of practice.'

The waiter shrugged and gestured around the room. 'There is almost no one here. Doesn't matter if you hit a wrong note.' He nodded and disappeared back behind the bar.

A wrong note? She'd definitely hit a couple of those this evening. In fact, her whole life felt out of tune.

She sat down at the piano and stroked the keys. Then looked around. The waiter had been right, there was hardly anyone here. Gently, she pressed one of the keys. It felt strange. And yet familiar. What should she play? There was some sheet music still in place. Schumann's *Kinderszenen* or *Scenes from Childhood.* Beautiful and simple sounding, but deceptively complicated. Would her fingers remember how to play it? She looked for the most famous piece: *Traumerei. Dreaming.*

Classical music is best known for its large symphonies and grand operas. But this was the kind of piece that Kate loved most: music which spoke quietly. When she'd studied Schumann, they'd discussed whether the music represented a child dreaming, or an adult looking back on a childhood dream. Either way, this gentle piece was rich with emotion. Each time the pattern of notes was played, the fourth note was higher as the music ascended, building to a moment of epiphany.

She had been tempted to play at the club Tim had taken her to. It was a jazz club, very relaxed. Most people there knew each other, and they were jumping on and off stage. Tim had encouraged her to have a go, but it had been so long since she'd played in public that she'd felt crippled with nerves. But she'd wanted to. The desire had been there. It had really been there.

But they had argued about the self-same thing. She and Tim.

He had tried to nudge her up on stage when the pianist took a break. 'Go on.'

She'd shaken her head. 'No. I'm fine just watching.'

He'd nudged again. Laughed at her. 'That's not the Kate I know. You would never have passed up the opportunity to play.'

Kate had shrugged and turned her body slightly away from him. 'Yeah, well. I've changed.'

Tim folded his arms and frowned. 'How often do you play?'

This was when she had started to become irritated. Why wouldn't he leave this conversation alone? 'Never.'

He'd laughed *again*. 'No, seriously. How often?'

Was she not speaking English? Should she speak more slowly? She looked him directly in the eye. 'Seriously. Never.'

'Why the hell not?' She hadn't expected him to understand. Music came out of Tim's pores. He continued to believe that he was going to get his 'big break' and the rest of his life was *still* on hold until he did. There was never going to be a mortgage, marriage, children, until his music career was established. Now Kate had some distance from him, she could almost admire his tenacity. But the older he got, the less likely it seemed that he would get his big break, and then what would he be left with?

She, on the other hand, had a life that was very full. 'I'm just too busy.'

He had looked at her differently, then. As if he had a bad smell under his nose. 'Doing what?'

'Looking after my family.' For years, it had been impossible to play at home. If the children were napping, the piano was too loud. If they were awake, they would want to sit beside her and pump away with their podgy toddler fingers. It was very cute, but not so good for her practice. Eventually, she had just given up on it.

'But you said they are at school now. Can't you play whilst they are at school?' Clearly, Tim couldn't understand what she would do with her day that would stop her from practising the piano. To be honest, she wasn't really sure what she did that sucked the six hours between school drop off and collection. The tidying, shopping, cleaning was one thing. Then there was all the other life laundry like running errands for her mother-in-law or picking up Luke's dry cleaning. Add Melissa and her frickin' bake sales into the mix and there was no time left at all.

Now she was completely out of the habit. It wasn't instinctive for her to lift the lid and start to play. It almost scared her. What if she'd lost the knack? Couldn't remember how to play? The old urge to play had deserted her completely, leaving only… what? Exhaustion? Boredom? Anger?

But she hadn't wanted to discuss any of that with Tim. How could he possibly understand? How dare he judge what she did all day? People without children had no idea what it was like. No idea at all.

'I just don't, okay?'

But he wouldn't let it go. 'That's insane. How can you call yourself a musician if you don't play every day?'

Kate's face flushed. She clenched the fingers of her free hand. 'I *don't* call myself a musician. I'm a mum. Just a mum. That's all I am!' She'd slammed her drink onto the table, ripped her coat from the back of the chair and left. Tim had called after her, but he hadn't followed. Leopards and spots.

She hadn't planned to see him again after that. He was the same old Tim that she had wasted eight years on. What had she been thinking, meeting him like that? Occasional coffees at the hospital were one thing, but a jazz bar? She had invited Luke knowing he wouldn't come: live music wasn't his thing. When she'd added that she could meet up with some old music college pals there, he had encouraged her to go with them. Which had made her feel even more guilty.

Now, sitting here, she couldn't believe that she had left it so long to play. Her back straightened instinctively as she positioned her fingers. Then, as she began to pick out the melody with her right hand, her whole body relaxed into it.

For several minutes, she was lost in the music. Pure escapism. Playing this piece, which had been played by so many other people before, somehow gave her a sense of her place in the world. She made mistakes but it didn't matter anymore; she didn't have to be perfect. Her fingers were a little tight, but they would loosen. She *needed* to play. She needed to remember what she loved about it. This was about her. Not Tim. Not Luke. Not even the kids. This was Kate. This was where she'd been hiding.

As the music ascended, Kate's chest rose and she breathed deeply and freely. Once she'd played the final notes, she paused, eyes full, fingers still resting on the keys. *Childhood dreams.* An image of Alice and Thomas lying in bed came unbidden into her mind and made her heart ache. They looked like tiny babies again when they slept. Pouting lips and soft eyelashes. She would give anything to be home right now, kissing them gently good night.

And Luke, too. What must he be thinking? He must think his wife had gone completely mad. Should she call it all off? She had been a fool to do this. A complete fool. A fool with a romantic dream that if she could just get Luke here, back where they'd had their honeymoon, back where she had been herself, that somehow she could…

She should call him. Tell him not to come. She couldn't call right now because he would be sleeping, but she would call him in the morning. Tell him she had overreacted and that he should stay home.

And then she needed to make up with Shannon.

CHAPTER TWENTY-NINE

Shannon

Shannon hadn't packed much for a one-night stay, but throwing things into a suitcase was still mildly cathartic. Reception had given her Kate's room number but there had been no answer from her door. Maybe she needed time to cool down? Shannon sent a text: *I'm so sorry. Please forgive me xxx*

As Shannon lived in Paris, there had been no real reason for her to stay in the damn hotel at all, but Robert had insisted. He'd wanted her to be on site in case she was needed through the night. What did he think was going to happen? An emergency PowerPoint situation? 'We're losing the animations on Slide Four. Repeat, Slide Four is down!'

As usual, he had got his own way. Telling people what to do. Ordering them around. Controlling them. It was a way of life to him. Well, he could think again if he believed he was going to control Shannon Ryan. She was her own boss. Time to pack up her things and get a cab home right now.

She paused with a spare pair of pants in her hand – she always brought extra. She needed him to not be her boss any more. She needed to move on. She threw the pants into the case. Her laptop was on the desk where she'd left it earlier. She would email her resignation right now.

Shannon had written more than one of these letters in the last ten years. Thankfully, most people changed jobs every couple of years in the IT industry, so her CV didn't look out of the ordinary because she'd moved around so much. Thanks to Irish grandparents, she had a European passport and had worked in England for over eight years. The job she'd had with Kate in London had been the longest she'd ever had. Probably why Kate was still one of her closest friends. It was only when Kate had met Luke that Shannon's feet had started to itch again. Since Kate had had the baby, Shannon had worked for two other companies in the UK before moving to France.

Baby. Even the word was making her feel queasy. Was she really going to have this baby? And was she going to have to do it on her own, without Robert?

An old business card fell out of her laptop case. SHANNON RYAN. PA TO THE SALES DIRECTOR. Her new card didn't have a job title because no one could work out how to describe the many random parts to her role. She had been a damn good PA; everyone Shannon had ever worked for had remarked on how organised she was. Every event under her watchful eye went seamlessly. She had an instinct for the details, but she was also a people person. People came to her if they weren't happy and she sorted it out. That's what she did. So why couldn't she organise her own life?

She opened the minibar and looked inside. Wine? Off limits. Toblerone? Disgusting. Nuts? Could you eat those when you were pregnant? She had no idea what the rules were. It would have to be the sparkling water. The bubbles were the most excitement she was likely to get. She poured it into a glass and took it back to the laptop.

Was resigning a dumb move? If she was going to have a baby, she would need a job. And getting a job in Europe was difficult enough as an American. Doing it pregnant was likely to be impossible. Maybe she should hold off for now?

She clicked open the last email from Adam and skim-read the contents. It was pretty much the same as his voicemail.

Hi Shannon. I don't know how to tell you this but I guess I'm just going to say it. Faye is in Paris. She knows everything and she is determined to hunt you down. She has your address. I couldn't persuade her out of it. Please call me. Adam.

Shannon let her head fall back on her shoulders. There was nothing else for it but to call Adam and find out what the hell was going on. What exactly did he mean by 'she knows everything'? What in the name of all things holy had he told her? Could that mean he had given her Shannon's home address too?

It looked like Shannon would be staying here tonight after all; Faye wouldn't be able to track her to the hotel. Would she?

There was a knock on the door.

It was followed by a loud whisper. 'Shannon. Are you in there?' Robert.

She toyed with the idea of ignoring him. Letting him wonder if she was even still there. But that would be childish. 'I'm in bed. I'll talk to you tomorrow.'

There was a soft thump, as if he had knocked his head onto the door. 'Please, Shannon. We need to talk. I'm sorry. I reacted badly. It was just a shock.'

What did he think it had been for her? A minor surprise? 'I know. And you're right, we need to talk. But not now, Robert, not tonight. I'm tired.'

That wasn't a lie; she felt exhausted. But she also needed to call Adam and find out what the story was with Faye. And there was no way she wanted Robert in earshot of that.

There was a rustle, which must have been Robert's back sliding down the door. When he next spoke, it sounded like he was speaking from the floor. 'Are you absolutely sure you're pregnant? Have you done a test?'

Now she was cross again. Did he think she was a dumb teenager? 'Of course I've done a test. Look, I'm sorry I told you like

that. That I just blurted it out. I was angry. My hormones are…
No, that's not an excuse. I shouldn't have told you like that. We
will talk about it, I promise. But not now. Definitely not now.'

There was a silence on the other side. Had he gone? She was
about to open the door to check when he spoke again. 'I'm
sorry about my daughter. About telling her she could turn up
at the boat.'

Shannon took a few deep breaths before she answered. *Stay
calm.* 'That wasn't fair, Robert. Not fair at all.'

'I know.' There was another long silence before he said, 'I
just wanted to make it happen. I wanted you to realise that I
was – am – serious about us.'

This was exactly what had made her so mad. It was what *he*
wanted. 'And what about what *I* want, Robert? I never pretended
that I wanted something serious between us. You are the one
changing everything.'

'I know. I know.' His voice was muffled. Was he crying?
She felt bad if he was crying. And then irritated. Was he just
manipulating her?

'You have to go, Robert. One of the sales team might walk
past and…'

'Then let me in!' His voice was back at head height again.
And forceful.

Shannon gritted her teeth. 'No. I will talk to you tomorrow.
Just go.'

'Why are you being like this? You are impossible!'

She heard him walk away. He was stamping so loudly, the
whole floor probably heard. She breathed out. Now Adam.

What was the time in Chicago? It didn't matter. This was an
emergency.

Adam had given her his mobile number and a landline. She
tried the mobile, just in case Faye had come back. She couldn't
risk her answering the phone.

The phone rang an agonising amount of times before the call connected. Shannon's heart was beating along with it. Getting up from the bed, she paced the floor and counted the rings. *Seven. Eight. Nine.* 'Hello?'

It was so strange to hear his voice. So familiar, yet so unreal. Shannon was almost grateful that she could blame the pregnancy hormones for the tears at the back of her eyes. 'Adam.' It came out like she was being strangled. She coughed. Tried again. 'Adam. It's Shannon.'

There was a silence at the other end. Maybe he was shocked to hear her, too. 'Shannon. I'm so glad you called. I've been trying to reach you for the last two days. Longer, actually. Do you not read your emails?'

'I know. I've been… er… tied up with work.'

'Did you get my voicemail? About Faye? She's in Paris and she knows where you work.'

'Yes. I read your messages. That's why I'm calling. It was a bit of a shock, obviously.'

'Yeah, I can imagine.' The international line was so good she could hear him scratch his head; a habit he'd had even when she'd first known him nineteen years ago. 'She's an impulsive one, that girl. I guess she gets it from her mother.'

Shannon stiffened. 'Jessie doesn't strike me as the impulsive type.'

Adam sighed. 'I meant you.'

CHAPTER THIRTY

Laura

Opening her eyes very, very slowly, it took Laura a few moments to take in where she was. With relief, she recognised her hotel room, although something about it looked different. Were the ceilings higher? As she rolled onto her side, the carpet greeted her. She was lying on the floor.

On the plus side, she was alone and fully dressed from the night before. Gingerly, she raised her head, waiting to see if there was a hangover about to pounce. So far, so good.

What time was it? Eight a.m. That gave her an hour to have a shower and get ready before the breakfast meeting at nine. What had Paolo called it last night? Croissants at dawn. Officially, this was supposed to be an informal social session before the formal presentations began, but everyone knew that Robert would be circling, probing, ensuring they felt as uncomfortable as possible before they had to stand up in front of the whole team and defend their activities for the previous three months.

Slowly, she peeled herself up from the floor. Was there time to lie down on the bed for just ten minutes? It looked so inviting and soft. What had she been thinking, spending the night on the floor? Clearly, she hadn't been able to get herself any further into the room, although this was strange as she'd managed to find her way here and get the key card to work in the lock.

Working out the shower took a couple of minutes; she was consecutively scalded and then frozen before managing to find a happy medium. Standing, head back, allowing the water to massage her forehead, she tried to piece together the night before.

When she'd got back to the bar, everyone was already pretty drunk and they'd made her drink quickly to catch up. All of the talk had been about travelling; places they'd been and those they'd like to visit. Laura had always had a bug for travel. She'd always wanted to live in another country for a while; experience another way of life. Kate had said yesterday that she'd spent a year living here in Paris. Laura would have loved to do that, but James had ruled it out because of his job. Paolo had talked about being certain he'd do some more travelling at some point, but didn't mention what he'd do about *his* job.

At some point, someone had decided it would be a good idea to buy shots. Had they started with sambuca? There had definitely been some tequila in there at some point too. Laura's stomach rose at the thought. Maybe the only reason she didn't have a hangover was that she was actually still a little drunk. She remembered someone had made a joke about forming the three a.m. club, so they must have been at it for a while.

The phone call! Like an icy bullet, she remembered leaving a voicemail on James' phone. What had she said? She put her forehead against the cold tiles. It all came back in a rush. She had told him his time was up – if he couldn't set a date for getting married then obviously she wasn't the right person for him. Had she actually said it was all over? Had she? What was she thinking?

She and Paolo had been flirting terribly; holding hands at one point. She remembered walking back to the hotel room. Paolo had been with her. He'd walked her to the lift, up the corridor, to her door. She felt a burning sensation in her chest, the heat rising until her face was glowing. Her eyes closed as she remembered.

Paolo had kissed her. And she had kissed him back. They had kissed. She was living with one man and had just kissed another. Passionately. What had happened to her? Who was she? A cheater?

Technically, it wasn't cheating. She had broken up with James first. Although, were they broken up if he hadn't yet listened to the message? Did that make it worse? Or better?

Shutting the shower off, she stood and let the water drip from her body. Focus. It was time to work out exactly where she was and what she needed to do next. What were the facts?

1. She had left a voicemail on James' phone to say that she was leaving him.
2. This would mean she had nowhere to live.
3. She had been snogging someone who was (a) her work colleague and (b) quite possibly a complete philanderer.
4. She had to give a sales presentation this morning to the European Sales Director (Robert), which was not going to rock his world, which meant:
5. She could also be out of a job; and
6. The hangover from hell was just about to arrive.

Not bad work for one night, really.

Pulling a large fluffy towel around herself, she peered into the mirror above the sink. It wasn't a pretty sight. Thank goodness there was no one here to see her looking like this.

Was that a knock on the door?

She listened. There was the knock again. She held her breath. Should she just ignore it? Then there was a voice.

'Laura! Laura! Are you there?'

Breathing out in relief, Laura opened the door to Shannon. 'Thank God it's you.'

Shannon smiled broadly. 'Well, well, well, and what have you been up to?'

How did she know? What had been said? 'What do you mean?'

'I was in the corridor in the early hours. I saw Paolo "walking you back to your room."' Shannon made mock quotation marks in the air for the last part. 'You were being *very* affectionate.'

Groaning, Laura sat on the bed and put her head into her hands. 'Shannon, I have a boyfriend. What have I done?'

Shannon wasn't picking up the vibe of panic and fear in the room. She sat down next to Laura on the bed, crossed her arms and gave her a mock serious face. 'Anything you want to tell me?'

Laura's head shot up. 'Nothing happened. It was just a kiss. Nothing else.' She prayed that her memory was serving her well and shook her head at Shannon's raised eyebrow. 'Nothing!'

Shannon shrugged. 'Oh, well. Good for you. You know I think you and Paolo would be a good match.'

'Are you crazy? Apart from the fact I actually already live with someone – or at least I think I still do, and' – Laura raised her finger to stop the predictable interruption – 'that Paolo lives in a whole other country.'

Shannon shrugged again. 'Long distance relationships can be fun. I've tried it a couple of times. Have you never heard of phone sex?'

Laura shuddered at the sex comment. Her delayed hangover had really started to make its presence felt and she could feel the beginning of a headache lapping the edge of her brain. All she wanted was to lie down. Not face Paolo. Not think about James. And definitely not present her sales figures to Robert in about two hours' time.

Shannon was still looking at her. 'There was another reason for me coming to see you.'

Laura's heart sank. She knew exactly what Shannon was going to say. 'The Machon order?'

Shannon nodded. 'I checked this morning. They sent it late yesterday.'

Yesterday evening, Laura had had other things on her mind. Plus, she'd been checking her emails, not the internal reports. Damn. Damn. Damn. 'I don't suppose we can keep this from Robert?'

Shannon shook her head and squeezed Laura's hand. 'He'll be checking it this morning too. But it'll be okay. Explain to him what happened. It wasn't your fault. He'll understand.'

Laura very much doubted that, but she didn't have any other option. 'Okay. Thanks for letting me know.'

Shannon stood up. 'I'll go and let you get ready. I just wanted to check that you were okay and give you the heads-up on the return.' She looked at her watch. 'You have about half an hour left of breakfast and then we are starting in the Renoir Room. Do you need me to do anything?'

Laura shook her head. She'd checked her presentation a thousand times; there was no conceivable way to make the figures look any better than they did, whatever colour she made the bar charts. Especially now she'd have to factor in the return. 'No, I think I've got everything, thanks.'

'Okay. I'll leave you to it.' When Shannon got to the door, she turned back. 'Seriously, though. Don't rule Paolo out. He's a good man.'

As she closed the door, Laura allowed herself to fall back on the bed. She hadn't thought about calling James once.

The best cure for an impending hangover was a whole plate of carbohydrates in the form of every type of pastry from the breakfast buffet. Another reason to love Paris.

Paolo had already been snared by Robert when Laura arrived and the conversation didn't look like fun, so she didn't interrupt. Thankfully, Gabriella was nowhere to be seen, so she joined Sylvie, Andre and Henrik at their table. According to the schedule, they had about twenty minutes before their team meeting began.

'All ready for the lion's den?' Henrik grinned at her over a large plate of cured meat and cheese.

Laura shrugged. 'No. I'm just hoping one of you has worse figures than mine so that Robert leaves in anger before he gets to me.'

Henrik nodded in Paolo's direction. 'I think the Italian numbers are the worst. I wouldn't want to be in Paolo's shoes at the moment.'

Laura chanced a glance in Paolo's direction. He was nodding at Robert, who was clearly expounding one of his many theories of sales strategy. Poor guy. Was his hangover as bad as hers?

Shannon arrived at their table with a sheaf of papers and a smile. 'Good morning, everyone. How are the heads this morning? There's been a last-minute change of plan to the proceedings this morning. Robert is going to meet with you all individually. There won't be a nine a.m. group meeting, so you can take your time over breakfast. Paolo will be first, Robert's telling him now, and the rest of you just need to turn up to the Renoir Room at your appointed time.' She handed out agendas.

This was new. Normally they all had to sit through the presentations from each country, in the interests of learning from good strategies or bad. Paolo and Robert were getting up from their table and leaving the breakfast room. Were they starting already? She hadn't even had a chance to smile at Paolo, much less actually speak to him. There was something worrying about all this. Ominous.

Henrik had noticed them leave too. He nodded in the direction of the exit. 'Judging by their faces, you might get your wish about sales figures, Laura.'

Now she felt sick. And it wasn't the hangover. After Paolo, she was next.

CHAPTER THIRTY-ONE

Kate

That morning, as usually happened when a new day dawned, everything seemed a little less bleak. Kate couldn't remember the last time she'd had a full night's uninterrupted sleep and, as her mum would say, she felt a lot better for it. After a long shower, she dressed slowly and carefully; she wanted to look perfect. She took care to apply just the right amount of make-up. Luke had always said that he didn't like make-up on women, although every time Kate had been made up for a night out he would remark on how pretty she looked.

It was still early and she wasn't ready for breakfast yet, so she wandered outside. The air smelled new as she left the hotel. Hand in hand, a young couple passed and smiled at her. A hangover was rumbling threateningly somewhere at the back of her head. Maybe she should head back inside and get some coffee. She really wanted to find Shannon and apologise for last night. By the time she'd seen her text, it had been too late to call her back. Far better to wait till the morning and apologise in person.

In the breakfast room, she could see Shannon with a large group who must be the sales team. She waved at Laura and then found a seat off to the side, not wanting to interrupt Shannon while she was working.

A kind waiter brought over a small cafetière of coffee and filled her cup before placing it on the table. She smiled at him. 'Don't go too far. I'll be needing another one of those very soon.'

Was it only yesterday morning that she was dropping the kids off to school? And only the night before that that she had conceived this whole plan? What had she been thinking? The whole dramatic plan seemed ridiculous now. She wanted to cancel everything, go back home and pretend that none of it had happened. But it was too late. Luke would be on his way. Well, if he had decided to come, that was. There was no guarantee.

She was just going to have to face up to it. Tell him that she had changed. That she had been wrong. She was going to have to be honest. But how honest should she be?

Shannon strode over from the other side of the restaurant and slipped into the chair opposite. 'How are you feeling this morning?'

Kate screwed up her eyes. 'A little bit delicate.' She reached over and squeezed Shannon's arm. 'I am so sorry I flounced off like that.'

Shannon patted her hand. 'Hey, please don't apologise. I was out of order. It's not my place to tell you what to do. I have zero experience with parenting.'

Kate felt a twinge of shame. In light of what she now knew about Shannon, she really shouldn't have thrown that one at her last night. Alcohol hadn't used to make her such a bitch. 'I don't think you need parenting experience to be able to tell when your friend has lost her way.'

Shannon poured herself a black coffee from Kate's cafetière. 'Is that how you feel?'

Kate started to pull pieces from the brioche roll on her plate. 'I don't know how it happened. When did I become this person? I don't even recognise myself.'

Shannon blew on her coffee, sipped it, grimaced and put it down. 'Don't be so hard on yourself. It sounds like having a baby can be pretty all-consuming.'

Kate nodded. 'Yeah it is. But it can be great, too. Honestly. I don't want to put you off. I was very drunk last night. Clearly, I can't hold my drink these days, either.'

'Tell me about it.' Shannon rolled her eyes and then winked. They were going to be okay.

'I'm so sorry about what I said about…' Kate stopped. She had a sudden memory of her text message to Melissa last night. She felt the colour drain from her face. 'Oh, God.'

'What's the matter? Are you going to be sick? Let me tell you, you'd be in good company this morning and I didn't even drink last night.'

Kate put her hands up to her burning face. 'I sent a message to Melissa last night.'

Shannon sniffed at her coffee and put it down again. She took a piece of bread from Kate's plate. 'Is that the Bake Sale Mother? What the hell did you message her for?'

Kate spoke through her fingers. 'I didn't. She sent me another message about the bake sale. And I let her have it, both barrels. I'm so embarrassed. How will I face her?'

Shannon shook her head. 'Here you go again. Why do you care so much what people think? I thought we were going back to confident, pre-baby Kate?'

'I know, I know. You're right. But I was actually pretty rude to her.' *Pretty* rude was an understatement. Poor Melissa had got the full force of Kate's post-dinner wrath.

Shannon frowned. 'Does this woman hound everyone as much as she does you about the damn bake sale?'

Kate shrugged. 'I don't know. Maybe not. I'm not sure.'

Shannon put the nibbled piece of bread onto the side plate in front of her. She looked a little green. Kate remembered how that felt. 'Have you considered that this woman might actually want to be your friend?'

Her friend? Melissa? Did that woman even *have* friends? She did persist in inviting Kate to her house, but Kate had assumed that it was just so she could show off about her daughter's table manners and the fact that she put each toy away in the cupboard before she got out a new one. Unlike Alice and Thomas, whose playtime aftermath made a hurricane look half-hearted. 'I hadn't considered that.'

Shannon picked up Kate's orange juice, smelled it and then put it down again. 'Maybe Super Mother is a little bit lost in Mama-land too?'

Melissa had mentioned once that they had only moved to the area a year before because of her husband's job. Kate couldn't remember what he did, but it was something very important connected with the European Parliament. He travelled to Brussels a lot. Which is why he had wanted to live close to the Eurostar. Was Melissa lonely?

'Maybe you're right. I'll invite her to come over more – it'll be my penance for being so rude to her. And on the subject of friendship, have you spoken to Laura about Paolo this morning? I'm just wondering where she ended up last night.'

Shannon smiled and leaned forwards. 'Well. I did see the two of them in the corridor late last night and they looked *pretty* friendly. I had a quick chat with her about it this morning and I have a feeling that things might turn out just great. Speaking of which, I really need to go and wander around with the sales guys, check no one goes into meltdown before their meetings, while trying to also avoid Robert.' She pulled a face. 'Once they go in, I'll be free. Can we catch up then? I really need to talk to you about something.'

'Of course. You go. I need to do a quick bit of gift shopping, so just call me when you're done.'

Back in her room, Kate began to repack her case. It was very strange, only having her own things to worry about. No searching under the bed for a favourite toy or forgotten shoe. Life was a lot faster without the kids in tow, that was for sure.

She tried to call Luke again. Still no answer. Why wasn't he picking up? She had a fluttering feeling in her chest. If something had happened to one of the children while she was not there, she would never forgive herself. She started to repack more quickly. Maybe she could get an earlier train home? But, if Luke did come out here, she would be leaving him standing at the Eiffel Tower waiting for her. She needed to see this through.

She zipped around the case and did a final check of the room, even though she knew she had everything. She would put the case into the storage room downstairs, check out and then meet up with Shannon. Hopefully, she wanted to tell Kate that she'd decided to keep the baby. For all her protestations, Kate knew her best friend really would make a great mum.

After that, it would be time to face the music. The Eiffel Tower. Two p.m.

CHAPTER THIRTY-TWO

Shannon

Being a professional woman meant putting on a work face and doing your job, even when you felt like you were dying inside. Shannon had stayed here last night so that she could be on hand in the morning to make sure that everyone had what they needed for the presentations after breakfast. And that's what she was going to do. What she was *not* going to do, was speak to Robert more than was strictly necessary.

Robert himself could have done with some tips about being professional this morning. When he had seen her arrive to breakfast, he had stood to speak with her, but she had only needed one glance to convey to him that it really wouldn't be a good idea. After that, he'd had a face like thunder.

Gabriella had made it down to breakfast and was sitting with Sylvie, nibbling on a fruit plate. Shannon felt sorry for her; she hadn't realised how much Gabriella must still be hurting about her break up with Paolo. But, when relationships didn't work out, you should be a grown up about it and move on. Shannon needed to get a move on herself. When should she tell Robert that she would be leaving straight after breakfast?

Fabienne arrived in plenty of time for the first meetings, elegant and efficient as always. Shannon kissed her on both cheeks. 'Thank you so much for coming here and taking over. I'll go back to the office and cover things there.'

Fabienne nodded. 'No problem, it's nice to get out for a change. But I still don't understand why you wanted to swap.'

For the first time ever, Shannon got to play the pregnancy card. 'I'm just tired. I need to get off my feet.'

Fabienne nodded and rubbed Shannon's arm. 'It's going to get much worse. You might want to buy some flat shoes.' She clapped her hands twice. 'Off you go then. Oh, I forgot. Someone came to the office today looking for you.'

'Really?' Shannon shivered. No one came in person any more without an appointment. Or at least a call or email first.

'Yes. She said she was a friend of yours and she was in Paris so she wanted to meet up. An American. Blonde hair. She said her name was Faye.'

Shannon froze for a moment. If Faye had been to the office already, she was getting closer. 'What did you tell her?'

Fabienne frowned. 'I told her you were here at the sales meeting, of course.'

Shannon took a deep breath. 'Did you tell her where the meeting was? The name of the hotel?'

Fabienne was looking at her as if she needed psychiatric help. 'Of course.'

As soon as she had given Fabienne the agenda and all the other paperwork she needed for this morning, Shannon called Kate. 'Where are you? I need to see you. I'll come to you.'

Shannon was greeted in song by one of the fishmongers as she walked along Rue Montorgueil. Buckets of fresh flowers lined the sidewalk and the smell of fresh salmon mingled with the stronger scents of flowers, fruits and ripe cheese. At a stall selling spiced bread, a shopkeeper was setting up a chess board, and he called out to Shannon to invite her to play. She smiled and shook her head. No time for games today.

Kate was in the queue at La Maison Stohrer. Shannon spied her through its elaborately carved storefront and Kate smiled and pointed out a gigantic display of cream puffs, arranged to look like a nun. Only in Paris.

'What did you get?' Shannon asked when Kate emerged from the crowd.

'Rum baba, of course. Why else would I queue so long? Although I was supposed to be looking for gifts for the children. What's going on? Has something happened?'

'Shall we get a drink? There's a nice bistro just up here.' Shannon wanted to wait until they were sitting down. If Kate had tripped at the pregnancy news, she might full on faint at what was coming.

As soon as they had a drink in front of them, Kate asked again. 'Okay, we're all settled. What did you want to talk about? Is it the baby? Have you spoken to Robert?'

Shannon picked up her glass of water – God, she needed something stronger – sipped and then stared into it, holding the glass with both hands. Might as well dive straight in. 'I've done this before. Pregnancy. It's not my first time.'

Kate was silent for a few moments, then she leaned forward and placed a hand over Shannon's. 'You mean you had a termination? Shannon, that's not…'

But Shannon was shaking her head. 'Not a termination. No.'

Kate kept her hand on Shannon's but her forehead creased. 'I don't understand.'

Shannon took in a deep breath, patted the hand of Kate's that was over hers and then sat back in her seat. 'Eighteen years ago, I had a baby. A little girl.'

Kate opened her mouth and closed it again. Opened it. Closed it. Made a strange sound.

Shannon smiled. 'Yeah, tough to get your head round, huh? I was nineteen. Well, twenty by the time the baby was born. The father was married. They adopted the baby. I went back home and told no one.' She paused and looked deeply into Kate's eyes. 'No one.'

But Kate was still getting her head around the first part. 'You were nineteen? He was married? How old was *he*, for goodness sake? And what the hell was he doing sleeping with a nineteen-year-old girl?'

Shannon could see how it might sound creepy. 'He was twenty-eight. His name was – is – Adam. He ran a bar off-campus. I had a fake ID – from my older sister. I told him I was twenty-two and in my last year of college. He told me he was single.'

Kate shook her head slowly. 'How did you get together?'

Shannon shrugged. 'How do these things ever start? We were drinking late at the bar; we drank there a lot, so I knew Adam to talk to. My friend hooked up with some guy, so Adam offered to walk me back to campus. It happened a couple of other times and then… one night… y'know. That's not the important part. The important part was six weeks later, when I realised he'd left me with a little gift.'

Kate opened her mouth and shut it again. She seemed to be deciding which of her queries was more important to ask, like a game of twenty questions. 'And no one else knew?'

Shannon shook her head. 'No one.'

'But your family? How did they not know?'

Shannon looked back into her water and swirled the ice cube around the glass. 'My college was a long way from home. I didn't have a noticeable bump until I was six months pregnant, so I just didn't go home for the last three months. Everyone at college was wearing sloppy sweaters and baggy pants, so it was very easy to hide a pregnancy. I just went to lessons and straight back to my room; told everyone I was studying hard because my dad had promised me my own car if I did well in my end of year assessments.'

'Wow.' Kate's eyes were wide. 'I looked like a war tank from six months. I would barely have been able to hide my bump under a four-man tent.'

Shannon wrinkled her nose. 'Yeah well, I wasn't eating particularly well and I was sick a *lot*.' Until she'd said that, Shannon had forgotten how sick she'd been the first time round. There had been days when she'd had to eat five ginger snaps before she could even get her head off the pillow. She'd started to leave two packets by the side of her bed. There had been no doting partner to get them for her.

'So? What happened?'

Shannon sighed. 'I told Adam I was pregnant. There was a part of me that thought… Oh, I don't know what I thought… It was ridiculous. What does anyone know at nineteen, right? That's when I found out he was married.'

Of course, Adam hadn't been going to leave his wife for a young girl he'd slept with twice. He'd said he loved his wife. They were 'just going through a difficult time.' Turned out his wife couldn't have children and was struggling big-time; had pushed him away. He'd cried when Shannon had told him she was pregnant. *If only it was Jessie*, he'd said. It had been ice through Shannon's heart.

Kate put her head on one side. Her eyes were full of sympathy. 'And then his wife found out?'

When Jessie had found out what was going on – and had calmed down again – she'd been the one with the idea. The plan. Shannon nodded. 'Yeah. Adam told Jessie what had happened and she suggested that they would raise the baby. Adam would be on the birth certificate anyway and, after it was born, Jessie would adopt it. I could just finish college and go back home. No one would ever need to know.' Shannon took a large gulp of her water.

'And that's what happened? You told no one else?'

Shannon nodded. 'I went to stay with them for the last three weeks of the pregnancy. Adam and Jessie. They were very kind.'

Kate pursed her lips and breathed out slowly. 'Oh, Shannon. That must have been so hard for you. And for Jessie.' She didn't mention any sympathy for Adam. He probably didn't deserve it.

'They were both there when I gave birth. I asked the nurse to give the baby straight to Jessie. I didn't want…' Shannon's throat was on fire and the backs of her eyes were stinging. 'I didn't want to see the baby.'

Kate's hands went to her face. 'Oh, Shannon.'

Shannon nodded. 'I know, right? Unnatural? What mother doesn't want to see her own child?'

'No. I didn't mean… I just… Oh, Shannon.' Kate leaned forward to put her arms around her, but Shannon backed off.

'Don't feel sorry for me, Kate. I couldn't bear it. I don't deserve it.'

'But you were nineteen, Shannon. Not much more than a child yourself. If you couldn't tell your family, then…'

Shannon put her hand to her forehead and started to rub it. 'From the moment I realised I was pregnant, life was all such a blur. I nearly walked out of college and went home a few times, to tell my parents everything. But I was so scared of how they would react. I was the first person in my family to go to college. My dad worked extra shifts to help with my tuition. It was real American Dream stuff. They were so proud of me. How could I tell them that I had ruined everything? That all their hard work and sacrifice had been for nothing? That I was just another knocked-up teenager.

'For months after the birth, I wondered if I had made a mistake. More than once, I thought about turning up at Adam and Jessie's house, asking to take her back. But then I saw them at the park together.' Shannon's throat was so tight she could barely squeeze the words out. She needed to finish. To explain. She forced down another gulp of water and looked into Kate's kind, non-judgemental eyes. 'They looked so happy, Kate. Jessie looked so happy. Pushing a beautiful pram, beaming at strangers who stopped to admire the baby inside. Her baby. She looked like… like a real mother. How could I compete with that?'

A tear made its way down Kate's face and dropped from the end of her chin. She wiped it away with the back of her hand. 'I can understand that you…'

Shannon took a deep breath and sat up straight. 'I made that choice, Kate. Me. No one else. No one made me. Adam and Jessie offered to send me updates. Photographs. They are good people. But I told them not to. Every time I move, I send Adam my new address and contact numbers in case of, y'know, if she needs a kidney or something, and I always write: "All okay?" And he replies: "All okay." That's our deal.'

This was the first time Shannon had told anyone this. Had she expected to feel a sense of unburdening? Because she didn't. If anything, she felt worse. Saying the words aloud, especially to Kate, a mother, made the whole thing feel more real than it had ever been.

'So when I say that I can't love a baby, that's what I mean. I am cold in a way that women should not be cold. How else can you explain what I did? And, even if, by some miracle, I could love a baby, I don't deserve to, Kate. I don't deserve it. Because loving another child would make what I did eighteen years ago so much, much worse than it is already.'

For a few moments, the two of them sat in silence. People chatted all around them. Happy people with straightforward, uncomplicated lives. What was Kate thinking of her right now? Whatever it was, she deserved it. Kate opened her mouth to speak and then her phone beeped.

She fumbled in her bag for her mobile. 'I'm so sorry. I just need to check this. I haven't been able to get through to L…'

As she swiped the screen and read the message, Kate's face turned pale.

Shannon frowned. 'Is everything okay?' It looked like bad news. Was it the children? *Please God, no.*

Kate stuffed the mobile back in her bag. Her eyes artificially bright. 'All fine, no problem.'

'Are you sure? Because it doesn't look like you're okay.'

Kate waved away the question, then leaned forwards and put her hand over Shannon's. 'You are a good person, Shannon. A kind, loving, generous person. You made the only decision you could at the time. And you were only just twenty when you had her! Almost still a child. You can't punish yourself for the rest of your life.'

Was that what Shannon was doing by not seeing Faye? Punishing herself? Or was she just a coward? 'She's here.'

Kate started and looked around her. 'What? Who?'

'Faye. My… the baby. The girl. She's in Paris. She's trying to find me.' Shannon tried to take a sip from her water but her glass was empty. When she looked up at Kate, her vision blurred. 'What the hell am I going to do?'

Kate took her hand again. 'It might be out of turn for me to say this, Shannon. But it's not too late.'

'To have a baby? Clearly not.' Shannon gestured to her midriff.

But Kate was shaking her head. 'To get to know your daughter.'

And then the tears really came.

CHAPTER THIRTY-THREE

Laura

Once, when Laura was at school, she had been called to the head's office. In the end, it hadn't been for anything serious at all, but those ten minutes, sitting on a hard plastic chair, waiting to be called in, had been agony.

This was a thousand times worse.

She got to the conference room at least twenty minutes before her allotted time and no one else was around. According to the schedule, Paolo would be inside right now and it took every ounce of self-control Laura had not to listen at the door.

But she'd only been there for five minutes when Robert strode out. He seemed surprised to see her and looked at his watch. 'You are not due for another fifteen minutes.'

'I like to be early and prepared.' Where was Paolo?

'Yes. Very good. I need a short break. I'll be back for your appointed time.'

He strode away with his mobile pressed to his ear. From the look on his face, she wouldn't want to be the person receiving that call. But where was Paolo?

'*Buongiorno.*' She turned and saw him walking across the lobby. She looked from him to the room he should have been in and back again.

He smiled. 'It didn't take very long. I am gone.' He mimed a plane taking off with his right hand.

Laura wanted to be sick and it wasn't just the hangover. 'What?'

Paolo nodded. 'Yes. Gone. I could have argued for my job but, I just didn't really want to.' He looked at her intently. 'It is time.'

Laura's head felt like the inside of a beehive. What should she say? She motioned towards the room of doom. 'It's me next.'

'I know.'

'And I don't have very good news for him.'

'You said.'

'What should I do?'

Gently, Paolo took her hand. 'What you should do is up to you. What I want you to do is say goodbye to Robert in there and goodbye to James over there,' he motioned in what she assumed was the direction of England, 'and then come travelling with me, anywhere you want to go.'

Laura felt as if her legs might give way under her. What was he suggesting? 'You want me to come with you?'

Paolo smiled his beautiful smile. '*Si*. You and me. Travelling the world together. What could be better?'

It sounded beyond amazing, but she needed to be sensible. 'But I want to buy a house. I want a family.'

'I want that too. Very much. And if we spend a year together, we will know.'

The beehive in her brain was in a frenzy. 'Know what?'

Paolo laughed. 'We will know whether we are a good fit.' He interlocked his fingers like a child playing a miming game. 'And then we can argue about whether to live in beautiful, sunny Italy or grey, rainy England and get married and have babies together.'

He made it sound so simple. How could it be so simple? Was he mocking her?

'Paolo. I am serious. I want to settle down, make plans.'

He drew in close to her. 'Laura, I am completely serious. I like you. I like you very much. We have… chemistry. But we don't know if this will work for ever. So we need to spend time together. That is what I am proposing. A year together. And then we make a plan.'

The beehive started to calm down. She looked at him. Deeply into his eyes. He was serious. What had Shannon said about him? *He's a family man.* Could he be *her* family man? Was this completely ridiculous? Or was it more ridiculous to wait around for an Englishman who, after twelve years together, still spoke in *maybe* and *could* and *perhaps*. And who never, ever used the word *plan.*

'Paolo, I…'

'Oh, you're still here, Paolo.' Robert strode back into the room and straight past them. 'Please will you follow me, Laura?'

She took a deep breath. And followed Robert.

After she had given Robert the explanation that Shannon had suggested, she watched him sit back and chew on his pen. He clearly wasn't happy. 'And why do they want to return so many units?'

'Because of their warehouse issues. Their software program showed no stock, so their customers bought elsewhere and they've been left sitting on a load of units.'

Robert shrugged. 'Not our problem.'

She had been waiting for this. 'I know. But they are one of the biggest distributors in the UK. If we want to maintain our relationship with—'

Robert interrupted. 'Relationship? If you had done your job and maintained a relationship, we wouldn't be looking at a huge stock return at the end of the quarter.'

Laura swallowed. *Relationships* seemed to be the key word in her life right now. Managing them. Maintaining them. Starting them? Where had Paolo gone? Was he packing right now? Would he wait to speak to her? And if he left, would they ever speak again? She needed to get her head back in the room. Robert was staring at her. Waiting for a response. 'I... er... I know what you're saying, Robert, but...'

Robert sighed. A big, deep sigh. 'I'm not happy, Laura, not happy at all. But I am also not prepared to lose another member of the sales team this week.' Laura wondered if that were true, or if Shannon had been fighting her case for her.

'Okay. So what happens now?'

'I want to closely monitor the UK for the next quarter. You need to schedule meetings with all your big customers in the next few weeks, which I will attend. Try to get them close together so that I am not going backwards and forwards to London too often. I will make sure these relationships are on track and then we can see how you manage them.'

Laura could feel a deep flush starting in her neck. This was humiliating. She would have to take Robert to all her meetings, like he was her dad coming to school to make sure the other children were playing nicely with her. 'I'm not sure that it's necessary...'

Robert coughed to interrupt her. 'It is necessary if you want to keep your job. With the quarter losses you've just shown me, I would be perfectly entitled to terminate your contract.'

Whatever cajoling Shannon had done on her behalf clearly hadn't stretched that far. Laura was failing and would need to accept the consequences. But she didn't want to. In fact, she had never really wanted this job at all. She clearly wasn't any good at it and, right now, she didn't give a fat flying fudge cake about having her contract terminated. What had Paolo said? *It is time.*

She sat up straight and looked Robert in the eye. 'It won't be necessary because I'm handing in my notice.'

He smiled and leaned back in his chair, legs stretched out in front of him. 'Really? There seems to be an epidemic of that today. Are you sure that is wise?'

She didn't care if it was wise or sensible or downright stupid, the thought of never having to talk about printers again was almost joyous. 'Thank you for the opportunity you gave me, Robert. But I'm not really cut out for a career in sales. I think it is best for both the company and me if I hand in my notice. I have loads of accrued holiday, so I think I can say that will be effective pretty much today.'

Robert's face changed. She knew that his American bosses would not be happy to find out that he had lost two of his sales team in one day. However, he soon regained his composure. 'I accept your resignation.' To his credit, he stood up and shook her hand.

As she left the room, she felt lighter than she had in a long time. Now she just needed to find Paolo.

CHAPTER THIRTY-FOUR

Shannon

Whatever she'd said to Kate earlier, giving up Faye was the hardest thing Shannon had ever had to do in her life. As soon as she could, she'd applied for her Irish passport and moved to Europe. Keeping several thousand miles between her and the memory of Jessie in the park that day had helped her to deal with it. That, and the knowledge that Faye was better off without her.

But her telephone conversation with Adam the night before had turned everything on its head.

'What's going on, Adam? Faye is in Paris? And you've given her my address? What were you thinking?'

'What did you expect me to do, Shannon? She's eighteen. She has a right to know who her mother is. I wasn't going to lie to her.'

Surely they hadn't kept it a secret from her all these years? Weren't you supposed to tell children if they'd been adopted? Be clear and honest about it from when they were small? Not spring it on them when they were older. Did Shannon have any right to have an opinion on that? 'You didn't tell her before now?'

Adam sighed. 'She knew that Jess wasn't her biological mother. We've always been honest with her. Answered any questions. Up until now she hasn't *had* a lot of questions. She's always been a happy, easy-going kid and she just accepted what we told her. But this last year, especially when she was approaching her eighteenth birthday, she's been asking a lot of questions. Questions about you.'

Shannon's heart thumped. 'What kind of questions?'

'What you looked like. Whether she looked the same as you. What your job was. Were you artistic like her?' He paused and Shannon fought the urge to ask him whether they did look alike. He lowered his voice. 'And, when Jessie wasn't around, she asked me if I'd been in love with you.'

Poor Jessie. She didn't deserve any of this. Shannon thought of the huge smile she'd worn in the park that day: the woman was born to be a mother. 'I hope you told her the truth.' The last thing the girl needed was some fairy tale about Adam and Shannon having been in love. At thirty-eight, Shannon could recognise the difference between love, infatuation and lust.

She heard Adam scratch his head again. 'Yes, I told her the truth. I said that we'd… cared about each other. But it wasn't love. It was her mum I loved. I love Jessie.'

Several thousand miles, and nineteen years away and that still hurt a little. 'And what does Jessie think about all this?'

'You can ask her, if you like.'

She didn't have time to say no before Adam had passed the phone over to his wife. Clearly he couldn't wait to be rid of Shannon. Again.

'Hi, Shannon.' Jessie's voice touched some long-forgotten place in Shannon. The place where she'd stored distant memories. The accusations. The hysterics. Then, later, the apologies and the sympathy. Jessie had cared for Shannon in her pregnancy. After the baby was born, she had held Shannon tight and whispered in her ear: *Thank you.*

Shannon swallowed and let her professional side take the lead. *Smile when you speak on the telephone and your customer will hear it.* 'Hi, Jessie. This is tricky, isn't it?'

Jessie sniffed. 'Yes, it's hard, but I think we all knew it would come someday. Faye's a very strong-minded young woman.'

'So Adam tells me.' Shannon had a weird feeling in her chest. Was that pride? That *definitely* had no right to be there. 'Jessie, you need to speak to her. Tell her to go home. I don't know what Adam was thinking, telling her where I live. We had an agreement.'

Jessie sighed at the other end. 'It's not as easy as that. She's there on an Art History trip. She knows that's where you live and she asked Adam for your contact details.'

It was such an insane thing to do. Shannon tried not to raise her voice, but it was a struggle. 'And he just gave them to her? How is that fair to me? Without warning?'

Jessie's voice was calm and soothing. 'To be fair to *him*, he has been trying to contact you for the last two weeks, Shannon. You haven't replied.'

That was true, but it was still a massive step to take. 'Surely *you* don't think this is a good idea? It's all so sudden. It needs to be thought out properly.'

There was short silence on the other end before Jessie replied. Calm and considered. 'I'd be lying if I said I was happy about it. But I knew it would come. She knows that I love her and…' Jessie's voice started to wobble at the other end. 'Be nice to her, Shannon. She's a really great kid. She's got a lot of you in her.'

Shannon's stomach flipped over. This was too much. She needed more time to think about this. 'Jessie, please. Talk to her. Maybe we can… I don't know… write first? Speak on the phone? Meeting face to face – it's just too fast.'

'It doesn't seem too fast to her. You remember what it was like to be young and impatient, Shannon.'

How was Jessie taking this so well? The woman was an absolute saint. Shannon's throat was tight. 'I'm not like you, Jessie. You're kind and patient and… you love her. I'm just not… I'm not like that.'

'You don't have to be her mom, Shannon. I've got that covered. You just need to meet her and answer her questions.' Jessie paused. 'She's going to think you're really cool.'

Shannon's throat was in danger of closing up altogether. 'How are you not angry, Jessie? If I were you, I would hate me right now.'

Jessie's voice was soft and broken. 'How could I hate you? You gave me the best gift any woman can give another woman. You gave me my child, Shannon.'

Shannon started to cry again. Once these waterworks got turned on, there seemed to be no stopping them. 'I can't do this, Jessie. I'm not like that. I just gave her away. What kind of woman does that make me?'

Jessie was crying openly now, too. 'It's going to be okay, Shannon. It's all going to be okay.'

When they'd finished speaking, Adam hadn't come back onto the phone. He'd seemed content to let the women deal with this. Once she'd hung up, Shannon had gone to wash her face in the bathroom.

And now here she was in the same bathroom, washing off the tears from her conversation with Kate. Yesterday, she had wished Kate had picked a different weekend to come. Now she was unbelievably grateful that she was here. Who else could she have talked to about all this? Certainly not Robert.

But what happened now? Should she just go home and wait for Faye to show up? Jessie had given her Faye's cell phone number: should she try to call her? What would she even say? *Hi. It's your birth mother calling. What's up?* Everyone – even Kate – seemed to think it was a good idea for Shannon to meet up with Faye, but what if it all went badly? What if Shannon upset her? What if Faye was angry? Or disappointed?

Whatever she did, she needed to reapply her make-up first. Shannon hadn't faced the world with less than foundation and mascara since she'd turned twenty-one. How did you dress to meet the daughter you hadn't seen in eighteen years? Her stomach flipped again. Was she really doing this?

Somewhere, in the midst of her fear, was a prickle of excitement. What would Faye look like? How would she sound? Would she be serious, or quick to smile? For the last eighteen years, Shannon had always pictured her as a baby, but she was a grown woman now. What was she going to say to her? How was she going to feel? Terrified? Desperate? Would she feel... love?

There was a knock on the door. Shannon froze. Was it Robert? Kate?

Another knock. Shannon walked to the door and put her hand on it. She took a deep breath. 'Hello? Who is it?'

'Oh, hi. It's, uh, is Shannon there? I'm Faye.'

CHAPTER THIRTY-FIVE

Laura

Packing to go home was so much easier; you could just throw everything in. Packing to go somewhere was what Laura hated: choosing what to wear, finding shoes which coordinated with all the outfits, remembering to pack all the toiletries. And knickers – they were easy to forget. Laura had once spent a wet weekend in Corby going commando. She could have bought a pack of new knickers, but it would have cost the equivalent to two pints of beer and she was on a student budget at the time.

Today she was even happier to be packing up her belongings. It didn't feel like an end of something, it felt like a beginning. Soon she would be packing up a lot more when she got back to James' flat.

Funny how she still didn't think of it as her flat, even though she'd lived there for nearly two years. It has always been James' place. He'd chosen the furniture and furnishings before she'd even moved in. He hadn't let her add so much as a cushion or a lamp. There was one bedcover that that she'd chosen – with his approval – and that was it. Would she take that with her, too?

She checked her phone again. He still hadn't replied to her drunken message. Either he was angry or he just hadn't taken her seriously. She couldn't blame him. This wouldn't be the first time she'd made threats to leave and then not followed through.

This time, though, there would be no change of heart. Kate was right – some people just weren't the settling down type. James was never going to change his mind – it was time to give something and someone else a try.

There was a knock on her door. Paolo, already. As soon as she'd left Robert's meeting, she had found him in his room and they had excitedly made plans for their next step. They both needed to serve one month's notice so would have to return home for a while, but Paolo had already said he would come and see Laura the following weekend. He was certainly a man of action. They'd arranged to meet downstairs in the lobby as soon as they were packed, but he was obviously too impatient.

'I'll be one minute, hang on!'

But when she answered the door, it wasn't Paolo.

'What are you doing here?'

James smiled broadly. Wearing dark grey trousers and a pink shirt open at the neck, he looked as if he'd come straight from a work meeting. 'Well, that's a nice welcome when I've just paid an extortionate amount of money to sit on a stuffy train for three hours, just to surprise you.'

Laura stood back from the door. 'Sorry. Come in.'

What the hell was he doing here? Had he got her message? He didn't look heartbroken. Had she dreamed it?

James strode in with confidence. 'So, how are your meetings going?'

Why was he acting so calmly? He must have heard her message by now. 'Not terribly well. The order got returned last thing Friday night.'

James turned around and frowned. 'What order?'

The order she had been stressing about for the last two weeks. That had kept her awake late every night and woken her early every morning. 'Nothing. Nothing important. Sit down.' She motioned to the chair in the corner of the room. One of those bucket seats which were so uncomfortable it made you wonder why they bothered with them. Maybe it was for occasions like this. 'We need to talk.'

James sat down on the bed and patted it. 'I agree. That's why I am here.'

Laura sat down next to him. A good fifty centimetres from where he had been patting. This was the man she had slept beside the night before last and now she didn't want to touch him. It was an odd feeling. 'Did you get my message?'

James laughed. 'Yes. Just about.' He raised an eyebrow. 'It was rather slurred.'

Laura wrinkled her nose. She could possibly have been a little classier. 'Yes, I'd had a few glasses of wine.' She held up her hands. 'I am in Paris after all.'

James held a clenched fist to his mouth and coughed. 'Not like you, though, is it? Anyway, that's not what I wanted to talk about. You gave me a bit of a fright with your message. Where did that come from? Not that silly argument we had on the phone yesterday afternoon?'

It was only thirty percent the argument they'd had yesterday. The other seventy percent was the other tens of arguments they'd had on the same subject. If she was honest with herself, maybe five percent of it had been Paolo. Or maybe ten percent. It really didn't matter any more. She needed to take a deep breath and do this.

She turned to give James her full attention. He deserved that, at least. 'James, I think maybe we just want different things. I am ready to move things up a level. Make plans. Buy a house. I understand that isn't what you want. Maybe we just need to face that it's over.'

'That's nonsense.' James took her hands in his. 'I don't want to break up. I know I've been working a lot lately, that you have been on your own. But I will try and cut down a bit, spend more time with you.'

Laura swallowed. She would have jumped at these words just a few weeks ago. But now it was too little, too late. 'It's not that, James. It's the future. I need to know where I am going. It's just the way I am.'

James started to rub her back. It should have felt soothing. She just wanted to be sick. 'Our future is together, Lau. It always has been. You know that. Everyone says what a great couple we are. I love you, Laura.'

Laura's mouth nearly fell open. The 'F' word? 'I don't understand. You never want to talk about the future.'

'That's not true, Laura. Really, it's not.' He looked into her eyes with his familiar blue ones. How often had she looked into those eyes? Was this going to be the last time? A lump rose in her throat. They had been together since they were little more than children. This was harder than she'd expected.

But she owed it to herself not to back down now. 'It is true. Every time I mention buying a house, or getting married or having children, you change the subject.'

'Well, I'm sorry if I made you feel like that. It's not what I meant. Everyone knows we're meant to be together. We're going to have all those things.' James nudged her. 'Your dad has even promised to give me some DIY lessons when we buy a house.'

Thinking about her parents made Laura feel wobbly. Had James really spoken to her dad about them buying a house? She was tired, hungover and sitting here with James felt like going back to reality. It was home. Everything else felt a little ridiculous. Leaving her job? Travelling? Paolo? Maybe that kind of adventure was more for the Shannons of this world.

James put his arms around her and she let herself relax into them.

CHAPTER THIRTY-SIX

Kate

Luke still wasn't answering his phone.

The churning feeling had started at the bottom of Kate's stomach before she'd met Shannon that morning, but she'd pushed it down. It didn't mean anything that she couldn't reach Luke. He might not have mobile reception where he was, or he might have left his phone in a different room, or maybe he'd tripped and fallen and thrown the phone too far to reach, or he might be at the hospital because one of the children had had a terrible accident or... *Stop it.*

And then she'd got his text.

Shannon had been spilling her heart out and Kate had had to force all thoughts of Luke from her mind. How could she have stopped the conversation about Shannon's daughter – her daughter! – to start talking about her own problems? Problems she'd brought on herself.

It was impossible to overstate how shocked she'd been at Shannon's revelation. Of everyone she knew, Shannon was the least likely to have a baby. It was almost enviable, how certain Shannon had been about not settling down and having a child. Not for her the uncertainty of *if* and *when* and *who with* which plagued the thoughts of most thirty-something women. Shannon's life was full and varied and exciting.

And now Kate had a bombshell of her own to deal with. Luke's text had been factual and brief.

I found Tim's number.

Why hadn't she thrown it away? The first time she'd met Tim in the hospital, he had scribbled his number on a leaflet about counselling which he'd found in the canteen. So old-school. If he hadn't left his mobile in the car and she hadn't let her battery die, they would have typed their numbers straight into their contacts. There would have been no evidence.

I called him to see if you were with him.

Dammit. If she had answered just one of the seventeen calls and messages from Luke yesterday, he wouldn't have called Tim. Luke wasn't a jealous husband. He wouldn't normally check up on her. He trusted her. Maybe a little too much.

He told me everything.

Everything? What everything? What was there to tell? That they'd met for coffee at the hospital twice. For a drink once. Been to a jazz bar together. And then she'd been at his house. It was this last one that worried her. What had Tim said? *Shit. Shit. Shit.*

Her first instinct was to go home straight away. Face the music. The return ticket she'd bought was for late tonight, but maybe she could just change it? Whatever it cost.

But a visit to the Eurostar website showed no tickets available for the rest of the day and the airlines she checked were the same.

She couldn't leave yet, anyway. What if Luke was on his way here already? She might be going one way as he went the other. No. She'd made the plan; she needed to stick to it. But would he? Or would she be standing at the bottom of the Eiffel Tower like a jilted bride?

When Shannon returned to the hotel to check out, Kate resumed her guilt gift shopping for the children. Anything was better than sitting still. She was unlikely to find a suitable gift on Rue Montorgueil. So she headed over to the huge underground mall at Les Halles. There had to be a toy shop in there somewhere. Nothing said 'I missed you' like a huge piece of primary-coloured plastic that wouldn't be played with after the first twenty-five minutes.

As she walked she tried Luke's number again. Several times. Still no answer.

What had Tim told him?

After the jazz bar, she had decided not to see Tim again. It wasn't right. There was nothing going on between them, but Luke didn't know she was meeting him and that made it wrong.

But then Tim had sent her a message about some old CDs he'd found which belonged to her. Bruch piano concertos. She'd been cooped up in the house all day and Luke had come home late and decided to go to bed early because he had to get an early train the next day. Tim was offering an escape. Kate would just drop round to his house and collect the CDs. It would only take half an hour for the whole round trip. No big deal.

She wished she could have blamed the wine, but she'd only had one glass. He'd played one of the CDs and it had brought back so many memories of their time at university. They'd laughed about eccentric tutors and he'd regaled her with stories she'd never heard before about what some of the brass section boys had got up to in the intermissions of performances.

They'd been sitting close. Legs touching. It was a strange thing, being physically close to someone you'd had a sexual relationship with in the past. The frisson of familiarity mixed with distance: a heady cocktail. Where had Tim's girlfriend been that night? He hadn't even mentioned her.

Every shop she passed seemed to be a clothing store. There was nothing in these shops that would suit the children. She would be better off buying them something in England on her return. There was still a while until two o'clock, but maybe she should start making her way to the Eiffel Tower. She wished she'd said earlier now. The plan had been to give Luke time to get here, but this waiting around was killing her. If he wasn't going to come, she'd rather know now.

Still no answer from Luke.

It was the kiss that had done it. Well, the almost-kiss. At that moment, Kate had felt really good. Laughing at something Tim had said. Sipping at her wine to make it last. Feeling light. Young. Free. And then he had stopped laughing and tried to kiss her.

Did it count as a kiss if your lips touched for less than a nano-second? Kate had jumped up so fast, the wine had been spilled on his cream sofa. She hadn't stopped to apologise. Just grabbed her coat and escaped to the car. Hadn't even taken the CDs with her. She'd been so distracted on the way home that she'd got lost. She was making a habit of that: literally and metaphorically.

That was why she'd come here. Somehow, she'd taken a wrong turn and got lost. When she was a kid and had lost something, her dad always said, 'Go back to the place you last had it.' So she had.

But nothing about this weekend had gone to plan. And not just the wild night out with Shannon, who had turned out to be both too busy and too pregnant for such a thing. It had been good to see her friend, but right now Kate wished so much that she hadn't come.

Her phone beeped and she snatched it out of her bag. It was a photo of the Eiffel Tower with a message: *I'm here. Where are you?*

CHAPTER THIRTY-SEVEN

Shannon

Faye was absolutely beautiful. Clear skin, long blonde hair, white teeth. She was like an American teenage poster campaign. Looking at her took Shannon's breath away. Was this how men felt when they looked at a beautiful woman? It was intoxicating.

Faye was framed in the doorway like a work of art. A rucksack on her back, wearing khakis and a white vest top, she smiled. 'You must be Shannon?'

Shannon nodded and held the door open for her daughter to come in.

Faye walked through the door and turned around to face Shannon again. 'I guess my dad told you I was in Paris?'

Shannon nodded. She still couldn't speak. *Her dad.* Adam. Faye looked a lot like him. She had his mannerisms too, tucking her hair behind her ear, twitching her nose.

'So, I guess, uh, this is a bit of a surprise. Me turning up, I mean?'

Shannon nodded a third time. God, she wanted to touch her. To hold her. To pull her close and breathe her in. It was overwhelming. She coughed, in the hope that some words might magically appear in her mouth. 'He said you were here, but he didn't know if…'

Faye looked down at the floor, hooked her thumbs into the straps of her backpack and ran them up and down it. 'Yeah. I told him I wouldn't just look you up without telling him. I nearly didn't but, you know, seize the day and all that.' She stared up at Shannon through her eyelashes, studying her face, as if gauging her reaction.

Seize the day? Maybe this goddess had a little bit of Shannon in her, too. It was so hard not to search for any physical resemblance; she didn't have that right. She took a deep breath. *Speak, you dumb woman.*

'How was your flight here?' What a ridiculous and inane question to ask. Especially when she actually wanted to ask her about the last eighteen years of her life.

Because she did. Suddenly, she wanted to know everything about this amazing creature standing in front of her. What did she like to do? What were her friends like? What was her favourite flavour of ice cream?

Faye frowned and scratched her head. She looked just like Adam when she did that. 'Yeah, it was cool. I came over with a group from my school.' She looked around Shannon's room. 'Our hotel is nothing like this, though. Why are you staying in a hotel when you live here?'

Shannon laughed. She liked the girl's directness. 'My boss wanted me to stay here.'

She watched Faye take in the room. Her bright blue eyes darting from the TV to the desk to the bed. She could just watch her for ever. Every tiny movement. Every blink. Should she hug her? Could she?

A couple of times, Faye's eyes rested on Shannon and then she looked away again. Her fingers tapped on the sides of her legs. Shannon wanted to say something that would put Faye at her ease, but she didn't want to rush her either. Eventually, Faye turned to face her. 'So, you're my birth mom?'

Shannon nearly lost her footing. 'Yes. I am.' Her heart was fluttering, her temperature rising. Was it the baby hormones or was she about to cry? Again. She took a deep breath and opened her mouth with no idea about what she was going to say. 'I am so sorry, Faye. For everything. So, so sorry.'

Faye bit her lip and her eyes filled. 'Don't apologise. I'm the one who appeared from nowhere. I just wanted to meet you and…'

All Shannon wanted to do was throw her arms around this girl and pull her close. Where had these feelings come from? This was the first time she had seen her in eighteen years – since she was barely born – and yet she felt as if she'd known her for ever. Did Faye feel the same way? *Slowly. Slowly.* 'Shall we sit down?'

Faye nodded gratefully. 'That's a good idea.' She perched on the edge of Shannon's bed.

Shannon wanted to sit next to her, put an arm around her. But she settled for pulling over the desk chair instead. Once she was seated opposite, she realised it had been a bad decision. It looked as if she was about to conduct a job interview. 'Are you enjoying being in Paris?'

Faye nodded. 'Yeah, I love it. I'm an art major so this is, like, Heaven to me. When Dad told me you lived here, it felt like fate, y'know?'

Shannon was worried about Jessie. Kind, thoughtful, unselfish Jessie. 'And how does your… mom feel about you coming?'

Faye rolled her eyes. 'You know mothers. Wanted to check I had enough underwear, that I hadn't packed anything inappropriate, that I had the hotel details and money for a cab in my purse at all times.'

Shannon smiled. 'No, I meant about you coming here. Meeting me.'

Faye traced the design on the bed quilt with her finger. 'I didn't tell them I was coming today. I know I said I would, but it was kind of a last-minute decision.'

Shannon tried not to laugh. The naïvety of the young. 'I think they may have guessed.'

Faye looked up. 'Really? I wanted to keep it secret for now. I don't want to hurt my mom. I mean, she is my mom. I love her. She drives me crazy sometimes, but that's just being a mom, right?'

Shannon nodded. Jessie was definitely Faye's mom. And judging by what she'd seen so far, she'd done a pretty good job. So where did that leave Shannon? Where did she fit in?

'Is there anything you wanted to know from me?'

Faye looked at the floor again, shrugged one shoulder, then looked up again. 'I don't know. I just felt like I wanted to see you. Obviously I've looked you up on social media, I knew what your face looked like, but I just wondered, y'know, if you were like me in any way. I can see you have my hair.'

'I think you'll find that *you* have *my* hair.' Shannon was trying to keep it light. But even saying this made her voice catch in her throat. She put a hand to her mouth to try to stop her chin from wobbling. It must be the damn hormones. Her tear ducts were going to run dry.

'Ha! I guess you're right.' Now Faye put her hand to her mouth and her eyes began to fill.

Shannon no longer cared what the protocol was. She moved to sit on the bed next to Faye – her daughter – and pulled her close. Faye clutched at her and they sobbed into each other's hair. No longer able to tell whose was whose. Shannon began to rock gently; she pressed her lips to the side of Faye's head and breathed her in. This was her baby. The child she'd never held. She was in her arms and she never, ever wanted to let her go.

After a few moments, Faye pulled back slightly and looked at Shannon. 'I was so scared that you wouldn't want to see me.'

Shannon wiped a tear from Faye's cheek with edge of her left thumb, keeping her right arm still wrapped around her, unable to tear her eyes from her face. 'Of course I wanted to see you. I wanted to see you so much.'

Faye searched in the pocket of her khakis and Shannon reached across to the tissue box on her bedside table and offered it to her. Faye smiled a watery smile and took one, blowing her nose loudly. 'It's just that Dad said…'

Shannon needed to go carefully. She had to be honest, to accept her mistakes. But this also meant being honest with herself. 'Your dad was telling the truth. But it wasn't that I didn't want to see you. I just thought it was the best thing for everyone if I didn't. You have two great parents.'

Faye nodded. 'The best.' She looked down at the bed, where she was tracing the quilt with her finger again. She took a deep breath. 'Have you ever thought about me?'

Had she thought about her? Shannon had spent the last eighteen years trying *not* to think about Faye. It was like a wound that never healed, but when she pulled the bandage back to look at it, the pain was unbearable. It would have been better not to look. But that was impossible.

'I thought about you every single day.'

Faye looked up and her face crumpled. Shannon pulled her close and held her tightly as she cried, her own tears dropping onto the top of Faye's head.

'I knew that Adam and Jessie would be great parents, that you'd be happy. But every time I saw a child who was about your age, I wondered how you looked, what you'd be doing, what made you laugh. When it got really bad, I just kept telling myself over and over that I made the right decision. That you had the best life possible?' As the words came out of her mouth, Shannon realised this was not a statement, it was a question.

'Oh, Shannon.' Faye leaned forward and put her arms around her again. 'You made the right decision.'

And, just like that, a million weights that Shannon hadn't known she'd been carrying, fell away.

*

Shannon had a thousand questions for Faye, who had about two thousand of her own. As Faye talked about her school, her friends, her passion for art, Shannon drank in every word, every movement. She hadn't known what Faye would be like, but she was exactly as she should be. Her heart felt as if it might burst. She was perfect.

Then Faye looked at her watch and groaned. 'I really want to stay here and talk more, but I can't. My course tutor is going to go *ballistic* if he realises I have split off from my travel buddies. We're supposed to stay in a three at all times. I don't care for me, but I don't want to get the other two girls in trouble.'

Rebellious but loyal. She really was a chip off the old block. Shannon squeezed Faye's hand. She couldn't keep from touching her all the time. 'That's okay. Maybe we can ask him if you can meet me for dinner tonight? With your parents' blessing, of course.'

After swapping cell phone numbers, and insisting she pay for a taxi to take Faye back to her friends, Shannon waved her off and came back into the hotel. She needed to see Robert. There was a lot she needed to tell him.

CHAPTER THIRTY-EIGHT

Laura

When James released her from his hug, Laura sat back on the bed and looked at him. He was handsome. And kind. And safe. And this impulsive side to him was new. He usually had to plan trips well in advance. And he'd told her that he didn't even like Paris. Actually, that part didn't really add up.

'I can't believe you came all this way to talk to me.'

He had hold of her arms and was smiling into her face. 'You were upset and, anyway, I have a client out here that I can see at the same time so it seemed to be the sensible thing to do.'

Laura's heart sank a little. So he hadn't flown out here just to see her. Still, at least they'd managed to have this conversation about the future. Did it matter that he was seeing a client as well? Surely the working out was irrelevant if you got the answer you were looking for?

'I'm glad you came. That we've talked. I just wanted to know that we are going to start making plans. Think about buying a house. Talking about having children.'

James stretched his arms above his head and yawned. 'And we will. We will. Let me get this financial year wrapped up. Then we can talk about it. Maybe look into a small house somewhere.' Well, that would please her mother.

Whilst they were talking like this, Laura wanted to get everything cleared up. She remembered Kate's question yesterday in the café. 'And kids. You do want kids?'

He nodded slowly and scratched his nose. 'Of course. At the right time. Someday. I mean, everyone has kids eventually, don't they?' He laughed and took her hands again.

A strangely familiar feeling started to bubble in the bottom of Laura's stomach. 'But I want to plan, James. I want to know what we are going to do and when.'

James sighed and pulled his hands away. 'Here we go again. I've said yes to everything you want. What else can I do?'

But he hadn't. Everything was *maybe* and *possibly* and *someday*. Laura couldn't work in vague adverbs. She wanted an actual plan. After ten years, was that unreasonable? She let her head droop down onto her chest. 'It's never going to happen, is it?'

James stood up and began to pace, running his hands through his thick, blonde hair. 'I don't know what's got into you, Laura. We're young, we're having fun. My God, we've barely left our twenties. Why are you so keen to get us tied down?'

She could tell him. She could explain that she wasn't asking for marriage and babies tomorrow, that she just wanted to know that it'd happen at some stage. That she didn't want their relationship to turn out like Kate and her ex-boyfriend. That if they wasted another ten years on 'fun', she would be forty-two. But there was no point. They'd had this argument so many times before, she could have acted it out. Both parts. Sometimes familiarity really did breed contempt. 'But I'm not having fun any more.'

James clenched his teeth and breathed out through his mouth. 'Let's not do this now. We're in Paris. Look, I'll go and meet with this client and then we can have dinner somewhere. Maybe we could book this room for another night? Travel home tomorrow, perhaps?' The look on his face wasn't so much hopeful as determined. He was expecting this argument to go the way of all their others. With her capitulation. But the adverbs hadn't changed. Someday, maybe, perhaps...

Laura looked down at her hands. 'Never.'

'What?'

She took a deep breath and looked up at him. 'It's over, James.'

James began to run his fingers through his hair again. 'This is getting ridiculous, Laura. We both know that we're going to kiss and make up. We always do. You're making more of this than you need to. Look, I'll get on to the estate agent on Monday. Will that make you feel better?'

Paolo had said she was beautiful, not ridiculous. He told her she deserved to be begged to be married, not just made to feel better. He had offered her travel across another continent, not a visit to an estate agent in South London.

She was being unfair to James. She was being unfair to herself. She was one hundred percent sure this time.

'I'm sorry, James, but you need to go. I have somewhere to be.'

And someone to see.

Paolo's face lit up when he saw her, but crumpled into confusion at her question.

'What's your plan?'

'My plan? What, right now? Maybe lunch or…'

'No. I mean us. What's happening now?'

'What do you mean?'

Laura's heart sank for the second time that hour. Was this just going to be a repeat of the conversation she'd just had? This time, she wasn't going to waste twelve years. He was in. Or out. 'Paolo, if we're going to do this travelling thing, I want to know where it's headed. I'm not about to just wander the globe for the next however long.'

Paolo's face cleared. 'Oh. Okay. Let's sit down.'

Laura's stomach was clenched tightly. She had never been this forthright in her life before. Although her lack of confrontation hadn't exactly worked out well.

They sat on chairs beside a small table in the hotel atrium. His was royal blue and hers was yellow. They were designed for aesthetics over comfort. But Laura wasn't planning on sitting here for long. It was time for doing, not talking.

Paolo's legs were splayed lazily in front of him and he leaned forwards so that his elbows rested on his knees. Then he pressed his fingers together as if he were about to pitch a marketing plan.

'So, we go back home for one month and both work out our notice to Sentek. I have saved those stock options that we got as a bonus last Christmas. If you still have yours, and we're careful, that should give us enough money for at least the first six months. I will visit you in England next weekend and we can make a plan of the countries we want to visit. Start looking at tickets. Then, in the next two weeks we can book the first leg of the journey. After that, we can plan each destination as we go along. How does that sound?'

Great. And he'd clearly thought this all through. But it wasn't what she meant. She needed more. 'And after?'

Paolo sat back up in his chair. Laying back, legs still splayed, he looked like a model from the front page of *GQ*. 'After twelve months, we will decide if we want to go to Stage Two.'

Laura held her breath. 'Which is?'

'Decide where to live. Maybe Italy. Maybe England. Maybe somewhere else altogether.' When she tried to interrupt, he took hold of her hands. 'Then when we want babies. And how many to have.'

Laura's heart bounced down to her toes and back up again. She could barely get the words out of her mouth. 'Are you serious?'

Paolo looked deeply into her eyes. She felt as if she was slipping. 'Completely serious. I want it too, Laura. A family.'

She needed to keep a grip on reality until she had everything nailed down. 'But what will we do? What jobs will we have?'

Paolo shrugged. 'I could go back to teaching.'

That one came from nowhere. She hadn't known about his previous job. There was a lot she didn't know about him yet. 'Teach what?'

Paolo turned one of the hands he was holding and kissed her palm. 'Mathematics. I have a PhD.'

Laura had to stop her mouth from falling open. 'A Mathematics PhD?'

Paolo stopped before he kissed her second palm and frowned. 'Yes. Why? Do you not think I am clever enough?'

Laura just wanted him to go back to the kissing thing. 'No, no. It's not that, I just, thought you would have done something more… interesting or… creative.'

Paolo smiled as he leaned in to kiss her mouth. 'If you don't think Mathematics is interesting and creative, my Laura, you've been doing it all wrong.'

As their lips touched, Laura had to agree. She had been doing it all wrong. This time, everything seemed to be adding up just right.

CHAPTER THIRTY-NINE

Shannon

The Pont des Arts used to be covered in padlocks which were attached by lovers to the bridge. They would lock a padlock etched with both their names and then throw the key in the Seine. Eventually, the weight of the padlocks got to be so much that it was destroying the bridge, so they'd all been removed by officials. This had been the subject of much debate around the world, and opinions were very mixed, but now the view of the Seine was clear and unimpeded as Shannon leaned on the side of the bridge and looked up the river. How nice it must have been for the bridge to be freed from all that weight. She took in a large breath. The city was beautiful in the sunshine.

Robert had barely spoken the whole way here as she had told him everything: Adam, Faye, the baby. He had listened as carefully as if she had been expounding her plans to market a new range of printers. She had tried to gauge his feelings, but his face was giving nothing away. Now he was leaning with his back against the bridge, his arms folded.

'So, after fighting me so hard about meeting my daughters, I am going to meet yours?'

Daughter. Even the word felt strange. Shannon shook her head. 'I don't know. I guess we'll talk tonight, but just seeing me might be enough for her. She might have satisfied her curiosity and I'll never hear from her again.'

Robert put his head on one side. 'But you would like to?'

Shannon had spent the last eighteen years trying everything to *not* think about Faye. And failing. Every birthday had been a struggle. She had tried so hard to lock away any feelings in a box at the back of her mind. But now that lid was off and it was all rushing out. 'Yes, I hope that she will want to know me. I know she doesn't need a mother. But whatever she wants, I want to be that for her.'

Robert nodded slowly; he seemed to be taking these revelations remarkably well. 'And what about our baby? How do you feel about that?'

Our baby? *Our?* Shannon's stomach flipped. This one wasn't quite as straightforward. But she had made one decision. 'I am going to have the baby. I want to have the baby. But I am not expecting anything from you. However much you want to be involved is fine by me.'

Robert reached out and held her elbows. 'I *want* to be involved, Shannon. I have always wanted to be more involved. It was you keeping me at arm's length. And, as for the baby, I will be his or her father. It was a big shock. I thought my days of being with a little one were over. But now I have had a chance to think it all through, I think this is going to be a good thing. For both of us.'

Shannon still wasn't convinced. 'But you said that babies were' – she paused for second to get the correct wording – 'the end of civilised life. You hate babies. Their noise, their mess, their… babyness.'

Robert nodded slowly. 'Yes. It is true. I am not a huge fan of babies. But that's other people's babies. This will be *our* baby. He or she will be a mixture of you and me. How could I not love a child like that?'

Shannon bit her lip. 'Really? You really mean it? Because, I'll be honest with you, I'm a little bit freaked out by the whole baby thing myself.'

Robert placed his hand on her cheek. 'You forget, I've done this before. I have two daughters. I'll help you through it.'

'Ha!' Shannon coughed out a laugh. 'I have heard about your parenting skills. You forget, I've met one of your daughters now. She told me how keen you were when they were small.'

Robert held out his hands and shrugged. 'Well, maybe. But that was twenty years ago. I was too young. I am a different man now. You've changed me with your strange American ways.' He smiled at her and then his expression changed. Became serious. He looked directly into her eyes. 'I will be a good father, Shannon. I promise. I will look after you both.'

Tears were burning the backs of Shannon's eyes. Was this all going to work out? Could she be that lucky? 'And what about work? How will everyone react?'

Robert took both her hands in his. He was smiling again. 'It's not a problem. I've already told my boss that we are dating – don't get cross, it would have been unprofessional not to – and I don't think Fabienne has been quite as discreet as you think she has. I doubt it will be a huge surprise to anyone in the office that we are together and I'm sure they'll be pleased for us about the baby.'

Shannon allowed a smile to turn the edges of her mouth. 'Well, then. I think it is going to be a good thing, too. Scary. But a very good thing.'

Robert's smiled widened. 'And maybe we could talk about getting m—'

Shannon put a hand over Robert's mouth. 'Hold on there, Mister. I'm having a baby, not a full frontal lobotomy. Let's just see how this works out, shall we? I'm not the marrying kind.'

Robert raised an eyebrow and threaded her arm through his. 'We'll see.'

They started to walk slowly back to the hotel. From the look on Robert's face, the sales people he would be seeing this afternoon might be getting a much easier ride than they'd envisaged.

He stroked Shannon's hand gently with his thumb. 'At least we have everything out in the open now. There's no more surprises, are there?'

'Actually, there is one more terrible thing.'

Robert stopped in his tracks and looked at her.

Shannon stuck out her bottom lip. 'I'm really afraid that I might have gone off coffee.'

CHAPTER FORTY

Kate

The Eiffel Tower could be seen wherever you were in Paris. It was intriguing how something so modern and stark could also be so beautiful. A kind of architectural Kate Moss. Kate had a picture of it in her hallway at home, which had been taken on their honeymoon. Hidden in the foreground of the picture, which Luke had taken from a distance, was Kate sitting on the grass. If you didn't know she was there, you could easily miss her.

Due to being terrified of heights, Kate had never been to the top of the Eiffel Tower; not even halfway up. When she'd made the plan, she'd considered whether to meet Luke at the top, like in *Sleepless in Seattle* with the top of the Empire State Building. Conjured visions of her clinging to the sides like Spiderman with vertigo were hardly romantic, though. She'd opted for underneath, in the middle, instead.

The river was full of tourists embarking on water tours of the Seine. Up and around Île de la Cité and back again. Families, couples, coaches of tourists. There was someone standing still in the middle of all that bustle, directly underneath the tower. Standing and waiting. It was him.

'You came.'

His face relaxed as he saw her. Then tensed again. 'Of course I came. You asked me to. Did you think I wouldn't?'

It was so unbelievably wonderful to see him. 'I didn't know for sure.'

On this bright and sunny morning, in a different country, he looked different. Her husband. Luke. 'Kate. What's going on?' His eyes looked concerned, worried, confused.

Kate took a deep breath. 'I'm sorry.'

'What for? I don't know what's going on, Kate. I just don't understand. I had no idea there was anything wrong. When I saw Tim's name, I thought… Well, I'm sure you can imagine what I thought. But when I spoke to him he said you'd just been meeting for a drink. Why didn't you tell me?'

'Can we sit down?'

Luke nodded, and they walked away from the tower and towards the Champ de Mars. The unexpected warmth of the October afternoon had brought people out with their blankets and picnics. The two of them found a space and sat down.

Luke crossed his legs and sat in front of her. 'Okay. What's up? Why did you just leave like that? If you wanted to come and see Shannon, I wouldn't have had a problem with it.'

Kate shook her head. 'It wasn't about seeing Shannon, although that has been great. I left because I felt lost. I didn't know who I was any more. And I wanted you to see what it was like. Not being able to suit yourself. Having to look after the children on your own.'

Luke frowned. 'Okay. But I have had the children on my own before. I still don't see what's going on.'

How could she make him understand how she felt? 'I want to be a good mum, Luke. It's my job. But some days it's just… overwhelming. And I've been angry. Really, really angry. Every day I have felt like I was fighting someone. The kids. You. Bloody Melissa. And then Dad died and I…' Her voice croaked and she stopped to get control of herself.

Luke squeezed her hand. 'If you needed more help, I could have…'

She held up a hand to stop him. 'That was the problem. I did need help. But I didn't ask. I wanted you to just realise. But even if you had offered, I'm not sure I would have taken you up on it. I've been on some kind of mission.' She shook her head slowly as the truth of her words – Shannon's words – began to truly sink in.

Luke nodded. He was trying to understand. 'And what about Tim? What was going on there? And why didn't you tell me?'

Kate put her hands up to her face and rubbed it. 'I don't know why I met up with him. I could get all deep and psychological and say that he represented my youth or something. But I think it was just because it was fun. And then it wasn't fun any more. I realised what I was doing. And I realised that I did want to have fun. But I wanted to have fun with you.'

Luke reached out and took her hand. His kissed her palm and she brushed away a tear that had collected in the corner of her eye. He pulled her in close and she rested her head on his shoulder. It felt good.

She turned her eyes up at him. 'I want to play the piano.'

He frowned. 'You already do play the piano.'

She shook her head. 'No, I don't. I haven't played in years. But I am going to start. Every day. And if the house stays a bit more untidy because of it, then so be it.'

'Okay.'

'And I might start giving lessons. Or playing in public. Or just playing to please myself. But I am going to play. And I need you to guarantee me one night a week when you will be home in time for me to do that. When you can have the kids and give them dinner and I can just leave and do what I need to do.'

Luke raised an eyebrow. 'Even if I take them to Café M's?'

She smiled. 'Even if you feed them Weetabix and Easter eggs. It'll be your night, your rules.'

Luke held her arms and pushed her away gently so that he could look in her face. 'Really? Whatever I want?'

When she nodded, he grinned and flicked his sunglasses back down over his eyes. She could see her reflection laughing in the lens.

There she was.

A LETTER FROM EMMA

I want to say a huge thank you for choosing to read *One Way Ticket to Paris*. If you enjoyed it, and want to be kept up-to-date with my future releases, just sign up at the following link. Your email address will never be shared and you can unsubscribe at any time.

www.bookouture.com/emma-robinson

I took a lot of the inspiration for this novel from some of my own past experiences. When I was twenty-nine, I ran away to Paris. I left my job and long-term boyfriend and moved to a very very small apartment in Montparnasse, attending a language school on Rue Victor Hugo every morning and wandering around Paris alone in the afternoons. It was one of the scariest, loneliest and most liberating things I have ever done and has given Paris a special place in my heart for ever. If I ever want to run away again, that's where you will find me.

Motherhood can be overwhelming. Like Kate, I lost my dad when my first child was very young and it was hard. I know from the followers of my blog that this is not an uncommon experience and I hope that I have done those feelings justice in my description of Kate's thoughts. I hope, like me, that those people are able to see their lost parent in their own children. I also hope, like Kate, that we realise that it is important to take care of ourselves as well as our children.

Please help me to tell others about *One Way Ticket to Paris* by writing a quick review. This is only my third book, so I'd love to hear what you thought of it and which parts you enjoyed. Reviews make a huge difference in helping other people find my book and I am grateful for every single one.

I also love hearing from my readers. Come and join the fun on my Facebook page Motherhood for Slackers. They are a friendly bunch and we even let boys in. You can also find me on Twitter or my website.

Stay in touch!
Emma

        motherhoodforslackers

        @emmarobinsonuk

        www.motherhoodforslackers.com

ACKNOWLEDGEMENTS

First thanks, as always, must go to my brilliant publisher Isobel Akenhead whose knowledge of many subjects continues to astound me (sorry for making you cry!). More kisses for Kim Nash for her fantastic PR and friendship and to the whole Bookouture family for being flipping brilliant, particularly Susie Lynes for talking me down branch by branch from the top of the crazy tree when necessary. Thanks chick.

Gratitude again to Kate Machon, Elizabeth Symonds, Martin Ross and Marie Dentan for reading early chapters and for inspiring weekends in Southampton. Extra thanks to Marie for checking my French and suggesting locations.

Thank you to Kirsty Ireland for accommodating me at Walton Hall Farm at very short notice so that I could focus on editing. You saved me! Huge gratitude also to Carrie 'Eagle Eyes' Harvey for her amazing proofreading skills.

The best thing about being a teacher as well as a writer, is the subject specialists you can call upon. Thanks to Alexi Williams for sharing her love and knowledge of classical music with me for Kate (any mistakes are mine) and to Neville Dennehy for talking me through all things mathematical for Laura (and for plugging my book during your wedding speech!). More general thanks to Brendan Ryan for brainstorming plots, titles and characters when we should have been marking and to everyone in the English Department Vortex at Coopers for your support – especially my Life Twin, Heidi Smith and Super Reader, Sophie Edmeades.

Apologies and thanks to all the friends whose life experiences I have shamelessly plundered for material, particularly Sarah Martin, Kerry Enever and Tracy Mullen for your stories.

To my wonderful mum for all her continued support and to Dan for keeping me grounded and making me laugh.

And lastly, another big thank you to everyone who read and reviewed the last two books. I really hope you like this one too. x